JO JAKEMAN

THE VANISHING ACT

CONSTABLE

CONSTABLE

First published in Great Britain in 2025 by Constable

1 3 5 7 9 10 8 6 4 2

Copyright © Jo Jakeman, 2025

The moral right of the author has been asserted.

A CIP catalogue record for this book is available from the British Library.

ISBN: 978-1-40871-842-1 (hardcover)
ISBN: 978-140871-843-8 (trade paperback)

Typeset in ITC Stone Serif by Hewer Text UK Ltd, Edinburgh
Printed and bound in Great Britain by Clays Ltd, Elcograf S.p.A.

Papers used by Constable are from well-managed
forests and other responsible sources.

Constable
An imprint of
Little, Brown Book Group
Carmelite House
50 Victoria Embankment
London EC4Y 0DZ

The authorised representative
in the EEA is
Hachette Ireland
8 Castlecourt Centre, Dublin 15,
D15 XTP3, Ireland
(email: info@hbgi.ie)

An Hachette UK Company
www.hachette.co.uk

www.littlebrown.co.uk

*To James, Alex and Danny for their love,
support and patience while I play make-believe.*

Part One

Chapter 1

Eloise

Eloise Ford was a Small Pond person. And within that pond, she wasn't even a big fish.

She didn't suffer from wanderlust, nor grass-is-greener syndrome. She didn't hanker after what everyone else had, and when life inevitably tested her, she never asked, 'Why me?'

Eloise had never believed that her life was a series of happy accidents or a bitter twist of fate. She'd nudged and nurtured her way to this safe and simple way of living that suited her so well, and she could predict what would happen in her day with impressive accuracy.

Those who pitied her small life were looking at it all wrong. If they simply followed her lead, it would save them so much trouble. In her opinion, comfort zones weren't something to be pushed or set free from; they were where you retreated to when life was tough. Her friends seemed to wear their lives like an ill-fitting bra that they couldn't wait to unclasp at the end of the day, but Eloise had carved out this sheltered, comfortable life to be devoid of danger and rid of risks.

And it was nothing short of blissful.

When she walked down the streets she knew so well, she invariably bumped into people she could stop and pass the time with.

'How're the kids? Has your mum had that hip replacement yet? I see there's a new wine bar on the high street – let's go next week.'

Her life was richer due to the familiarity of having lived in the same town for over half her life. She'd lived in the same narrow house for twenty-two years and been married to the same dependable man for twenty-five. She still drank the same branded tea bags and the same coffee. It was only her choice of wine that had changed. Now, it came in hand-picked crates from small, organic, sustainable vineyards instead of boxed in litres by the lowest bidder. It had taken a while, but Eloise had finally become the woman she'd been pretending to be when she'd first met Kit. Eight years older than she was, Kit had seemed sophisticated and wise. He'd taught her about music and love, but more than anything, he'd taught her what it was to feel safe.

Eloise rinsed out her favourite yellow mug and left it turned turtle on the draining board before scraping out her son's cereal bowl and placing it in the dishwasher. She'd given up explaining to him that proximity to the dishwasher was not enough to clean the pots. The same was true for laundry and the washing machine. *There's no such thing as cleaning by osmosis, Edward.*

Maybe she shouldn't have done so much for her children, because Edward was now unable to do anything for himself, stricken as he was by an acute case of Overbearing Mother Syndrome. Ready or not, that was all about to

4

change when he left home to go to university in a couple of weeks and Eloise became the reluctant caretaker of an empty nest. She was going to need a new project. ✓

She hitched up her yoga pants and walked into the pantry to grab a protein bar. She paused by the catering-sized packs of rice and a bumper pack of toilet rolls, where pen-drawn lines made piano tiles up the wall. Edward at two years old, at four, at six. Meghan at seven and three quarters, at nine, at thirteen. They'd stopped measuring when Edward had overtaken his older sister in the height stakes, but Eloise still tracked their growth by the number of steps they took away from her towards independence.

And by that rationale, they had finally outgrown her.

Being a mother had been such a large part of her identity for more than twenty years that she wasn't sure what else she had to offer the world. But she wouldn't go to pieces, because it was her job to get her children safely to this point. If only they weren't so keen to be free of her. Though they couldn't see it, she still had some uses, and one day they would realise she *did* know better.

Her daughter, Meghan, no longer returned Eloise's calls from her white-walled flat, with its soft cream sofas, shaggy-dog cushions and neatly stacked pile of home interior magazines on a smudge-free glass table. Even her partner, Charlie, had a face that looked like it had never had a spot, blemish or wildly sprouting eyebrow hair. Eloise didn't feel comfortable there. Homes should be messy, chaotic places where spills and scuffs were part of the decor. Too much cleanliness made her think that someone was hiding something. And if anyone should know, it was Eloise. She was a connoisseur of concealment, a doctor of deceit. Though everyone said it was the quiet ones you had to watch, they never did, and that was why she sailed through life without a care.

She glanced at the contraption on her wrist, which logged her heart rate, steps and poor night's sleep. She was going to be late for yoga, and by 'late', she meant she would only be ten minutes early.

Wherever possible, Eloise liked to arrive for appointments at least twenty minutes ahead of schedule. She had to factor in being caught in a traffic jam caused by a broken-down vehicle, or an unscheduled stop to fill the car with diesel if the tank showed less than a quarter full. At this thought, her heart rate spiked. The more she watched the numbers on her wrist climb, the more panicked she became. This blasted thing was going to kill her.

She closed the pantry door, grabbed her car keys and water bottle from the little table in the hall, and then she was outside, squinting against the glorious sunshine and wondering where she'd left her sunglasses. She was almost at the car before she realised she'd forgotten her bag and yoga mat.

'For goodness' sake.' She turned and jogged back to the house, imagining the ten-minute window narrowing. She picked up the mat and her bag, then remembered the toy for Wendy's grandson, and the surprisingly spicy book Jan had lent her. Goodness, where was her head today?

Once again she walked out into the sunshine and closed the door. This time, she took a moment, took a breath and took in everything around her. All was as it should be. That was the beauty of living such a small, predictable life – absolutely no surprises.

Truth Seekers UK Facebook Page

Where true-crime fans search for the truth
Missing but never forgotten

Patty Hansen

Have you seen the news about that missing woman in Scotland? Cake in the oven, phone, keys and purse still in the house?? Something suss there. The husband keeps changing his story. I say lock him up now.

Niki Hunter

Praying for her safe return.

Andy Pickford

The last time I was in Scotland, I was nearly eaten alive by midges. Have we checked their alibis?

Patty Hansen

Andy, do you take anything seriously?

Marsha Pirolo

If you watch the body-cam footage from the police, you can see a ghostly figure in the doorway. She died in that house for sure.

Sally Ann

Every time I read about a woman going missing, it makes me think of my aunt, Elizabeth, who disappeared before I was born. It tore our family apart. How can people vanish off the face of the earth like this? My mum has never stopped hoping that she'll get answers one day, even if it's just to know her final resting place.

Holly Bobs

Sorry about your aunt, Sally Ann. You can't walk down the road without being caught on CCTV. Phones and bank cards can be tracked. Every transaction you make is traced. It takes serious effort for someone to vanish completely. They don't do it on their own. Someone knows something and they'll crack eventually. Keep the faith, hun.

Chapter 2

Holly

Holly Bond had far too much to be getting on with, and so she took a deep breath and did precisely nothing.

She'd tried to go back to sleep. Couldn't.

She'd considered getting up. Wouldn't.

Instead, she lay on her bed, studying the cracks and watermarks on her ceiling, making them into shapes and patterns while she listened to cars speeding past her bedroom window. She imagined those people going to work, going out, doing something with their lives, and she hated every last one of them.

Holly's friends were working in cafés or packing to go to university to follow their dreams or, at the very least, get away from home, but Holly had nothing to look forward to. She was even jealous of Lola McFee for being pregnant, as disgusting as it was, by a bloke thirty years older than her with a gold tooth. No wonder she threw up each morning. At least Lola knew what she'd be doing for the next eighteen years. Holly didn't know what she'd be doing in eighteen days. No plans, no future, no hope. And more importantly, no clean underwear.

Holly missed her mum for a thousand reasons, but today, the reason was knickers. Mum had always made sure she had clean clothes, but her stepdad, Liam, didn't even make sure there was food in the house. Apparently, she was old enough to take care of herself, even though all the evidence suggested otherwise.

She sat up and checked her phone. She lifted it higher, pulled her vest lower, and pouted. She smiled as she sent the picture to Eddie, but her face fell as soon as she looked at her laptop. She couldn't put it off any longer. She needed a job.

She didn't know why she'd bothered taking her A levels. She'd always known she wouldn't go to university. Where would she have gone? What would she have done? She didn't want to be a vet, an accountant, or anything that required formal training, and she couldn't leave Cornwall, or else Lisa wouldn't know where to find her. She'd only done her exams to put off the inevitable race to the bottom and because she and her sister had promised each other that they would make something of themselves. And that made them both liars.

The only good thing Holly could say about college was that it was where she'd met Eddie. He never took himself seriously, never took anything seriously, and that was one of the things she liked most about him. He was a skinny geek who talked about politics, foreign films and computer games, but he listened as well as spoke. He made her laugh like nobody else, cared what she thought, and never called her stupid when she got something wrong. But like everyone else in her life, he was leaving her.

They'd talked about travelling together and doing bar work or fruit picking while exploring places they'd only seen on the telly. But that was all forgotten when he was offered a place to study computer science in Sheffield. He said she could visit him when he was settled, but she knew better than that. She was fun to hang out with, but she wasn't the kind of girl that guys like Eddie stuck with. And yes, she was sad about that, but she wouldn't go to pieces over a lad. She'd miss spending time with him, but more than that, she would miss being at his house with his typical family, a fridge with food in it and an actual biscuit jar with the fancy chocolate biscuits.

She flipped open the laptop and watched it flicker to life. Holly was expanding her CV and attempting to find creative ways to dress up her lack of tangible experience. Though she was intent on looking for a job, she got sidetracked every ten minutes or so and fell back into reading those true-crime Facebook pages where they shared pictures of people who'd disappeared or turned up dead. Some people offered prayers for the safe return of loved ones, while others were convinced of wrongdoing. There was a lot of finger-pointing and blame. *The husband did it*, they said. *A serial killer, for sure. Trafficking!* They would pass judgement on the pictures of missing girls. *Look at her eyes!* they'd say. *Drugs*. And, *Is it any wonder?* All the while patting themselves on the back for being above such things. A guy in one of the American groups kept telling people to *Wake up!* Couldn't they see the obvious answer to all these missing people? Alien abduction. She'd laughed. They all did. But the truth was, she'd rather accept that aliens had abducted Lisa than a serial killer. It was all about what you were willing to believe to preserve your sanity.

11

Each of these missing people posts hit Holly hard. Some had only gone missing last week, and some hadn't been heard from in two months, two years or two decades, but no one was giving up their quest to find the truth. Holly admired their resilience.

'Huh,' she said aloud. 'Resilience.' And then she added it to her CV under *Attributes*.

Sometimes there were stories about unsolved murders, people hoping they could finally get answers. Other times, the people were missing without a trace. But without exception, when the families asked for information about a missing person, they were fooling themselves that there could still be a positive outcome. After a certain amount of time, you had to accept they weren't coming back. Holly just didn't know how long a 'certain amount' of time was, and whether she was fooling herself too.

She scrolled the photos and the posts, looking for a familiar face. She knew she wouldn't find Lisa there, smiling under a headline saying that she'd hit her head, got amnesia, and forgotten her name. She also knew she didn't want to see an artist's impression of an unidentified female. *Do you recognise this young woman whose body was found washed up on a beach?*

She knew she shouldn't do this to herself, but the sites made her feel less alone. Only these people knew what it was like to be so desperate for answers you turned to Facebook, of all places. Every day without news meant there was a chance that Lisa was living happily ever after with a hot new boyfriend and a cat called Mittens.

Holly's sister wasn't officially missing, but she clearly wasn't here and hadn't been for months. She had argued with their stepdad, which led to Liam throwing a punch at her, which she expertly dodged. Unfortunately for Liam, he connected with the door frame and broke a bone in his hand. Lisa left quickly after that and said she'd be in touch, but her phone was no longer in service and her social media accounts hadn't been updated in months.

The way Holly saw it, there were three ways to view this situation. One was that Lisa was doing just fine and was having too much fun to remember her younger sister. Another was that Lisa was in trouble, and Holly was the only one who could help her. The least favourable – and perhaps most likely – option was that Lisa was already dead. Sometimes Holly believed all those things at once. She didn't know if it was better to remain in the dark or to discover a truth that would destroy her for ever. Hope was all she had left, but it was a slimy little sucker that slipped from her grasp if she held on to it too tightly.

She had told the police everything she knew, which wasn't much. Her sister had argued with Liam before going to London to stay with friends while looking for work there, but Holly hadn't heard from her since. No, she didn't know which friends. No, she didn't know where in London. It happens all the time, the police officer said. Lisa was an adult who had left of her own free will. They told Holly to sit tight and maybe get her mum or dad to call them if they had any concerns.

It was just Holly and Liam now, and he wasn't happy at being landed with her. Though Holly wouldn't admit it, she couldn't help but wonder if Liam had . . . God, how to put it? Played an *active* role in Lisa's disappearance.

13

Probably not.

Almost certainly not.

But there was no doubt that Liam lost control when he'd been drinking, so she had to make sure she didn't make him angry. She had to keep out of his way until she could find somewhere else to live. First, though, she needed a job.

Chapter 3

Eloise

Late. Eloise was never late. It was practically unheard of. Temporary lights and a burst water pipe meant she hit traffic no matter where she turned. She might have cried if there'd been any moisture left in her body, but she was sweating so much she was basically a husk.

By the time she'd found a parking space on the hill behind the yoga studio and power-walked fast enough that her rasping thighs almost ignited the flammable material of her leggings, she knew the game was up.

She paused at the entrance to the Salutation Studios and considered turning around and going home. She could pretend she'd had a flat tyre or a debilitating bout of diarrhoea, anything but admit to the cardinal sin of being late to Monday-morning yoga. She could, of course, sneak into the back of the class and mouth 'sorry' before taking her place – the class had started only six and a half minutes ago, after all – but she didn't want to risk annoying Mimi again.

The best thing she could do was draw a line under the challenging morning and ensure everything went smoothly from now on. She made her way around to the café in the courtyard at the back of the studio, where she would take a moment to gather herself, wait for her friends and try to get a grip on her day.

Usually Monday was Eloise's favourite day of the week. Whereas schoolkids and office workers felt a sense of dread on a Sunday evening, Eloise positively revelled in it. She laid out her sports kit, filled her water bottle, and went to sleep knowing the following day was all hers. No errands, no paperwork, no expectations. Her husband, Kit, would be out at work, the gallery would be closed, and no one would dare lay claim to her time. It was an entirely guilt-free day.

On Mondays, she went to yoga with her oldest and closest friends, Mimi and Jan. Then, on sunny days, the morning would slide into lunch and tumble into cocktails quite effortlessly. Other times, she'd take herself off to the harbour after her post-yoga coffee to let the icy water snatch her breath away so she could emerge refreshed, invigorated and ready to take on the world. Or she'd take a dog-eared book to the beach and not speak to another soul as she napped, swam, read, and treated herself to an ice cream, a toastie or a cake. Because Monday was *her* day, and calories didn't count on a Monday. Fact.

She secured her favourite table under the sea-glass and shell windchimes, placing her yoga mat by her chair and water bottle on the table before hugging her oversized bag to her chest and heading back to the window under the sun canopy.

'No yoga today?' asked Wendy, pouring syrup into an iced coffee. Her rosy cheeks suggested high blood pressure rather than good health, but she had unlimited energy.

'Not today,' replied Eloise. 'The universe had other plans for me.'

'Anything exciting?' asked Wendy.

'My need for granola and cappuccino was deemed to be greater than my need for tree poses and savasana.'

'Shall I make it a double, love?'

'You're an angel. Oh, and I've got something for Henry.' Eloise reached into her bag and pulled out a plush toy penguin. 'Didn't you say he was obsessed with them? I saw it in a shop window and—'

'Oh, bless your heart! That's so kind of you. He'll love it.' Wendy wiped her hands on her apron and took the toy from Eloise. She smiled and stroked its fur before placing it on a shelf under the counter. 'That's made my day, that has. I don't care what anyone else says, you're bloody lovely, you are.'

'Oh,' said Eloise. 'Do other people—'

'Joke,' laughed Wendy. 'I'm joking, love. I've literally never heard anyone say a bad word about you. You're golden.'

Eloise wrinkled her nose and turned her head. She often felt like she was missing the punchline. 'How did Henry's first day at school go?'

'Worse for us than him,' Wendy said. 'Henry were as good as gold. Loved everything about it. He thinks his teacher walks on water. I'm having him this weekend while our Melanie's away. I'm thinking of taking him to the Seal Sanctuary at Gweek. Have you been? I really want to take him to Scotland over half-term if Mimi will let me have the time off. I tell you what, it's lucky I moved down here

17

when I did, because God only knows how she'd cope without me.'

'Mimi or Melanie?'

'Both. But between you, me and the gatepost, I'm in the doghouse with Mimi.'

'That makes both of us,' said Eloise. 'What are you in for?'

'I forgot to lock up. I was sure I had, but the door was open when she got here this morning.'

Eloise grimaced. 'Was anything taken?'

'Nah. But why would anyone break in? I don't even lock my own back door. If someone wants in, they're going to do it whether I lock up or not, aren't they? I don't want to come home to broken windows and splintered door frames, so let them have at it, I say. I don't own anything that I can't live without.'

'Won't it invalidate the insurance if the doors are unlocked?' asked Eloise.

Wendy waved her hand. 'Who bothers with insurance nowadays? Anyway, I've got to keep Mimi sweet if I want time off with my grandbaby, so put in a good word for me when you see her, would you?'

Eloise watched Wendy grab a flapjack with tongs and place it on a small blue plate on a napkin. 'I still find it hard to believe you're old enough to be a grandmother.'

'Family tradition,' Wendy said. 'Mum was sixteen when she had my sister and eighteen when she had me. I couldn't wait to have my own kids, and our Melanie was the same. Family is everything, isn't it?'

Eloise's gaze was momentarily caught by a fly buzzing weakly in a spider's web beneath the sunshade canopy. As the spider darted towards it, she said, 'It depends on the family.'

'Do you want to take a seat and I'll bring your coffee over,' Wendy said. 'I'm on my own this morning, so it might take a while.'

'Sure. No rush.'

Eloise weaved her way through the tables and sank into her seat. She sipped her water, which was already warming up, and checked her phone for an update on that burst water pipe. She needed to know if she'd have to take a longer route home. There couldn't be any more surprises today.

But on the local news website, it wasn't the headline about the water pipe that caught her eye, nor the fact that the reservoirs were running dangerously low. It was the third article down that made her sit forward in her seat. She clicked on it and tapped her fingers as she waited for it to load. She wiped the sweat off her top lip.

Human remains, she read. *Old Engine House.* And there, under a photograph taken at least thirty years ago, was a name she'd hoped never to read again.

Elizabeth King.

Truth Seekers UK

Sally Ann

OMG, you guys! Remember how I said we were looking for my missing aunt???? Well, human remains were found in these ruins in Cornwall at the weekend – and they belong to Elizabeth!!! I can't believe it. They still need to do DNA tests to confirm it, but someone called the police and mentioned her by name, so we're as sure as we can be that we've finally found her. The article below says it better than I can.

It's not the outcome we'd hoped for, but it's the one we've long expected.

RIP, sweet Elizabeth. #ForeverNineteen.

From *The Beacon*

In the early hours of Sunday morning, a dog walker discovered human remains in an abandoned engine house in Cornwall. Following an anonymous tip-off, we can exclusively reveal that they belong to Elizabeth King, a teenage runaway. The 19-year-old was last seen hitchhiking by the side of the M1 near Nottingham in February 1994. How she came to be in Cornwall is a mystery. The area remains sealed off while officers search for evidence . . . *See more*

Niki Hunter

Prayers for your family, Sally Ann. May you know the peace of the Lord.

Patty Hansen

She went missing in Nottingham?? But her body was found 400 miles away in Cornwall?? WTF??

Marsha Pirolo

The article says she was hitchhiking, so they probably drove her there and ditched the body after she was unalived. Sally Ann, condolences at this sad time. I sense that her soul is still restless. I hope you get answers.

Holly Bobs

How has the body stayed undiscovered there for THREE DECADES?? Those engine houses are sealed off but that doesn't stop people from exploring them. Something not stacking up here.

Sally Ann

Mum doesn't talk about her much, but I know Elizabeth had a big bust-up with their parents. It sounds like she was a complete nightmare by all accounts. She hung around with a bad crowd – parties, boys, drugs . . . She was going to stay with her boyfriend in Wales, but she never turned up. He was under suspicion for a while, but police never got enough evidence to charge him. Mum still thinks he had something to do with it, though.

Patty Hansen

Your mum's 100 per cent right. It's always the boyfriend or husband who did it. What's his name? I bet I can track him down. It only took me seven minutes to find the tart who was sleeping with my husband, and only another two to find her boss. Within fifteen minutes, even her kids' teachers knew what a dirty little whore she was.

Andy Pickford

Damn, Patty. Just . . . damn.

Sally Ann

All we know is that he was a football coach from Rhyl. He was a couple of years older than Elizabeth, and his name began with a G. Mum thinks it was Gary or Gavin. She said his surname started with a G, too, but I'd take that with a pinch of salt because she just said it was Gary Glitter. Sorry. It's not much to go on, but that's all she remembers.

Patsy Hansen

Leave it with me. I'll see what I can do.

Holly Bobs

So sorry for what your family is going through, Sally Ann. It's not even closure, though, if you don't know what happened to your aunt. I hope you get answers soon.

Sally Ann

I know, right??!! Everyone says, 'Well, at least you know', but we don't know anything apart from the fact that she's dead. But we already knew that, or we'd have heard from her by now. I won't rest until I find out what happened to her and who's responsible. I owe it to my mum. We're the only ones left. The rest of Elizabeth's family are long dead. We need to work out her last movements, but I'm not sure where to start, and the police aren't being any help at all.

Holly Bobs

I live close to where the remains were found. Do you want me to go to the site and see if I can find out anything?

Sally Ann

Really? Are you sure? OMG, that would be amazing!! I'll try and get down to Cornwall as soon as I can, but I've got a little lad who needs looking after so I need to stay put for now and see what the police say.

Andy Pickford

Your aunt was HOT. What a waste.

Holly Bobs

Piss off, Andy, you lowlife. Sally Ann, leave it with me. Maybe Patty can use her sleuthing skills to look for leads on the Welsh boyfriend, and I'll see what I can find out from the scene. And speaking from experience, don't believe everything the police tell you. They'll try to cover up the fact that they missed clues for thirty years. Who knows how many other victims there've been, thanks to their incompetence. Women go missing every day, and we're the only ones who care.

Chapter 4

Eloise

Eloise fanned her face with a laminated menu. She was glad she was already sitting down because she didn't think her legs could have held her up.

Despite the sweltering day, she felt chills up her arms. A curious numbness radiated from her heart to her fingertips and sent prickles across her scalp.

Though she had hoped she would never hear Elizabeth's name again, a part of her had always suspected this day would come. She clenched and unclenched her fists and put one hand on her chest as if soothing a frightened animal. She was surprised to feel her heart still beating to a steady rhythm.

She tried to cross her legs, but the shiny material of her patterned leggings made it impossible, and her thigh slipped straight off again. She leaned forward with her elbows on the table and her chin in her hands until her arm slid off the table with a jolt and she felt her teeth pinch her tongue. She put the back of her hand to her mouth but didn't see the blood she was expecting.

She picked up her phone again, hoping she'd misread the headline.

25

Elizabeth King was 19 years old when she was last seen hitch-hiking on the M1 on 24 February 1994 with a friend. It was thought she was on her way to visit her boyfriend in Wales, but she would never reach her destination. Witnesses said—

'Greek yoghurt, coconut granola and a double-shot latte.'

Wendy set the coffee on the table, causing some to spill into the saucer, as Eloise flipped over her phone.

'Thanks, Wendy. That's . . .' Eloise didn't know what she was meant to say. Lovely? Not what she ordered? The least of her worries?

Wendy stepped closer, her broad hands on the table between them. 'Is something up? You look a bit peaky. It's the heat, isn't it? It's been making me come over all peculiar too.' She flapped her zebra-print shirt and blew her fringe out of her face.

'No. I'm fine. Just fine. I'm feeling a little . . .' Eloise paused. She wasn't sure how to explain the crushing feeling in her chest. Eventually she said, 'Out of sorts,' though that hardly seemed adequate. She was shocked, scared and desperate for someone to tell her this was all a sick joke.

'Oh love,' said Wendy. 'I'd sit and chat a while, but . . .' She glanced over her shoulder at the two women standing at the window, ready to order.

'It's okay,' said Eloise. 'You go. I'm just having one of those days. It's probably low blood sugar.' She gave what she hoped was a reassuring smile.

'Okay. I'll be keeping an eye on you. You'll shout if you need anything, won't you?'

Wendy walked towards the kitchen while Eloise wiped her clammy hands on her Spandex and took a deep breath.

She touched the back of her phone case, wondering if she dared look again.

She'd worked hard to keep her family safe and protected, and she wouldn't let a headline in the local news jeopardise that. Kit referred to them as a pod, like dolphins. For their children, there were no uncles or aunts and only one living grandparent, though dementia meant she wasn't present in the way she used to be. It had been crucial for them to forge the kind of family neither she nor Kit had been part of growing up. And it had been surprisingly easy. She'd built a home, kept everyone safe and revelled in every smug moment. She'd been too busy to give much thought to the past. Nothing could be gained from wondering if she could've – should've – done something differently.

She couldn't resist. She had to find out what the police knew. She had to read on.

Police investigating Elizabeth's disappearance made the grim discovery of human remains in an abandoned engine house in Cornwall following an anonymous tip-off. They are appealing for anyone with information to come forward.

EL

Yes, Eloise had information, but no, she would not be 'coming forward', whatever that meant. She squinted at the picture accompanying the article. She zoomed in, but instead of becoming clearer, it lost all focus. At first she thought it was a black-and-white photo, but then she remembered the home-dyed black hair, pale face and fierce black eyebrows. A homage to Siouxsie and the Banshees back when good hairspray and a bad attitude were all a girl needed.

Before she could consider whether the remains could be traced back to her, she heard the doors of the yoga studio open. She mustn't let her friends suspect anything. If they found out about the circles she used to run in, it would destroy everything she had worked so hard for. They were clever, accomplished women, but not worldly-wise like she was. They'd never understand.

She took a deep breath and turned to them with a smile.

'Sweet Jesus,' said Mimi. 'Who the hell died?'

Eloise let the conversation wash over her as she sipped her second cup of bitter coffee. This time, she'd had it with oat milk so that she wouldn't feel judged by Mimi, who wore her vegan credentials like a badge. For a woman who encouraged peace and love, she certainly was quick to judge anyone whose views did not align with hers. And no matter what she said, Eloise *could* taste the difference.

She'd told Mimi that the only reason she looked awful was because she was so terribly sad to have missed her yoga class. Mimi was conceited enough to believe it, but Jan stifled a laugh and shook her head while Eloise raised a finger to her lips.

The café was busy, with every table occupied. To everyone's surprise, it was proving extremely popular, and it was keeping the rest of Mimi's business afloat when many of the classes were struggling to reach full capacity. It was a beautiful space, an oasis away from the bustling world, and Eloise could see why people kept coming back. Mimi had worked hard to renovate the old sail loft. Even Arthur, her curmudgeonly landlord, treated the café like a second home, and he certainly wasn't the kind of man to take oat milk in his tea.

28

Eloise listened to her friends but didn't know how to get involved. It was like watching a skipping rope loop around and around while waiting for the right moment to jump in. Jan was untwisting her bra strap while discussing the state of her youngest son's schooling, while Mimi was sitting cross-legged on her bench with her tattooed wrists upturned towards the sunshine muttering about the woeful state of her sex life. Neither seemed to notice or care that they were talking about different topics.

'And don't get me started on uniforms. I don't under-stand the point,' said Jan. 'It doesn't help them to learn anything, and it's such a faff to iron the shirts.'

'It's the socks that kill me,' said Mimi. 'I don't care how cold his feet get. Just take them off. There isn't a man alive that can make that look sexy. God, I wish I were gay.'

'And when do they get time to be kids? To play? Why do they need that much homework?'

'Every Thursday night. It gets monotonous, you know? Same old moves, same old saggy bits. I'm seriously consider-ing taking a lover.'

Eloise had been friends with Mimi and Jan since that first baby class in the church hall. Different personalities from different worlds, they would never have met if they hadn't fallen pregnant in the same year. They would never have been friends if they hadn't been through so much together. They'd helped Eloise survive the sudden death of her first son. While all the other parents backed off as quickly as they could in case the grief was contagious, Mimi and Jan sat and held her. They said they were there for as long as she needed them. And then, when Eloise gave birth to Meghan, they indulged her neurosis up until the point where they told her to snap out of it and appreciate her beautiful baby girl. That didn't stop her from panicking at every rash, sniffle and fever, but her friends were always there to advise her and tell her when her concerns were justified. Which was hardly ever.

Jan had five children, all boys, and would have had more if Chad hadn't booked himself a secret vasectomy. Mimi, on the other hand, gave birth to Moonbeam – who now called himself Mark – and declared that she'd done her bit for procreation.

Eloise marvelled at how large her friends lived their lives. They threw themselves head-first into everything and knew exactly who they were and what they desired. Eloise thought she knew what she wanted – a happy family life, to love and be loved, and an art gallery that turned a profit. She supposed two out of three wasn't bad, but she wasn't sure what came next. Everything was changing around her, and she was powerless to stop it. All she wanted to do was keep her head down and be content, and for the most part, she was. Until she'd read the name Elizabeth King in the news.

She put her hand on her chest again. This time she could feel the jitters. The past was reaching out. All she needed to do was stay out of it and not be tempted to investigate the story further. She wouldn't even look it up online because this had nothing to do with her.

Nothing at all.

'Right. That's enough,' said Mimi, slapping the table and making her jump.

Eloise sat up straight. 'What is?'

'You. Your face. You expect us to believe there's nothing wrong with you today?'

'Honestly, it's nothing,' she said with a flap of her hand and a smile.

'In my experience,' said Jan, 'if one of the kids starts a sentence with "honestly", it means they're lying through their teeth. I've known you for twenty-odd years and know when you're hiding something. Is it Kit? One of the kids? Oh God, it's not that dodgy mole, is it? Have the doctors said something?'

'No, it's nothing to do with . . . Hold on, what mole?'

'The one on your left shoulder,' said Mimi. 'And you really should get it checked out. But if it's not that, what is it?'

Eloise gently placed her cup down, stalling for time. She leaned forward on the table, and Jan and Mimi leaned in too.

'So, the thing is,' she said, lowering her voice even though no one could overhear their conversation. She paused, still undecided about which way to jump. She didn't know whether the truth would set her free or land her in chains. These women knew her better than anyone, even better than Kit did, but there was so much about her they wouldn't understand.

On the other hand, a problem shared . . .

'I read something in the news this morning about human remains being found in an old engine house on the road going out towards Helston. There was something about the name . . . I thought maybe I recognised her. And looking at the photo . . . well, I'm pretty sure she's someone I used to know.'

'Oh darling!' exclaimed Mimi. 'That's terrible.'

'Ah,' said Jan. 'I'm so sorry, El.'

Eloise didn't meet their eyes. 'It's okay. It looks like she died a very long time ago.' She looked down at her hands. 'It was a shock to read the name, that's all. It's made me feel quite unsettled.'

'Do the police know what happened?' asked Jan.

Eloise shook her head. 'It doesn't say anything in the news article, but I guess her body's been there for a while.'

'Do you think she was murdered?' asked Mimi.

'Why would you ask that? How would I know? I've told you, she was just someone I knew a long time ago.'

Mimi got up and stood behind her. She threw her arms around her, and Jan did the same, kissing the top of her head and swaddling her with bosoms and Lycra.

'What's happening?' Eloise said, lifting her head in search of oxygen.

'It's called love,' said Mimi.

'It feels more like a hot flush,' said Eloise. 'Do you mind?'

The women returned to their seats, but reached out to each hold one of Eloise's hands.

'Really,' said Eloise. 'It's okay. Don't make a fuss. I hadn't thought about her in years.'

'Still,' said Mimi. 'Were the two of you close?'

'God, no. She was nothing but trouble.'

'Well, I hope they find out what happened to her,' Jan said.

Eloise smiled weakly. That was one thing she disagreed with her friend on. She'd do whatever she could to make sure no one found out what had happened to Elizabeth King.

32

Holly Bobs

I'm making it my mission to discover what happened to Elizabeth King. I'm on my way to the place where they found the remains. I've just got off at the closest bus stop and am walking the rest of the way now. I can see the outline of the engine house chimney on the hill. I've always found these things a bit creepy, if I'm honest. The countryside is littered with them around here. I don't know why they weren't knocked down and the mines filled in when they stopped being used.

The first thing to note is that this place is remote. There are no cameras and barely any passing traffic. I have a notebook and will find out what I can. Sally Ann, is there anything you want me to ask when I get there?

#JusticeForElizabeth #ForeverNineteen

Sally Ann

I can't thank you enough for this! I doubt the police will tell you anything that isn't publicly available, but please find out everything you can. I owe you big time.

Andy Pickford

Take photos of everything and anything, even if it doesn't look relevant right now.

Patty Hansen

Also take photos of the people who are hanging around. Killers often return to the scene of the crime. They just can't help themselves. They love to relive the drama and feel that rush of power.

Chapter 5

Eloise

Eloise drummed her fingers on the steering wheel and lowered the car window. She stuck out her head, craning to see what was causing the hold-up, but there was nothing but a curving bank of brake lights like angry fire ants up the hill. A dozen or more drivers sweltering as they watched their morning slip away. There was rarely heavy traffic on this road. It wasn't used as a shortcut, wasn't on the way to anywhere particularly special, and the summertime tourists had all gone home.

She only came this way if she was going to the beach where they used to take the kids surfing, and even then, only if someone else was driving. The road was too narrow and the hedges too high for her gossamer nerves. Cornish lanes were the one aspect of living here that Eloise could never adjust to.

She had claimed she had a migraine so that she could skip lunch with Mimi and Jan and take some time for herself to think about what the discovery of the bones in the engine house meant. Still, the universe had a great sense of humour, and she was already feeling that familiar pinching pain behind her right eye. At least in this she wasn't a liar.

35

She sank back into her seat but left the window open, hoping to catch a breeze. She imagined pressing a cool ice pack to her forehead. Despite the late-summer heat, the air smelled like autumn was on its way. Crisp leaves, earthy undertones, a hop, skip and a jump from here to pumpkin spice season. She popped open the glove compartment and fished out a pair of bejewelled sunglasses that Meghan had bought her for her birthday. She wondered whether her family had any idea what she actually liked, or if they simply purchased items they wanted and would eventually take for themselves.

She touched the phone charging in the centre console in a nest of sticky chocolate eclair wrappers. As the sound of ringing filled the car, she noticed movement ahead. Brake lights were extinguished and cars began inching forward again. The ringing stopped abruptly, and Eloise was about to speak when she heard the familiar voice.

'Hey, this is Megs. Leave a message after the tone and—'

She cut off her daughter with a jab of her finger. It had been nearly two weeks since they'd last spoken, and in that time, she'd left two phone messages and sent three texts. She knew Meghan was busy, but would it hurt her to pick up the phone occasionally and tell Eloise she was alive? Was it time to send out the search helicopters? Sniffer dogs? Navy Seals? A SWAT team? Drones? How selfish must a person be to not even respond to a text from a worried mother?

She rubbed her temples. But of course, she wasn't annoyed with Meghan, she was upset with herself for driving this way home despite knowing that no good could come of it. Now that the traffic was moving, she could see a police van and a white tent on the crest of the hill next to the familiar sight of a conical red-brick chimney splitting the sky. A few onlookers had gathered, though there was nothing to see. Some people were sitting in cars in the lay-by next to an overflowing bin, and Eloise wondered what had brought them here, because it couldn't be the same reason that had compelled her.

No matter how much she wanted to, she would not stop the car. She would simply drive by the site at an appropriate speed while paying her respects. She wasn't the only person in this traffic jam who'd been brought here to see the circus. No accident was blocking the way, no tractor, nor hill-tired cyclists. These people were doing the same thing as she was. They were hoping to be part of the drama and see something to satisfy their morbid curiosity, all while staying at a safe, sterile distance.

She didn't know what she hoped to find and equally didn't know what she was so scared of seeing. She was level with the site now, gawking and staring like the rest of them and sweating more than the warm day warranted. As she edged her way forward, she heard a *smack*. Her body jolted forward and then slammed backwards.

Her car stalled, and she screwed up her eyes and laid her forehead against the steering wheel.

'Stupid, stupid idiot,' she muttered to herself.

She looked up to see the man in the car in front of her getting out of his white Audi. She slid down in her seat until she was hidden from view, but she had very little choice but to face him or leave tyre marks on the tarmac as she sped away down the wrong side of the road. But bright yellow Fiat 500s did not make good getaway cars. Though Eloise did not believe in such things, there was every indication that today was cursed. Everything in her life had been going so well until someone disturbed those bones.

The man from the other car looked at his bumper with his hands on his hips. This was Eloise's first ever car accident. She was usually such a careful person. She had never had a bump, scrape, speeding ticket or parking fine.

She reached for her phone and threw her sunglasses onto the passenger seat. She'd have to give this man her details, call the insurance people, and explain to Kit why she'd gone miles out of her way instead of coming straight home. And then she'd have to come up with a plausible reason why she hadn't noticed that the car in front of her had stopped.

'Are you okay?' she asked the man as she closed her door. 'You're not hurt, are you? I don't think I hit you too hard.'

He spun around to face her. 'Didn't you see me? It's a big enough bloody car. Do I need flashing lights and a fucking siren?'

He was wearing a suit, but his hair was messy and there was dirt under his raggedy nails. His true self wasn't far beneath the surface.

Eloise folded her arms. 'Look, I can't apologise enough,' she said. 'I didn't realise that you'd stopped, and—'

'Looking at that, were you?' he said as he nodded towards the phone in her hand. 'Typical.'

'No, I . . . God, no. I'd never . . . I'm not that kind of person. If you tell me a rule, I will follow it to the letter, and the rule is never to look at your phone while driving. Even if you're only going five miles an hour in slow-moving traffic. See? Rule follower.' She jiggled the phone at him, but he wasn't convinced.

He pinched the bridge of his nose. 'The police will be able to check your phone records, you know, and see if you were texting at the time of the collision.' He suddenly winced and put his hand to his neck. 'Whiplash,' he said. 'I'll have to go to the doctor. For all I know, you did this on purpose.'

'Hold on,' Eloise said, drawing herself up to her full height but not quite meeting the man's eye. 'I did say I was sorry. And I don't mean to be rude, but this was an accident. You do know what an accident is, don't you? It's something unexpected and unintentional.' She unfolded her arms and put her hands on her hips, but that felt ridiculous, so she crossed them again.

'I'll need your insurance details,' he said. 'And a little less of your attitude.'

'A little less of my . . .? Wow, you really are something.'

She took a deep breath, refusing to lose her temper. Her head was swimming; she was unsure how her day had gone so spectacularly wrong. She narrowed her eyes and allowed herself a moment to imagine driving her little yellow car straight at the obnoxious man in front of her.

'I saw it,' a woman shouted. 'I saw everything.'

'Perfect,' said Eloise, turning away. 'And here was me thinking my day couldn't get any worse.'

She looked behind her at the line of vehicles waiting impatiently, the drivers glaring at her for holding them up even more than necessary. She mouthed 'sorry' at the nearest one, and bent to check her car for damage, but

39

thankfully, she saw none. She looked at the other car and saw there was a slight dent.

'You were rubbernecking,' the woman said. 'I saw you.'

Eloise squeezed her eyes shut. There was no point denying it.

'And you knew other people were doing the same. You stopped suddenly, causing this lady to hit you from behind.'

She looked up suddenly as she realised the woman wasn't talking to her.

'I bet you do it all the time to claim for whiplash.'

The man stepped backwards as if affronted. 'How dare you say such a—'

'You say the police can check whether she was on her phone. Well, they can also check whether you make a habit of claiming for whiplash on your insurance.'

'I can assure you—' he began.

'Yeah, well, assure me of whatever you like, mate, but I saw what I saw, and I'm happy to provide a witness statement.' The woman looked at the Audi's bumper. 'And you know what? That damage looks old to me. How do we even know this happened today?'

The man's nostrils flared. Eloise stood in silence with her mouth open, unsure whether she should say anything at all.

'Do you want me to go and get one of those police officers?' the young woman said, pointing behind her. 'You have to report a car accident by law, right? I mean, I'm no expert, I don't even have a car, but I know what I saw.'

'I don't have time for this,' the man said. 'We're holding up the traffic, and I have better things to do with my morning.' He turned to look at Eloise, who still hadn't spoken. 'Look, I stopped abruptly and you bumped me. I think we can agree that we both contributed to the incident, so there's no need to involve the insurance companies, eh?'

She nodded. 'Fine by me.'

'And you . . .' he said to the other woman, pointing a finger in her face. Then the fight left him, and he dropped his arm. He shook his head and got back in his car without finishing his thoughts aloud.

Eloise watched him drive away, then turned to her saviour, who was smiling broadly.

'All right, Mrs F?' the woman asked.

'Yes, thank you, Holly. Fancy seeing you here.'

Chapter 6

Holly

It was the first time Holly had been in the front seat of Mrs Ford's car and one of the few times she'd ever been alone with her. There had been times when Eddie would leave them to chat while he finished his college work or popped to the bathroom, but Holly would never choose to be by herself in a room with her boyfriend's mum. And now, ten minutes into the journey back to Eddie's house, she remembered why.

'Thanks for the lift, Mrs Ford,' she said. 'I appreciate it.'

'Please, Holly, I think you've known me long enough to call me Eloise.'

'And I'm sorry about your sunglasses. I didn't see them. I might be able to reattach the arm.' Holly held up the two pieces of black plastic, and a lens fell onto her lap. 'Or not.'

She noticed the muscles in Eloise's arm stiffen.

'It's fine,' Eloise said. 'Besides, I should be thanking you for helping with that idiot back there. I was so taken aback by seeing the police and the tent by the engine house, and I must admit I was distracted. Luckily I was only going at a snail's pace. You don't really think he was trying it on to get a payout for whiplash, do you?'

Holly dropped the pieces of sunglasses into the door pocket. 'Yeah, you hear about it all the time. Blokes like that are always chancing it, aren't they?' She put her feet up on the dashboard, then, on hearing a sharp intake of breath from Eloise, put them down again.

'Well, I would've admitted full liability if you hadn't come over and put him in his place, so thank you.'

'I wrote down his licence plate, if it helps?' Holly said. 'I put it in my notebook.'

'Did you? I don't think it'll be necessary, but maybe send it to me anyway.'

Holly smiled. Eddie's mum didn't like her, not that she *Hol* cared, but knowing she'd done something useful for a change felt good. She glanced around the vehicle without making it too obvious. It was a shock to find that Eloise's car resembled a skip on wheels. There were slippers in the foot-well of the passenger side of the car, sweet wrappers in the door and the central console. Empty drinks bottles rolled around the back seat every time the car accelerated or slowed, and inexplicably, there appeared to be a box of bathroom tiles behind the driver's seat.

'Have you been working out?' Holly asked.

'Who, me?'

'I just thought ... with the sports kit and everything ...'

'Oh.' Eloise looked down at her thighs as if surprised to see what she was wearing. 'Kit says I have all the gear but no idea. I didn't get a chance today because I was running late, but I usually go to yoga with friends on a Monday morning.'

'Yeah? Where do you go?'

'It's a place called Salutation Studios.'

'I know it. My sister used to work there, but the woman who owns it was an absolute bitch. She was always on her case about something or other, expecting her to be grateful for minimum wage.

'Right.'

'I'm surprised the place is still going, to be honest, because I heard that a lot of the businesses around there are being knocked down to make way for a new housing estate. Not that I care about yoga, actually, I hate it, but there won't be any community spaces left at this rate.' Holly chewed the side of her thumbnail. 'Though you can't say we don't need more affordable housing, so . . . but then who's to say it'll *be* affordable housing and not an estate for second-home wankers?'

Eloise didn't say anything or change her position, but Holly thought she'd detected a slight cooling of the air temperature despite the dashboard showing it was twenty-seven degrees outside. That woman must love her yoga.

They travelled the next mile in silence until Eloise said, 'So, you were at those tents where the police vans were, were you?'

'Yeah. A friend mentioned it to me and, you know, I didn't have anything better to do with my day, so I went up there to see what was happening. Get the goss.'

'And did you discover anything interesting?'

Holly suppressed a smile. Though Eloise had her eyes fixed on the road ahead, it was obvious she was dying to know. Something in her forced casual nature suggested more than a passing interest. Holly shifted in her seat so that her back was against the door and bent one knee.

'Well,' she said. 'Did you hear that they found human remains in the engine house?'

Eloise nodded. 'Now you mention it, I think I might have heard something on the news this morning.'

'Yeah, so this all happened yesterday. God knows how long she's been there. Someone called the police with an anonymous tip-off, but I was talking to this guy called Ken and his sister's husband's friend . . . or was it his friend's sister's husband? Anyway, whatever, they're in the police force, and Ken says they didn't take the first call seriously at all. This police officer looked in on his way home, shone his torch around a bit and couldn't see anything. But then, a couple of days later, a woman phones the police in a panic, saying her dog ran into the old engine house and was gone ages. She was worried he'd fallen down one of the mine shafts or something. She was about to call for help when the dog came back with a bone in his mouth, and it turned out to be part of a foot.'

'A foot?'

'An actual human foot. Just bones, though. I mean, the police tried to mug her off by saying it was probably from a sheep or something, but once they realised she wasn't completely bonkers, there were police and forensic scientists everywhere. And then, of course, they found the body that matched the foot, like a twisted version of Cinderella. Though did you know that in the original Cinderella, the ugly sisters cut off their toes to fit their feet in the glass slipper?'

45

Eloise was stealing glances at Holly and then snapping her focus back to the road. 'I don't know what to say. That's . . . horrendous,' she said.

'I know. But a lot of kids' stories are darker than you realise.'

'I was talking about the foot.'

'Oh.' Holly twisted in her seat. 'Yeah. Grim.'

'And the man you were talking to,' said Eloise. 'Ken, was it? Did he have any other information about the young woman?'

'Ken, yeah. He said that the police would be lucky to get much DNA evidence because she's basically a load of bones wrapped in a carpet.'

'A carpet?'

'Yep. And she didn't roll herself up in a carpet and fall down a great big hole, did she? It's proof she was murdered. Not that I was ever in any doubt about that, but the police will probably try and paint it as a suicide so they don't have to investigate it. You know what they're like.'

Eloise frowned and slowed the car, but she said nothing, so Holly carried on. 'What I want to know is, how can they properly identify her body if they can't get enough evidence? If she's this woman who's been missing for, like, decades, can they still get DNA from her hair and stuff?'

'Didn't I see that the police had already identified her? I'm sure I read a name in the news.'

Holly shrugged. 'I guess. But only because someone phoned them and told them who it was. It's not like they've done any real detective work, is it? But you know what I can't stop thinking about? The person who made the call must be the killer, right? One hundred per cent. So why alert the police? They've got away with it for this long. Why say something now? Why stoke it all up again?'

'It's strange,' said Eloise. 'Definitely strange. But I don't think we can assume that the caller and the killer are the same person.'

Holly snorted. 'How else would they know her name? It's not like someone stumbled across her and recognised her from a missing poster. And if they're not the killer, they know who the killer is, at the very least. All the police need to do is find out who made that phone call, and they'll find Elizabeth's murderer. It might be thirty years late, but there shouldn't be a time limit on justice. Elizabeth King's killer deserves all that's coming to them.'

Holly Bobs

Hey, Sally Ann, so, I found out LOADS. For one thing, the police had a tip-off they ignored before the dog walker found her. Is anyone surprised? Nope. Me neither.

If I were you, I'd be asking the police how they managed to miss her in the first place. Are they covering something up? Or covering up FOR someone?

About six or seven people were hanging around. I managed to get photos of all of them. None of them looked particularly dodgy. I ruled out anyone under the age of forty, as they wouldn't have been old enough when she disappeared.

And I was talking to this guy who seemed a bit of an expert in these things – I've told him about this page actu-ally because he might be of some use, so if anyone sees Ken on here, say hello – and he says there won't be much DNA after all this time so I don't know if you'll be able to find anything that links Elizabeth to her killer. Our best bet is to learn everything we can about her last movements. From that first newspaper article, it sounds like she lived near Nottingham. Is that right? Why was she in Cornwall? Did she have any links here? Are you sure she never made it to Wales? Patty, did you manage to get any leads on the Welsh boyfriend?

Marsha Pirolo

I hope this doesn't sound insensitive, but having eyes on the ground is so exciting. If you think it would help, I'll happily go to the place where the remains were found and see if I can sense anything from the departed soul. It goes without saying, I wouldn't charge my full fee.

Niki Hunter

I know there's a lot of pain and frustration here, but there are a couple of things to be mindful of. Firstly, the police still haven't confirmed that these are Elizabeth King's remains so let's not get ahead of ourselves. Secondly, we need to work with the police, not against them. They don't have the numbers to check out every phone call and anonymous tip-off. I'm sure they're doing their best.

Patty Hansen

Are you, Niki? Are you? The police will be covering their arses for sure. Elizabeth will only get justice if we do our own investigating. Talking of which . . .

Guess who I've found? Say *bore da* to Gavin Gallagher from Rhyl!!

Chapter 7

Eloise

Eloise turned up the volume on the radio on her kitchen window ledge. She tapped her foot and made circular movements with her hand as if it would speed up the newsreader. It had been two days since she'd driven past the engine house, and every day she'd listened to the local radio, desperate for an update while also praying that there wouldn't be one.

She'd checked all the news websites but was careful not to put anything into a search engine that might look suspicious if anyone were to investigate it – not that they would.

She would have spoken to Kit about it, but they'd barely had any time together, and whenever they found themselves alone, she couldn't find the words to broach the subject. Sometimes he looked at her in a way that made her think he knew exactly what was on her mind, but if he did, he didn't say. And the more time that passed, the easier it was for her to say nothing. Besides, it looked like the problem had simply vanished, much like Elizabeth had done thirty years ago.

On today's news, they'd mentioned the building of the bypass and shared their thoughts about the rise in parking charges, but there was no talk about the body in the old engine house. Yesterday's chip paper, as her grandmother used to say. Funnily enough, Eloise once saw her dad's face on the newspaper around her chips and battered sausage when she was around five years old. The neighbours talked about it for the rest of his life, so Gran turned out to be wrong about the longevity of these things.

She switched off the radio as a song came on, sampling something from her youth and passing it off as new music. She'd heard enough, or rather, she'd not heard anything, which was even better. She was losing sleep over the news article and the remains in the engine house. Panicked that the police would follow the trail back to her and her carefully curated life. No good would come of it. The only way she could maintain what was left of her sanity was to ignore the problem until it went away. So that was decided, then. She would stop listening to the news reports. What else was there to say? The dead couldn't tell tales.

Hearing footsteps overhead, she rolled her eyes. Holly had arrived an hour before Edward was due to get home from work and Eloise could hardly ask her to wait outside in the baking hot sun. Hold on. Could she? She shook her head. It was too late for that now. Since Holly had scared off that man in the big white car, and not asked any questions about why Eloise was driving that way home, she could hardly say no to her anyway.

Edward and Holly had been going out for eight months. It was the longest relationship Edward had ever had, but Eloise didn't think they were serious. Her son was so laid-back, it was hard to know what he was thinking. She

51

suspected the relationship had only lasted this long because he couldn't be bothered to end it. He'd be going to Sheffield soon, so the romance would reach its natural conclusion in a matter of days. She hoped the girl wouldn't be heartbroken. It wasn't that Eloise disliked Holly, but she didn't like anyone else being in her house. She felt like she couldn't quite relax, drop her guard, couldn't break into song and dance in the kitchen if the mood took her. She felt judged on what she cooked, how clean her oven was – all things Holly probably didn't even notice, but still . . .

She missed being able to laugh at silly jokes, in-jokes, and talking about things that outsiders wouldn't understand. Now they had to politely ask about each other's days and remember not to swear or put their elbows on the table. You'd think Holly would have become part of the family by now, but the girl wasn't easy to warm to. As his mother, Eloise thought Edward was the most handsome boy on the planet, but there was no mistaking the mismatch between him and Holly. She was into fashion and make-up, whereas he was the kind of person who still wore jumpers his grandmother had knitted for him and watched space documentaries for fun.

For the first time in over twenty years, it would be just Eloise and Kit in the house. It would be a lot quieter around here, that was for sure. First Meghan and now Edward. She wondered if she should get a puppy, but as soon as the idea popped into her head, she dismissed it. The local community pages on the internet were full of lost dogs, found dogs, and aggressive dogs without leads. That was an added stress she didn't need.

Though it wasn't ideal, she had to admit that she was looking forward to learning to be a couple again. They could take spontaneous weekends away, have meals out, and stay in bed all day if they wanted. It was a chance to get to know the people they'd become.

When they first met, she told Kit that if they were going to have kids, they had to promise they would always stay together and give the children a stable background. No running off to find themselves or falling in love with some-one at work. This was it. For life.

But once the kids had left home, would Kit feel the need to stick to their agreement? Because if they weren't being overinvolved parents, what were they – a pair of middle-aged empty-nesters marking their cards until retirement? Things were changing too fast, and Eloise hadn't prepared for this new chapter, which was unlike her because she usually planned for everything.

She placed her hands on the fridge door and bowed her head. Edward leaving home marked the end of their happy family set-up. She kept telling herself that going to university was an excellent opportunity for him. She herself had never had the chance. Her teenage years had been too chaotic to even consider her future. Survival didn't depend on grades. And she hadn't just survived, she had thrived. If her parents and sister could have seen her now ... well, they would never have recognised her, which was the point.

She opened the fridge and looked at the slim pickings. Half-empty jars of capers, mustard, miso paste and jam. A tub of crème fraiche two days past its best. A heel of Parmesan, lettuce, and an orange pepper that was showing its age. She assumed that Holly would be staying for dinner again, but all Eloise could conjure up was a pasta dish. And a side salad. She thought that maybe she had some garlic bread in the freezer. She was always amazed by how much Holly ate. She couldn't shake off the image of the girl as a locust, moving through the house eating all their food, depleting their resources, consuming her son; and of course, there was that other problem that Eloise had been ignoring in the hope that it would go away.

Though she wasn't above misplacing things and miscounting the coins in her purse, she was certain that items had been going missing from the house over the past six weeks. She could be scatty at times, but she was sure this wasn't down to her.

She'd looked for a simple explanation, but unfortunately, there was only one conclusion.

Holly was stealing from them.

Chapter 8

Holly

Holly sat cross-legged on her bed, a chair under the door handle, and read through her CV for the final time. Eddie had put in a good word for her at the café where he worked, but they said they were unlikely to replace him over the winter months. They did, however, say that he could have his job back when he returned home next summer. Eddie was one of those people who would always land on his feet.

Holly knew they should talk about what his going to university meant for their relationship, but she was too chicken to broach the subject. He'd told her that he'd be home for Christmas and that she should keep coming around to the house in the meantime because his mum would love to have someone to fuss over, but he obviously hadn't noticed the tension between them.

Holly liked his dad, though. Kit was possibly the sweetest man she had ever met, apart from Eddie. He was quieter than Eloise, a lot older, and had something to do with reopening one of the old Cornish mines. He could trace his family tree back through generations of miners, and it was the only subject she had ever heard him talk about at length.

That, and which were the best biscuits for dunking in your tea.

She pressed send on her email applying for an administrator role with the council, then logged into Facebook. Patty had done a great job tracking Elizabeth's old boyfriend, Gavin, from Rhyl. Holly had sent him a friend request, but luckily for her and anyone else interested in justice for Elizabeth, he didn't care much for privacy, so she'd already learned a fair bit about him. There was no helping some people.

His profile picture showed a grinning, round-faced man, squinting against the sunlight with the sea behind him. But who wouldn't be smiling if they thought they'd got away with murder? He worked for a construction company and coached a kids' football team on weekends. His profile said he was separated from his wife. Currently single, but in the market for women. He was in his mid fifties, had never lived anywhere but Wales and, crucially, he liked to holiday in Cornwall. What a coincidence.

Out of habit, Holly checked her sister's Facebook profile again. She knew there'd been no activity there for months, but that didn't mean anything. Lisa had given up on it ages ago. She was more of a TikTok person. Funny dances. Lip-syncing. Make-up tutorials. But she'd not posted anything there for three months either.

Holly clicked through the missing people pages she followed. Thankfully, there was nothing about Lisa on any of them. Perhaps it was time to craft her own post for the Truth Seekers page and hope that someone could help her in the same way that she was helping Sally Ann. There were plenty of resources out there if you knew where to find them. But the one thing that was stopping her from sharing Lisa's photo far and wide was fear.

As soon as she put this out there, she was admitting that Lisa wasn't off having the time of her life. She was admitting that she thought something terrible had happened to her sister. And as soon as she admitted that, she may as well admit that Lisa was already dead, because only a handful of these cases ever resulted in a happy ending after this long.

She was staring at Lisa's picture on the screen, wondering whether she should give it another week or try talking to the police again, when a notification flashed up on the laptop.

Gavin had accepted her friend request.

Chapter 9

Eloise

When Eloise heard Kit's key in the door, her shoulders relaxed and something uncoiled in her chest. From the first moment they'd met, Kit had always made her feel calm. Her friends commented that he had an aura about him, a presence that made you think everything would be okay as long as he was around. He was her rock, and she was the limpet that clung to him.

He'd been the DJ at the nightclub where she'd worked, though it was hard to imagine now. She'd often crashed on his sofa when she didn't fancy getting the night bus home. It was only a small thing, but the second time she'd stayed there, he had brought her a cup of tea in the morning, and he'd remembered how she took it. Strong, a dash of milk and sweet enough to give the dentist cause for concern. And he didn't once suggest she share his bed.

They'd been friends for months before they kissed on Polly Joke beach in the glow of the fire. She'd often sought out his company, but she hadn't seen him in a romantic way until that night. Firelight and cheap cider had a far better success rate than Cupid ever had. As soon as he leaned in for that kiss, she thought, 'Oh, so *this* is what I've been waiting for.'

At that time, she wore nothing but men's board shorts and band T-shirts, and never any make-up. She was surprised that Kit had even noticed she was a woman. Over the next two years, they'd split up and got back together more times than she cared to count. It was always Eloise who put the brakes on things. She hated the fact that she was falling for this man, hated how vulnerable it made her, but every time she tried to walk away, she found that the only person she wanted to talk to about her trust issues and her broken heart was Kit. Eventually she gave up fighting the inevitable.

She heard him throw his keys onto the table and kick off his shoes. She turned to greet him as he walked into the kitchen with his eyes glued to his phone screen.

'Hi,' she said. 'Why are you home so early?'

Kit jumped and took a step backwards. Recovering himself quickly, he said, 'Hello, love. I didn't realise you were home.'

Eloise wrapped her arms around him, smelling his familiar citrus scent and melting into him. 'Didn't you see my car out on the road?'

He looked back at the front door as if reimagining his journey from his car to the house. 'No, I completely missed it, but this is a lovely surprise. I wasn't expecting you back until six.' He leaned in for a kiss.

'I haven't had anyone in the gallery all day,' Eloise said. 'I closed at lunchtime. I thought we could walk down to the harbour and get a glass of something cold. I feel like I've hardly seen you this week, and it's such a gorgeous day.'

Kit glanced back at his phone before he slipped it into his shirt pocket.

'That sounds lovely, it really does,' he said. 'But it's been a long day, and I just want to crash out in front of the TV.'

'Oh.' Eloise tucked a strand of hair behind her ear and stepped away from him.

'If that's okay with you?' he asked. 'I've not been sleeping great, and—'

'Of course. No. An evening in front of the television sounds perfect. Who were you messaging?'

'What?'

'You were texting someone.'

Kit scratched the side of his nose. 'Oh. Just . . . work. There's a conference that I thought I'd managed to escape, but it looks like they need me after all. I'm seeing if I can make it work with my diary. Do we have anything on next week?'

'Apart from taking our son to university?'

'Oh,' he said. 'Yeah, I don't know whether I can do that now. Will you be okay to—'

'Kit,' Eloise said. 'This is important.'

'I know. I know. And I'm sorry. Let me see what I can do.'

Kit took a beer from the fridge as Eloise leaned on the kitchen counter.

'You didn't say why you're home early,' she said.

'I needed to use up some leave before the end of the year, so I took the day off,' he said. 'I'm sure I mentioned it?'

'Is everything okay?' she asked. 'You seem . . .'

'Yeah, sorry. I've been with Mum. Today wasn't one of her good days.'

'Oh, I'm sorry, darling. You should have said something. I would have come with you.'

'It was a last-minute thing. Besides, you do so much for other people that I thought I should take some of the load.'

'Were you there long?' Eloise asked.

'Most of the day.' He motioned towards the door with his beer. 'I'm going to grab a quick shower.'

After a moment, Eloise followed him out of the room. 'Kit?'

He was already at the top of the stairs.

'Yes?'

She studied his face for a hint of what he was thinking, but at that moment, she had never felt so unsure of him.

'I . . . I'm going to pop out for a bottle of wine. Do you want anything while I'm there?'

He shook his head. 'No. I'm all good, thanks.'

'Great. Okay then.'

'And sorry if I seem a bit off,' he said. 'By the time you're back from the shop, I'll be a brand-new man. I promise.'

'I'm perfectly happy with the old guy,' she said with a smile.

She watched him walk into their bedroom, then sank onto the stairs. A minute later, she heard the shower running. She knew that was where Kit did his crying; he didn't fool her. She knew everything about him, or she'd thought she did.

For one thing, she knew he hadn't spent the day with his mother, because Eloise had gone to see her on her way back from work and Kit hadn't been in all day. What she didn't know was why he was lying about it.

Transcript from local news station

Geoff: And finally, new information has come to light in the case of the human remains found in Cornwall over the weekend. Melody, what can you tell us about these developments?

Melody: Thanks, Geoff. I'm here at Ensley Mine, where you can see the distinctive silhouette of the engine house behind me. A familiar sight on the Cornish landscape, but no one expected it to be a scene of such tragedy. An anonymous caller identified the remains, discovered here at the weekend, as Elizabeth King, though police are yet to confirm this. Elizabeth was just nineteen years old when she disappeared on a cold February night while hitchhiking. No stranger to her local police, she had a record of petty theft and aggravated assault. Following an argument with her family, she stole money and was thought to have gone to Wales to meet with a boyfriend. Sadly, she never arrived. Many people are wondering just how she came to be in Cornwall.

Well, Geoff, in a shocking twist to the story, we're hearing that these remains have been moved to this remote location only recently. Though it certainly appears that the young woman has been dead for at least thirty years – tying in with what we know about when Elizabeth disappeared – she has only been here, in this ruined building behind me, for a few weeks at most.

What we have to ask ourselves is why would someone move her remains now, and why leave them here in this abandoned engine house?

It could still take some time for DNA testing to be completed, but whether or not this is the sad culmination of the search for Elizabeth, the police have opened a murder investigation and are currently looking into several cold cases to see if there are any links.

This is Melody Firewalker reporting for Southwest News. Back to you in the studio, Geoff.

Chapter 10

Eloise

'You're joking,' Eloise said. But from the look on Jan's upside-down face, it was evident that she was serious. Jan always was. 'When does she need to be out by?'

'And then slowly come back to standing position,' said Mimi from the front of the class. 'Imagine that you are stacking your vertebrae on top of one another, one by one, rounding your shoulders up to your ears, and . . .' she audibly exhaled, 'releasing them.'

As Eloise's head came up, she locked eyes with Mimi, standing at the front of the class with one eyebrow raised. Even above the ambient music and the cheap water feature at the back of the room, she had heard everything.

'Breathing in through your nose, take your arms back, and up and over, and stretch your fingertips to the ceiling . . .'

Exposed beams triangulated above them. Rusted hooks, a hangover from the loft's previous existence, reminded Eloise that this used to be a booming business back when the town relied on the fishing industry. The town still boomed, but for different reasons now. Students and holidaymakers were almost indistinguishable from the locals who had grown up here.

Feeling that she was gradually unravelling thanks to the events of the past week, Eloise had made sure she arrived in plenty of time for yoga this morning, but she'd still been too late to hear Mimi's news from the woman herself. Between sun salutations, Jan was trying to explain that Mimi had had a letter evicting her from the yoga studio.

'And on the out-breath, fold over and down towards your toes. If you can't touch the mat, soften your knees.'

Usually Mimi walked up and down correcting posture and reminding people to breathe, but today she needed her time at the mat as much as anyone.

For twenty years, Mimi had dreamed of her own studio. She'd eventually got the money to develop the old sail loft just as the pandemic hit. At first, she'd struggled, but it was finally breaking even. The building wasn't hers, but the rent was reasonable and wouldn't go up as long as she undertook the necessary renovations and didn't bother the landlord, Arthur. He said he was just glad someone could make proper use of the space. He'd turned down several offers from developers and rebuffed those who'd offered to pay a lot more to lease the space than Mimi could afford, but Mimi had charmed him with her energy and her plans to make this a proper community space. Arthur said he couldn't understand her love of green tea and green juice, but he knew a pure heart when he saw one.

'And this time, step your right leg back, and your left, into downward dog. Lowering into plank position. And on the exhale, bring yourself gently to the mat . . . up into the cobra pose, pushing through the floor to arch your back.'

Mimi had kept many of the old features of the sail loft, the patchy paintwork and the sliding doors. She'd only had to spend money on new floors and a kitchen. Arthur said the building was hers for as long as she wanted. They didn't need to bother with contracts and such.

And that was her first mistake.

'And now, moving onto your back . . .'

Eloise rolled over.

'. . . bend your knees, feet hip-width apart, and engage your core.'

She didn't tense the muscles that needed to be tensed, didn't suck her belly button into her spine, and she certainly did not engage her core. Though she heard every word Mimi said, she couldn't conjure the energy to do anything else except lie there. The sunshine was streaming through the high window, warming her bones, and she felt as if she was melting into the mat.

'With the palms of your hands flat on the floor at your sides . . .'

She had spent the past week in a constant state of high vigilance, poised to fight or flee, and now every muscle in her body ached. She had hardly spoken to Kit over the weekend, so was no clearer as to what he'd been doing that Friday. She could have asked him outright, sure, but if he was lying about where he'd been, she couldn't trust him to tell the truth when confronted. Instead, she'd busied herself with helping Edward shop for new bedding, towels and an air fryer. She'd slept fitfully, dreaming of her childhood home and people she'd hoped never to see again, lurking in corners like they'd been waiting for her.

The news that the remains in the engine house had only recently been moved there had unsettled her, but there was no one she could talk to about it. Not even Kit. Especially not Kit. And now she was on her own, trying to make sense of the news, and failing. She couldn't confide in her best friends, her husband or her children. She had done such a good job of creating the perfect persona that she couldn't tell them that everything was built on lies.

Kit had informed her that he was going away for that work conference he'd so casually mentioned on Friday. Until this past week, she wouldn't have thought to doubt him, but now she couldn't shake suspicion from her head. He wouldn't be around to drive Edward and his belongings to Sheffield after all, so the last time they would be together as a family would be at dinner on Wednesday night before Kit had to leave for the airport. She couldn't bear it. Every time she thought about their family disintegrating, she felt like she would be reduced to rubble. They held her together and gave her a purpose. What was she meant to do without them?

Eloise hated the fact that she was having to share her son with other people. She'd never been good at it. Growing up, she'd not had much to share. And it wasn't just because her family didn't have any money. Plenty of families were hard up but still managed to spoil their children at Christmas. Eloise and her sister would often get handouts from social services – dolls, and pretty notebooks with pencils and rubbers that smelled like someone's idea of a strawberry – but her mother would take them away and sell them down the pub before the tacky

67

decorations had even come down. And the few things she did have, which had been too old and worn to make money from, she'd had to keep hidden from her sister, because Deborah broke everything she touched. Eloise grew up knowing to hide the things you loved, or they'd be taken from you. Yet here she was, sending another child out into the world where she couldn't watch over them and protect them any more.

She'd been careful with her heart and could count all the things she loved on one hand. Edward, Meghan, Kit, Mimi and Jan. She would die to protect them all – or in Kit's case, she certainly wouldn't think twice before pushing him out of the way of oncoming traffic.

Things had been perfectly amicable between them, but every so often she caught him staring into space, his eyes glazed over, and now he was going away to a conference just as she needed him most. She was perfectly capable of driving Edward to university and helping him get settled in, but she couldn't believe that Kit was letting her return to an empty home with an empty heart. He'd always been in tune with her moods and her emotions, so how could he think she wouldn't need him now? ✓

She listened to Mimi's voice, the water and the music with images swirling through her mind. Why did life have to be such a challenge? It felt like everything was coming to an end – her time as a mother with children under her roof, her once strong marriage, and her freedom from her past mistakes. She'd barely had any time to think about what she would do next when she felt someone kick her sharply in the side.

She opened her eyes to find Mimi standing over her with her arms folded and Jan slightly behind her with her hand over her mouth.

The room was empty apart from the three of them.

'I suppose I should be flattered,' said Mimi. 'But next time, could you try not to snore?'

EL

Sally Ann

The police aren't saying much, but this is weird – apparently those remains haven't been in that engine house very long. They think that someone moved them there a month or two ago. What does that even mean???!!!

#JusticeForElizabeth #ForeverNineteen

Holly Bobs

I was just coming on here to ask about that! It was on the local news. How can they tell she's been moved? I don't understand!!

Ken Marchpane

Hello, this is my first time posting here. I met Holly at the site where the human remains were found and she invited me to join this group.

If it's okay to jump straight in – there are several ways the police might deduce that the remains have been moved. There could be evidence at the site of a body being dragged or carried. A forensic entomologist will be able to study the insects and larvae. From this, they can determine how long the person has been dead and the environment their body was kept in initially. The existence of different species of blowfly, for example, shows whether she has been kept in a warm or cold environment and whether it was urban or rural. Different stages of decay attract different necrophagous insects to feed on the body and lay eggs. I hope this helps. Kind regards, Ken.

Patty Hansen

I feel sick.

Andy Pickford

Just to be clear, Patty, you're happy to cyberstalk a woman and ruin her life for sleeping with your fella, but you draw the line at crime-fighting flies? Yeah, whatever. Women like you are the reason I'm single.

Patty Hansen

I seriously doubt that's the only reason.

Sally Ann

Thanks, Ken. I can't say I enjoyed reading that or understood half of it, but it was really useful. I hadn't realised they could do that. When you say they can use these insects to identify where the body has been kept for the past few years, how accurate can they get? For example, could they say that she was in Wales? (Are there such things as native Welsh insects?)

Andy Pickford

Yep. Welsh insects are easily recognisable. They all sing like Tom Jones and have an unnatural affinity with sheep.

Holly Bobs

See, I told you Ken would be helpful! (Hi, Ken. Nice to see you here, and please ignore Andy. We can only assume he was dropped on his head as a child.) And I know where you're going with the Welsh flies stuff, Sally Ann. Our friend Gavin is still looking like suspect *numero uno* to me too. I am ALL OVER HIM. I'm about the same age as Elizabeth was when she went missing. I'm going to see if I can jog his memory about what he was doing when he was my age – and who he was doing it with.

#JusticeForElizabeth #ForeverNineteen

Chapter 11

Holly

Eddie had given Holly a key to his house so that she could let herself in and shower, sleep or grab a sandwich while he was out working. He didn't like her being home when Liam was in the house, but her stepfather worked shifts and slept most of the day, so he wasn't hard to avoid.

Eddie's parents were out most of the week, and he was working every shift he could. His parents would help him with rent and food at university, but he'd have to earn his own beer money.

The Ford family looked perfectly well off from the outside – affluent even – with their art gallery and their two cars, but Eddie said the gallery was losing money and his dad's salary barely covered their bills and his grandmother's care costs. He'd seen his dad's credit card statement, and it wasn't pretty.

Holly tried to be sympathetic. Honestly, she did. But it always amazed her that people with a roof over their heads and multiple cars could consider themselves hard up. They didn't walk through Truro town centre eyeing up alleyways and doorways, wondering if they gave enough shelter to sleep in.

She made herself a peanut butter sandwich and a coffee with one of those pods in their fancy machine. Despite everyone being out of the house during the day, she wouldn't have a chance to come here once Eddie left. For one thing, they'd notice that the good dunking biscuits were missing.

In the past three weeks, Holly had applied for fifteen jobs. She could do maybe eleven of them, had relevant experience for possibly four, and had heard back from precisely none of them. She was starting to get desperate.

Over the past couple of months, she'd been rehoming things the Fords didn't need and wouldn't miss. She needed to sell them to make enough money for suitable clothes for a job interview – assuming she ever got one. She'd started with some dusty old vinyl she'd found in a box in the attic. The Stone Roses, Jamiroquai, Blur. She'd checked every room in the house and the Fords didn't even own a record player. Those albums were now bringing their new owners joy and had earned Holly some cash. There were no losers here.

Occasionally she found loose change in coat pockets or in messy piles on window ledges. She'd found a bag of clothes by the back door. The note on the plastic said to leave the bag outside on Tuesday for a cancer charity to collect, but that was weeks ago, and it had never reached the kerb, so Holly was doing Eloise a favour. She'd got a fair bit of money for those clothes on Vinted and was now ready to shop for some suitable work clothes.

This would be the last time she would get a chance to search through Eddie's house for buried treasure. She finished her sandwich, wiped the plate, and returned it to the cupboard. She took her coffee with her into the room at the back of the house, which could've been called a conservatory if it had been tidier but was partly a dumping ground and partly an art studio. Holly had never seen Eddie's mum with a paintbrush in her hand, but apparently she was a gifted artist. She used to sell paintings and prints from a market stall in Truro and did a roaring trade at the Christmas craft fairs.

She picked her way over boxes until she was standing in the middle of the room. She moved a basket of laundry, waiting so long to be ironed that the season to wear those clothes had passed and was close to coming around again, and opened a cardboard box full of Christmas decorations that had never made it back into the loft. She smirked at the Santa and angels that Eddie and his sister Meghan had probably made at school. Eloise didn't strike her as the tender-hearted type, but she hadn't thrown away any of her children's artwork or cards. When Holly had searched her bedroom drawers last week, she'd even found two small boxes of children's milk teeth marked *M* and *E*. She found it surprising that Eloise was so sentimental.

She was looking for items that Eddie's family never used and wouldn't miss. Something so insignificant that by the time they noticed it was gone, Holly would be long forgotten and only referred to as that ill-mannered girl their son used to date. By her reckoning, it took people precisely three months to forget she'd ever existed. Three months since her sister had left. Three months since her college friends stopped inviting her to join them for drinks. Three months.

75

Which meant that Eddie would have forgotten all about her by the time that toilet-roll angel was back on top of the Christmas tree.

She sat on a pile of cookery magazines, her knees almost up to her chin, and sipped her coffee. From her new vantage point, she could see a brown case under the sideboard. She reached in and dragged it out. It was dotted with dust and mould. There was an address label on it in the name of Christopher Ford. So that was what Kit was short for. She clicked the catch, and it sprung open to reveal six battered handbags, two pairs of shoes, and piles of photographs in frames.

She reached for the bags. Two were crocheted, two looked like leather, and two were cheap and shiny, but nice enough. She thought she'd be able to get some money for these. She slid the case back under the sideboard and stood up, looping the bags over her arm. She heard her phone buzz and placed her coffee down on the box of decorations as she checked the notification. Her screen was cracked, but she could still read most of the messages, and there, across the top of her phone, was what she'd been waiting for. A message from Gavin, Elizabeth King's Welsh boyfriend. He'd been reluctant to chat at first, but she'd lied her way into his confidence, and now it was time to find out what he knew about Elizabeth.

She felt a thrill course through her. She had sent him a message saying that she recognised the beach in his holiday photos and that she didn't live far from there.

His message read, *Went down in the van this summer for a few days surfing to clear my head. I go to Cornwall every summer. Do you surf? Perhaps next time, I should give you a buzz.*

Swapping her phone from one hand to the other, she wiped her sweaty palms on her jeans. He'd admitted to coming down to Cornwall and having a vehicle big enough to transport human remains wrapped in carpet. Surfing was the perfect cover. Holly couldn't work out why he had decided to move the body now, after all this time, but what did it matter? She had confirmation that he had been in Cornwall with a van at the time that Elizabeth was left in that engine house.

I'd like that, she typed. *But before you do, I need to ask you something. It's kinda sensitive.*

She waited. And he waited. She could see that he was still online. She was wondering how to broach the subject of Elizabeth when he responded. *What is it? You can ask me anything.*

She was getting excited now and was already imagining how she would triumphantly tell Sally Ann and the others on the Truth Seekers page that they'd only gone and cracked the case. Honestly, she didn't know what the police were doing. This was easy.

Were you a football coach in Rhyl in the early nineties?
Yeah. Why?

There was no doubt about it. He was definitely the right person.

I'm just going to come out and say it. I'm looking into Elizabeth King's murder. She was on her way to visit you when she disappeared. Can you tell me anything about what happened?

His message came back immediately. *I have no idea what you're talking about. I don't know anyone called Elizabeth.*

I think you do.

77

Nope, he replied. *You've got the wrong person.*

Holly sighed. He wasn't going to make this easy for her. *The police questioned you about her disappearance in 1994.*

I don't know why anyone would have thought she'd come to see me. We were only together for a week, the summer before. It meant nothing.

She smiled to herself. *So you did know her then? Maybe you've seen the news – her remains have been discovered in Cornwall, not far from where you were on holiday. Coincidence? I think not.*

There was a long pause, and she thought he wasn't going to respond.

I've told you I have no idea what you're talking about. Don't contact me again.

Immediately, he went offline, and Holly was left staring at her phone.

Holly Bobs

Have I got some SERIOUS updates for you guys??!! Sally Ann – we've got him. We've actually got him!!! Thanks to Patty's skills tracking him down, I sent Gavin a friend request and we've been chatting over the past few days. Here's what I've learned so far.

1) he is definitely Elizabeth's ex

2) he came down to Cornwall on holiday THIS SUMMER

3) he drives a van that could easily transport A BODY!!!

Sally Ann

Oh my days. That's amazing. I can't believe it. The power of this group blows my mind. I don't know what to do with that information. Should I go to the police? I don't want to do anything unless we're absolutely sure.

Holly Bobs

Yeah. I mean, we've done all the hard work for them now, but they'll take the glory. I'll send you the screenshots of Gavin's messages to show them. Tell them I'll talk to them if they want.

Andy Pickford

Not wanting to piss on your parade or anything but have you any idea how many men went to Cornwall with vans this summer? I bet half of them know someone called Elizabeth. Good luck convicting the poor mug on the back of that evidence.

Holly Bobs

Thanks for explaining that to us, Andy. What would we do without you?! He got really defensive when I asked him about her. At first he said he didn't know her and that I'd got the wrong guy, but then he let slip that they'd only had a week-long fling, told me never to contact him again and blocked me. Classic guilty behaviour.

Patty Hansen

Give the police the info and let them take it from here. Happy to have played a small part in bringing this scum to justice. Imagine how many other cold cases we could solve. #ForeverNineteen #JusticeForElizabeth

Andy Pickford

Solve? We've not solved anything. We have a guy who met the dead woman when he was younger. He drives a van and goes on holiday to Cornwall. Hardly cast-iron evidence.

Look, I'm not trying to be a dick here. I admit this bloke is our best lead, but you can't go around accusing people without proper evidence. As far as I can see, our man Gav doesn't have a clear motive. Maybe he wasn't happy that a holiday fling turned up on his doorstep, but that's no reason to kill her. We need some forensic evidence to link them. Have we got anything more from our resident mad scientist? Earth to Ken. Come in, Ken.

Niki Hunter

Andy's right. This is harassment and I will be no part of it. I am leaving the group immediately.

Patty Hansen

Ta-ra! Don't let the door hit you on your way out.

Niki Hunter

I mean it.

Patty Hansen

And yet you're still here. I hate it when people Announce and Flounce. Just leave already.

Ken Marchpane

I agree with Andy that this is circumstantial evidence at best, but it puts Gavin in the right place at the right time. The last anyone heard of Miss King was when she was on the way to see him. That doesn't prove he was the last one to see her, but when you put all the information together, it certainly does make a compelling case. She had no links to Cornwall as far as we know, so there was no reason for her to be here. But this means nothing without forensic evidence linking Miss King to Wales and Gavin. Kind regards, Ken.

Holly Bobs

Ha! In your face, Andy! Ken thinks we're on the right path. So what if plenty of people have vans and come to Cornwall? Not all of them are Elizabeth King's ex-boyfriend, are they? Please keep us posted, Ken.

And Sally Ann, will you let us know what the police say? If our investigation leads to a conviction, I think we should do more of this kind of stuff. In fact, I have another case I wouldn't mind your help with. This one's a bit closer to home, though.

Chapter 12

Eloise

At 3 p.m. Mimi called an EGM. For the rest of the world, EGM stood for Extraordinary General Meeting, but to Jan, Eloise and Mimi it meant Everyone Gather at Mimi's. It was an unmissable, drop-everything-at-once call to arms.

Eloise shut the shop early again and rushed to the yoga studio. The gallery was too quiet, giving her too much time to think, so she was glad of the opportunity to focus on someone else's problems for a while. When she arrived, Mimi was finishing a mother-and-baby class, and Jan was sitting at their usual table with her shoes off and her swollen ankles on display.

'Any idea what this is about?' Eloise asked.

'She was meeting with her solicitor today,' Jan said. 'It's probably about the eviction. I've ordered us a couple of iced teas. Hope that's okay?'

'Perfect.'

'How are things with you? Any more news on that dead friend of yours?'

'I told you she was just someone I used to know, not a friend. And no, I've not seen anything else in the news, but then I've not been looking, so . . .'

A large group of women moved through the studio in unison. Some had babies strapped to them and others had strollers. Two of them stopped by the café.

'What about you?' asked Eloise. 'What's new?'

Jan pointed at her ankles. 'This heat is making me swell up like a balloon animal. I've started keeping my underwear in the freezer.'

Mimi emerged, waving goodbye to someone, and made a beeline for Jan and Eloise.

'Good,' she said. 'You're both here.'

'I wasn't aware we had a choice,' said Eloise.

Mimi sighed and rolled her eyes. 'I have to be out by mid December. Three months.'

'They can't do that,' said Jan.

'Three months' notice is pretty standard,' said Eloise.

'Just because it's standard doesn't make it right,' Jan replied.

'Technically, they only have to give one month, so three is, as my solicitor told me, "more than generous".'

Wendy brought over their drinks and slipped away without a word. Eloise mouthed, 'Thank you.'

She took a sip of her iced tea. 'What does Arthur say about this?'

'Not a lot. It's his nephew who's driving the sale. He's only been in Cornwall for a couple of months, and let's just say he's making his presence felt.'

Jan sat back in her seat and folded her arms. 'Are you sure there's nothing we can do to stop it?'

Mimi shrugged. 'That's why I called you here. I want ideas. Anything you've got, no matter how ridiculous it sounds.'

'The only reason this building and land is worth anything is because of what you've done here. Do you get any of that money back if Arthur sells up?' Eloise asked.

Mimi looked away. 'I'll ask him about it when he comes in. He'll be here any minute, but I think I'm screwed.'

'And to be clear,' continued Jan, 'we're *not* allowed to call him a daft old twat or throw rotten fruit at him?'

'He's eighty-nine years old,' said Mimi.

'I didn't hear the word "no",' said Jan to Eloise. 'Did you?'

'I can't imagine Arthur going to his solicitor and then still coming in here every day as if everything's okay,' Eloise said. 'Does he understand what's happening?'

Mimi shook her hair out of her eyes. 'Like I said, Joseph is behind this. He's become very interested in his uncle's assets lately. Do you know what worries me the most? It's who is going to look after Arthur if I'm not here. He has never had to pay for a cup of tea or a toasted teacake even though he comes to the café three or four times a week. I've even offered him free classes, but he says there's no way he'll be able to get up off the floor once he's down there. Oh, there's an idea. I wonder if I could offer chair yoga for elderly people or those with injuries and mobility issues?'

Her shoulders sagged and she slapped her hand to her forehead. 'Think, Mimi! Of course I can't. Because I won't have a studio by Christmas, will I? God, I can't quite keep the idea in my head, you know? I could kill Arthur. Even though I love the daft old git. And let's not forget that I take him shopping every Thursday morning. Which, if I'm being honest, is really rather taxing because he stops to talk to every damn person in the shop. Do you know I once got a parking ticket for spending so long in Sainsbury's car park? That's how long he takes, but it's his only trip out, and you don't see Joseph taking him, do you?'

Eloise rubbed her friend's arm. 'I know this sounds trite, but we'll sort something out. We're going to put our heads together and come up with a plan. You'll see.'

Mimi's head jerked up and she got to her feet. 'They're here. I'll try and make them see sense while you come up with ideas.'

She walked to the other side of the café, but Eloise didn't turn to look. She couldn't bear it. She wasn't just upset for Mimi. This was her sanctuary too. She'd grown used to coming here every week. She was sure she would be able to find somewhere else to drink coffee and catch up with her friends, but she felt protective of this place. Perhaps it was just another sign that everything good in her life was coming to an end. Soon there would be nothing left for her here.

Today, the sun's heat was oppressive and uncomfortable. The geraniums in their terracotta pots smelled sickly. Something in the kitchen was burning and it caught in the back of Eloise's throat. A fly circled her head, dodging the back of her hand as she swiped at it.

'What do you think?' Jan asked. 'We must be able to block the sale of this place if we kick up enough of a stink.'

'Arthur stands to make a lot of money from it,' said Eloise. 'He might need to adapt his home so he can stay in it, or pay for carers, or a nursing home. We don't know his situation. We might be better off helping Mimi to start again somewhere else.'

'Or,' said Jan, 'maybe we could raise funds to help her buy it off him? Then he still gets the money, and she gets to stay.'

Eloise looked over her shoulder. 'Maybe. But it's going to be expensive.'

Mimi was talking to Arthur, who was sitting with his hands clasped over his walking stick. He looked frailer than usual. A tall man, whom she took to be his nephew, stood too close to Mimi as if he were trying to intimidate her.

Eloise's view was suddenly blocked by Wendy. 'Who's the dipshit with the attitude?'

'We think he's Arthur's nephew,' Jan said. 'Joseph.'

'And it's true that he's kicking us out?' Wendy asked.

'That's his plan,' said Jan. 'He's got developers interested, but we're not going to take it lying down. We need to help Mimi get the money together to buy this place. Maybe some sort of fundraiser? Get local news on it?'

Wendy nodded. 'Great idea. I really don't want to lose another job. Hey, there's a basket of lost property in reception that we can sell. An iPhone, yoga mats, a glass eye . . . We can have an open day and get the local paper to cover it. Something about local businesses being squeezed out while the fat cats destroy our towns. Make such a fuss that it'll put pressure on the developers to back out. What do you think?'

'Actually, I think that's a bloody brilliant idea,' said Jan.

Eloise got to her feet. 'I'm up for anything, but while the two of you brainstorm, I'm going to go and lend my support to Mimi. I don't like the look of that guy.'

Holding her iced tea to her chest, she sauntered across the café, listening to ice clink against the glass. As she got closer, she could hear the tall man saying, 'My only concern right now is that my uncle is well looked after and—'

'I am looking after him!'

'You're not even paying the going rate for renting this property. He was lucky I came along when I did.'

Eloise quickened her pace and didn't slow as she neared him. She bumped into his back and upended her ice-cold tea down his lilac shirt. 'Whoops,' she said.

The dark-haired man spun around to face her. 'You have got to be kidding me,' he said.

Eloise took half a step backwards. 'Oh,' she said. 'It's you.'

'Don't you ever look where you're going?' he asked.

She tried to smile, but on this occasion, there was no doubt that the accident was entirely her fault.

'Nice to see you again,' she said. 'I hope you managed to avoid whiplash this time.'

Chapter 13

Holly

Holly sold four of the handbags within twenty-four hours. The largest one went for thirty pounds, and the other three sold for fifteen each. She thought she might keep the final two. One was well-worn soft brown leather, the other crocheted with red tassels.

She'd been into town and got some black trousers, white pumps and a fitted pink shirt with black stitching. And now she had something to wear for that interview with the council. God, an actual interview. She was so nervous. Maybe Eddie could give her some tips when she saw him later. She'd bought him a going-away gift. It wasn't much. Just a photo of the two of them in a frame. It was a bit cheesy, and she hadn't yet decided if she would give it to him. Imagine giving him a gift like that, only to be dumped minutes later.

They still hadn't talked about whether they were splitting up the moment he left or if they would try and make it work every other weekend. If he asked for her opinion on the subject, she would tell him that it was clear they had no future, and yeah, whatever. If they happened to bump into each other when he was back for Christmas, it would be okay to see him, but she wouldn't sit around pining for him. But if he just so happened to beg her to try and make this long-distance thing work, well . . . she might be willing to give it a try.

She froze as she heard footsteps coming up the stairs. The handle turned, but she knew the door couldn't open. After a moment or two, a fist banged twice.

'Hols? Are you in there?'

She held her breath. Liam had to know she was in the room, because the door was locked with a chair under the handle. There were only so many times she could tell him she must have had her headphones on when he knocked. The door juddered as he tried to open it, and then she heard his footsteps move away. In fairness to Liam, he'd never raised a hand to her. Lisa had taken the brunt of that because she'd reminded him of their mother.

Holly almost couldn't bring herself to think about her mum because the pain was too much to bear. Crying about her wouldn't bring her back. Staying in bed wouldn't make the hurt go away. The sad fact was that she didn't know if there was anyone left in the world who loved her. To Liam, she was an inconvenience. Her dad was long gone, her mum was dead, and for all Holly knew, Lisa was too. As for Eddie, well, he probably didn't love her to begin with. It wasn't even as if she had friends who'd known her since primary school and loved her like a sister. She told herself she didn't mind. Fewer people in her life meant fewer people who could abandon her. One day she would be self-sufficient, but first she needed that job with the council.

Through an old school friend, she had heard about a room in a shared house becoming available at the end of

October. It was being held for her, tentatively, but she needed to prove she could pay the rent every month. She'd promised she was good for it, but they wanted to see confirmation of a monthly income before they would agree it was a done deal.

Once she was sure Liam had gone downstairs, she stood before the mirror and held the red bag against the pink shirt. Nope. She grabbed the brown leather bag and slung it over her shoulder. It could do with a wipe, but it would do. She needed to fill it with the kind of thing a perky admin assistant would take to an interview. Purse. Notebook. Pen. Tissues. Phone. Lipstick. The bag's lining was frayed, and the lipstick disappeared into the abyss within seconds. She rooted around for it and ended up turning the bag upside down and giving it a shake. The lipstick sprang free, but Holly wondered whether anything else might be hidden there, lost for years. A cheeky tenner, perhaps? A winning lottery ticket? She felt the pockets and the lining, and sure enough, something was lurking in there.

She pulled it out, disappointed to see it was only a tatty piece of green paper. When she unfolded it, she saw that it was an old driving licence. It took her a moment to realise what she was looking at. The address was unfamiliar, but that wasn't what struck her.

The name rang a bell.

Holly sank to the floor. 'Holy shit.'

She was holding Elizabeth King's driving licence.

Sally Ann

UPDATE: The police ruled Gavin out of their investigations years ago. I don't know if we've discovered enough to convince them to view him as a suspect again, so we're back to square one.

I suggest we post Elizabeth's photo all over social media. Please share her picture far and wide, especially if you have contacts in or around Cornwall. Maybe we can jog someone's memory. Someone knows something. They've been sitting on this information for thirty years. It's time for it all to come out into the open.

I can't let this go. I feel we're getting close now.

#JusticeForElizabeth #ForeverNineteen

Holly Bobs

We were definitely wrong about Gavin then? Do you think your aunt made it to Cornwall and was killed here? Because if you do . . . God. Can't believe I'm typing this. I *might* have found some evidence to back that up. I'm just not sure what it means yet.

Sally Ann

Really?? What is it? It looks like Wales is a red herring, so let's get Elizabeth's name and face everywhere in Cornwall. Let me know what you've found, hun!!

Holly Bobs

I don't want to say too much at this stage, but if I'm right about this, it could be a HUGE breakthrough. If I'm wrong, I could ruin someone's life.

Sally Ann

Absolutely. I get it, but don't leave me hanging. This is really important. We have to find out what happened to Elizabeth. Have sent you a friend request. DM me immediately!

Chapter 14

Eloise

For eight hours, Eloise couldn't see out of her rear-view mirror. Duvets, pillows, bags and boxes were crammed into every space. Though Holly didn't take up much room physically, her uncharacteristic silence filled the car.

Eloise hadn't wanted the girl to come with them, but what was she meant to do? Leave her at the side of the road when they stopped for a quick toilet break? Well, apparently not. Edward said that wasn't kind or funny and that she should be ashamed of herself for joking about it. It was sweet of him that he thought it was an attempt at humour.

But in the end, she had to admit that the additional pair of hands had been useful. Holly and Edward had carried all the boxes across the car park, the campus and then up three flights of stairs while Eloise unpacked clothes and books before making Edward's bed and slipping a fuzzy old teddy bear called Fidget under his pillow. He might be six feet tall with a patchy beard, but he would always be her baby.

The room was just as she had expected a single room in halls of residence would be. There was a bed without a headboard wedged in the corner, a good-as-new desk, and a squatting lamp that reminded her of the beginning of a

Pixar movie. Shelves ran the length of the neutral-painted room at head height, only stopping at a wardrobe so narrow you'd have trouble hiding in it. The carpet had seen better days, and the implausibly small sink in the corner barely had room for a toothbrush behind the taps, but all things considered, it was better than she'd had at eighteen. It was all Edward would need until he found a group of friends he could rent with next year, somewhere off campus. Eloise felt her stomach clench at the thought of these new relationships with people she didn't know. She envied him this new beginning, if not his well-used mattress. Understandably, he was nervous, but this could be the start of something amazing.

From the window, she watched students and parents stooping under the weight of boxes and cases. She was sad that Kit wasn't here to settle their son into his new life. She didn't know what was wrong with him. She could guess, but she didn't like the answers. She had to entertain the possibility that he was having an affair. But maybe that was preferable to thinking that his mood had something to do with Elizabeth King. Had he heard the news? Did he think everything was about to come crashing down around their ears? He had to know that she wouldn't let that happen.

She plucked a peace lily from a cardboard box and smoothed the shiny leaves. She didn't know why she'd bought it. Edward had never been into plants, but perhaps it would make his room look more like a home, and maybe he'd occasionally peer at it through a pounding hangover and remember that, to keep the peace, he needed to call his mother.

95

She was just wondering where to put it when the door opened and Edward came in carrying a crate of beer. He was sweating with the exertion of carrying it up the stairs as he dropped it onto the end of the bed.

'This is the last of it,' he said.

Eloise wondered how a young man of eighteen years old could be so unfit. She'd suggested, quite forcefully, that he join a sports team while he was here. His PlayStation pallor was out of place against the rugged teens she'd seen in the corridors.

'Is this okay here, do you think?' she asked, squeezing the white-speared plant onto a bookshelf. 'Do try and remember to water it, won't you.'

'Yeah, I think I should manage your expectations here, Mum. That's never going to happen.'

'Plants are like mothers,' she said. 'Oh, they're hardy enough and can cope with being ignored for a while, sometimes for weeks, but the time will come when they wither without attention. Some people say it helps if you talk to them.'

'Mothers or plants?'

'Both,' said Eloise.

'Got it,' Edward said with a smile that had always melted her heart.

'What have you done with Holly?' she asked.

Edward lifted the crate off the bed and onto the floor, where it hit with a thud. He scratched the back of his head as he stood tall. 'She said she'll meet you by the car in an hour but I'm to text her if you need longer than that.'

'Really? Why?'

'She thinks you might want to spend time with me with-out her hanging around. You know, so you can say goodbye properly. Tell me how awesome I am. Sob and wail. That kind of thing.'

'That's . . . incredibly nice of her.'

Edward flopped onto his bed and yawned. 'You still don't like her, do you?'

Eloise began rearranging Edward's books. 'I wouldn't be me if I didn't wonder whether she had a hidden agenda.'

'I think she just wants some time to herself,' he said. 'She's going to miss me. I am pretty awesome, you know.'

'Yes, you've told me that before.'

'By the way, she was asking a lot of questions about Dad, so you'd better watch out that she doesn't set her sights on him next.'

Eloise turned to him. 'What kind of questions?'

'I'm joking, Mum,' Edward said. 'She's not his type.'

'Seriously, though, what kind of things was she asking?'

'Where he grew up, where he worked . . . She seemed really interested in the mines, that kind of stuff.'

Eloise sat beside him. 'I'll be sure to keep an eye on them. Since you brought it up, what *is* going to happen to your relationship now that you're here?'

'I don't remember bringing it up,' he said.

'Good job I'm here to remind you.'

Edward sighed. 'I think we've split up.'

'You *think*?'

'We said we'd see each other around, so I guess that's . . . it. We agreed that I can't keep returning to Cornwall every other weekend, and she can't afford to make the trip up here. I need to make new friends, and though we didn't say the actual words, it felt like we were saying goodbye.'

Eloise patted his arm. 'It's for the best, darling.'

'Is it? Because I feel really shit.'

She leaned back against the wall. 'All break-ups feel bad. Even the ones where you know it's for the best. Even when that person has let you down or lied to you, or if the relationship was good but has just run its course. It's painful because either you're hurting, or the other person is, or the future you'd been so sure of has been snatched from you and it feels unjust. But you'll get over it. You're young, handsome and charming. I'm sure you'll meet someone better in time.'

'It's not just that,' he said. 'I feel guilty that I'm excited about my future and she's . . . well, she has nothing to look forward to. Could you maybe check on her from time to time?'

'Absolutely not,' said Eloise. 'I don't plan on seeing her ever again after today.' She thought about the money that had gone missing from the house over the past few weeks. 'I won't miss her, that's for sure. And don't feel guilty. If she cares about you – and for what it's worth, I think she does – then she'll want what's best for you. Although . . . for all we know, she's making the most of her spare hour by crafting an effigy out of your chest hair.'

Edward pulled at the neck of his T-shirt and glanced down. 'Nope. All five hairs present and accounted for.' He smiled before adjusting his glasses. 'Good luck with being stuck in the car with her on your own all the way back to Cornwall, though.'

Eloise looked up to the ceiling. 'That's going to make for an interesting journey. Why did you bring her all the way here if you knew you were going to break up with her?'

'She said she had nothing better to do, and I didn't have the heart to say I'd rather she didn't, so . . .'

'You will stand firm, won't you?' Eloise said. 'Make it a clean break. No messaging or Snapchat, or whatever it is you do. Don't string her along. Please don't respond to her texts. I promise you it's kinder that way. I love you, Edward, but if you mess that girl around, I will give you a thick ear.'

Edward smiled. 'And here's Holly thinking that you don't like her.'

Eloise smiled too, and stroked his hair. 'This isn't about whether I like her or not. It's about you doing what's right. I admit I'm glad to have her out of our lives. I never really warmed to her.'

'You don't say.'

'She reminds me a bit of myself when I was that age, and I didn't like myself very much back then. Given the hand I'd been dealt, I did the best I could, but I was brutal in pursuing what I wanted, and people got hurt because of it. I've spent my whole life making up for that.'

'When are you going to stop?' Edward asked.

'Stop what?'

He took off his glasses and cleaned the lenses with his T-shirt. 'You always try to be so perfect and have these impossible standards that the rest of us will always fail to meet,' he said.

Eloise folded her arms. 'No, I don't. I have high standards for myself, but I don't . . . at least, I don't think I put that on you, do I?'

99

'Maybe not intentionally. But we all feel it, Mum. Don't you ever get sick of it? Isn't it tiring being perfect?'

He said it with a smile, but his words hit Eloise hard. She never intended to set unrealistic standards for others. Quite the opposite. She was the only one who ever fell short. She was the only one she judged. Okay, no, that was a lie. Her biggest fault was being quick to judge others, though she was rarely wrong, so maybe it was her superpower.

Edward was mistaken about her wanting to be perfect, though. It was never about perfection. It was about safety. All her life was about staying safe, staying in control and creating order from the chaos. It was the only way she could breathe freely. He was, however, right about one thing – it was incredibly tiring.

She just had to wait a little longer for this thing with Elizabeth King to die down, and then maybe she could finally relax and set her mind on perfecting the art of imperfection.

Transcript from an interview with
Amy Thomas and Sasha Walters

Interviewer: Do you want to start from the moment you heard the news that Elizabeth's remains had been found?

Amy Thomas: Yeah, so, we saw something on the news and—

Sasha Walters: Actually, I heard it on the radio first, didn't I? And I called you up and—

Amy: Yeah, you called me and were like, 'Oh my God, have you heard about these remains they've found in Cornwall?' Sasha loves these true-crime cold cases, see?

Sasha: I do. I love them.

Interviewer: And what was it about the article that caught your eye?

Amy: Do you want to . . .?

Sasha: Okay. Well, I heard that the police had found these remains of a girl who'd been missing for thirty years, but then I heard that someone had moved her recently, and I thought, 'Well, that's a bit odd, that is. So I went on the internet to see what I could find out because, as Amy says, I love all those true-crime podcasts and like to see if I can solve them, see? At first, none of it jogged my memory or anything, I just felt sad for the girl. Poor thing was only nineteen. And then they said that she was on her way to Wales when she disappeared, and that's where we're from, so I thought, 'Oh, that's interesting.' Then they said that her body was found in

101

Cornwall and I remembered how we went to Cornwall for Amy's hen do back in '94, and then it hit me.

Amy: It did. It hit her. And that was when she phoned me.

Sasha: It was. I recognised her photo. All that mad black hair she had, and eyeliner. Not a lot of girls looked like that in Rhyl, I can tell you. She was sleeping in the waiting room at the coach station when we got there. It was like six-thirty in the morning, and she was shivering.

Amy: It was absolutely bloody freezing. There were eight of us—

Sasha: Well, there were meant to be eight of us, but Sheila—

Amy: Don't get me started on Sheila.

Sasha: So anyways, we get talking to her while we're waiting to get on the coach to Newquay, and she's upset because some pathetic excuse for a man—

Amy: Is there any other type?

Sasha: Well, she'd come to see him, but he'd already taken up with this other girl, so we said, 'Look, why don't you come with us to Newquay because Sheila bloody Brookes isn't coming, is she, and you may as well have her coach ticket.'

Amy: I can't believe I asked her to be my maid of honour.

Interviewer: You asked Elizabeth King to be your maid of honour?

Sasha (laughing): Oh my God. Can you imagine?

Amy: No, I asked Sheila Brookes to be my maid of bloody honour, but to be honest with you, I may as well have asked a complete stranger for all the good it did me.

Interviewer: So you met Elizabeth King at the coach station and asked her to go to Cornwall for your hen party?

Amy: Yeah, and I didn't expect her to come if I'm honest. Who agrees to spend the weekend with a bunch of people they've never met before? But she said she knew someone down there, so . . .

Sasha: Got to hand it to her, though, she was fun at first. Wicked sense of humour. But after a few drinks . . . well, she was a sloppy emotional drunk, and she latched onto us like nobody's business, didn't she? She was quite . . .

Amy: Intense.

Sasha: I thought we could drink, but that girl . . .

Interviewer: And when was this exactly?

Amy: Two weeks before my wedding. So it'd be the last Friday in February.

Interviewer: Can you tell me exactly what happened that weekend?

Sasha: It was what you'd expect from a hen weekend really. Amy had a veil and L-plates and we played daft games. I thought Wales was wet, but that weekend in Newquay . . . There was nothing else to do but stay inside and drink.

Amy: Look. We were drunk, all right? We couldn't be expected to babysit everyone.

Sasha: What Amy's saying is that we left the club and went for chips. It took a while for anyone to realise she wasn't with us.

Amy: She wasn't there the following day to get the coach back to Rhyl either. But she'd said she had friends in Cornwall, so I guess we assumed she'd hooked up with them. I mean, I did wonder if she was okay, but I felt a bit rough from the sambuca, and I was trying hard not to throw up.

Sasha: Not being funny, but you should've tried harder.

Amy: I apologised at the time, Sash.

Sasha: God, the smell . . .

Interviewer: And the last time you saw her was in the night-club on the Saturday night?

Amy: Yeah, about eleven, maybe? Not that late.

Interviewer: Did you notice her talking to anyone in particular?

Sasha: Only the DJ. She got into a bit of a spat with him about the music he was playing. Said it was all a load of . . . well, it was mostly Britpop and she wanted the Cure and the Smiths and all that miserable stuff.

Amy: I've got some photos here if you want to see them. She's not in many, but you'll see what we mean about the hair.

Interviewer: So as far as you're aware, Elizabeth King stayed in Cornwall?

Sasha: To be honest with you, I thought she'd met a fella.

Amy: Right? She was nursing a broken heart, and everyone knows that the quickest way to get over a man is to get under one.

Truth Seekers UK

Sally Ann: Thanks for all your help with Auntie Elizabeth. Those two women from Wales only came forward because of the local news coverage and everything we shared online. Patty found Sasha on Facebook (honestly, Patty, you are amazing! I can't thank you enough – and it has reminded me to be more careful with online security!!). They've spoken to the police, but I'm not holding my breath. We still need to keep pushing for answers.

#JusticeForElizabeth #ForeverNineteen

Ken Marchpane

According to my contact, forensics have confirmed that the remains are that of a female who has been dead for approximately thirty years. She was aged between sixteen and twenty-five at the time of death. Preliminary investigation shows she was kept somewhere cold and damp – possibly a cellar or outhouse. There is coal dust present on the carpet. So far, they have been unable to ascertain how she died. There were no distinguishing marks or jewellery. After this amount of time, they are unlikely to be able to find much more than this. Kind regards, Ken.

Sally Ann

Sasha emailed the photos of Elizabeth from the hen weekend. Please share them. We need to know if anyone saw her after she left that nightclub, or if they saw her leaving with someone.

Andy Pickford

What about the Welsh girls your aunt was with? Were they hot, too?

Patty Hansen

Reported.

Andy Pickford

It's violating community standards to say a woman is attractive now, is it? What a sad, sad world we live in.

Sasha Walters

Hello!!!!! OMG. I can't thank you enough for letting me join this amazing community. I see you've already read the interview that me and Amy gave. I couldn't believe it when Patty got in touch. Honestly, if there's anything I can do to help, please say. I feel just awful that we didn't make sure Elizabeth was safe before we left the nightclub. I've got a daughter that age now, and if anything happened to her . . . Sally Ann, can I talk to your mum and explain what happened? Or Elizabeth's parents if they're still alive? I just want to apologise. I'll never forgive myself for leaving without her.

Sally Ann

Oh, bless you, Sasha, that's so kind. Elizabeth's parents died not knowing what had happened to her. It's just my mum now, and this whole business has stirred up a lot of unwelcome memories for her. Mum and Elizabeth didn't have a great relationship. They had a huge argument the night Elizabeth disappeared. When she's ready, I know she'll want to chat with you, but can we leave it for now, hun?

Sasha Walters

Okay. If you're sure xx

Sally Ann

Right, so we know Elizabeth was last seen alive in Cornwall. Thanks to Sasha, we know it was in a nightclub called Bertie's in Newquay, talking to the DJ. Maybe we could track him down? Patty, can you do your magic to find out who the DJ was in 1994? Holly, you said you might have a new lead, but you still haven't accepted my friend request. Can you tell us more? I feel like we're getting close now.

Patty Hansen

I'll find that DJ. Trust me. Tracking down Gavin and Sasha has given me the boost I needed. It's been a long time since I felt like I was doing something that mattered, you know? Since my man-child of a husband walked out, I've hardly left the house. I never see anyone in real life. This hunt for Elizabeth's killer is helping me as much as it's helping you. To say I'm happy to help is the understate-ment of the century.

Chapter 15

Holly

Holly and Eloise had been driving for an hour before they stopped at a service station for something to eat. The sat nav said they would be home by midnight, and Holly was toying with the idea of asking Eloise if she could stay in Eddie's room for the night. Perhaps she'd be able to find more evidence to link Kit to Elizabeth or other young women.

She was still trying to get her head around the possibility that Eddie's dad was a murderer and the bags were trophies and . . . Oh God, what would she tell him? She didn't want to tear his family apart, but she had to get justice for Elizabeth King. She was going to find answers for Sally Ann and her mum, and then one day maybe the universe would reward her and give her some answers of her own.

Much as she tried, she couldn't come up with an innocent explanation for why a dead woman's bag was hidden in their house. She hoped the answer was as simple as that Eloise had picked it up in a second-hand shop. If that was the case, Holly could ask her which shop she'd found it in, and then she would take the bag to the police, because this could be the kind of evidence that could lead to them finding Elizabeth King's killer. But even as the thought crossed her mind, she knew that it was a coincidence too far. Kit Ford knew something about Elizabeth's disappearance, and maybe Eloise did too.

Holly had done her research. One hundred and seventy thousand people were reported missing in the UK each year – one every ninety seconds. Many were found within a month. Some disappeared without a trace, but according to the Missing Persons Unit, some were discovered and never identified. There were over six hundred nameless bodies waiting for someone to claim them like lost luggage.

Holly took a seat at an empty table halfway between WHSmith and Burger King, watching pink-eyed people rush to empty their bladders and refuel on carbs and sugary food that would only make them more tired, then get back out on the road before that lorry they'd passed half an hour ago managed to get ahead of them.

Eloise slipped into the immovable plastic chair opposite. 'I got sandwiches and crisps. I hope that's okay. There wasn't much choice.'

'Thanks.'

'And a Coke, because if I'm going to be awake for the next God knows how many hours, you are too. We need to stay alert.'

'Sure.'

While Eloise had been saying goodbye to Eddie, Holly had been reading the interview with the two Welsh women who'd been among the last to see Elizabeth King alive. Sally Ann had posted the link on the Truth Seekers Facebook page, and now it was all anyone was talking about.

Holly had been so sure that Gavin was guilty. Everything had stacked up. He knew Elizabeth, he'd been to Cornwall over the summer, and he had a van to easily transport a dead body. But as Andy had pointed out in the Facebook group, Gavin had no motive. The two women in the interview had taken Elizabeth to Cornwall and left her there. There was no reason for her to return to Wales or for Gavin to follow her to Cornwall. This meant that Elizabeth King had stayed in Cornwall, and not long afterwards, she'd been killed – which brought Holly back to the driver's licence, in a bag inside a suitcase with Kit Ford's name on it.

Now, when she thought about her boyfriend's kindly dad, his friendly nature seemed unsettling, his silences calculated and ominous. What did she even know about the man? He was the kind of person neighbours would say kept himself to himself.

'You and Mr Ford,' she said suddenly. 'When did you two get together?'

Eloise ate a prawn cocktail crisp while she thought. 'It was . . . 1996? No. The summer of '95. We were quite young. Well, *I* was. He seemed quite sensible and grown up at the time. But I suppose compared to me, everyone was.'

Holly nodded. 'And how long after that did you get married?'

'Oh, not for a few years. We split up a couple of times because I was young and foolish, so it took a while for us to get to the same place emotionally.'

Holly couldn't believe she was seriously considering the possibility that lovely, kind-hearted, biscuit-dunking Mr Ford was a killer.

'How well did you know him? I mean, you got on well with him and had known him for a few years by the time you married, but how could you be sure what kind of person he was?'

Eloise was looking at her with her head tilted like a confused dog.

'What I mean is, did you live with him first?' Holly asked. 'Or speak to his ex-girlfriends? Ask his parents questions about his past?'

Eloise laughed. 'I know you've been applying for jobs recently, Holly, but some things in life don't require two references. Thank God. I think you know when someone is good. Or good for you, at least. I don't think the past is necessarily a reliable indicator of someone's future. Just because they've done something they're ashamed of doesn't mean they will repeat that pattern. Sometimes it's the exact opposite. It can drive them to make amends and right those wrongs ten times over.'

Holly took a sip of her drink. Was Eloise hinting that she knew about her husband's dark past? Was it possible she knew what he was capable of, yet she'd married him anyway? She remembered the day she had seen Eloise by the engine house. Perhaps she had already known about Elizabeth, and that was why she was there.

Eloise motioned towards Holly's untouched sandwich. 'Aren't you going to eat that?'

Holly pushed away her tray. 'Not hungry.'

Eloise sighed. 'Ah. I see.'

'You do?'

'All these questions about Kit and me . . . Well, I think I can guess what's on your mind.'

111

Holly's throat was inexplicably dry, and she took another swig of Coke. 'You can?'

'Holly,' said Eloise, 'you're still a teenager. You have your whole life ahead of you. This is not the time to settle down. You and Edward are too young. Maybe in the future, when he's finished his studies—'

'I'm not talking about me and Eddie,' Holly said.

'You're not? Then what's with all the questions about—'

'Look, I'm just going to come out and say it. I think it's better to be direct, don't you? The thing is, I found something, and I think Kit . . . Mr Ford . . . I think he's hiding a secret. A big one. And, well, if it were me, I'd want to know. But now you've got me wondering if you already know. And if you do, I suppose the question is, what are we going to do about it?'

Holly looked at Eloise's startled face. This was turning out to be one of the worst days of her life, and considering everything else she had going on, that was saying something. If Eloise didn't know about her husband's seedy past, this was going to be a very uncomfortable conversation, with life-changing repercussions. And if she did know, she would likely deny it and get angry with Holly for bringing it up. Either way, Holly's big mouth was about to get her stranded in a motorway service station hundreds of miles from home.

'What are you trying to say, Holly?'

She tightened her grip on her bottle of Coke. 'I guess I'm asking if you're ready to admit the truth about your husband.'

Truth Seekers UK

Patty Hansen

Hey everyone. No joy tracking down the DJ yet, but we're getting closer. The manager of Bertie's told me to go away. FYI, these were not the words he used, but I don't want to get a Facebook ban for inappropriate language. I thought the Cornish were supposed to be all scone-making, pasty-baking, apple-cheeked sweeties, but so far all I've been met with is sarcasm and attitude – and if I'm honest, it only makes me like them more.

The manager – Bertie Big Balls – said they didn't keep electronic records from the nineties, and when I pushed him for paper copies, he told me it was a breach of GDPR. Like that even existed back then!! Anyway, I told him that he was protecting a murderer and he got all defensive and hung up on me.

Next, I joined a Facebook group about how Cornwall used to be so much better 'back in the day', and I asked for memories of Bertie's from the early to mid nineties. I used those photos Sasha gave us of Elizabeth at the hen party to see if I could jog a memory or two. Unfortunately, none of the pictures shows our guy, but one woman says there was a DJ called Chris who was free and easy with his disco balls back then (if you know what I mean). I'm looking forward to seeing where this one leads. Will keep you posted.

Let me tell you, though, that club sounds like a hoot. I think we might need a field trip to retrace Elizabeth's steps. We could take flyers with her face on them to see if anyone remembers her. What do you all think?

I'm also looking at the cost of getting T-shirts made up with 'Truth Seeker' across the back in big, bold letters and on the front a small logo on the top right saying '#Forever19'. Any thoughts?

Andy Pickford

Hold your horses, love! No one said this was going to be a real-life group. The whole point is that we don't have to leave the comfort of our bedrooms! I'm totally up for some merch, though. Can mine be a hoodie?

Patty Hansen

Tell me you still live with your mum without telling me you still live with your mum . . .

Marsha Pirolo

Love it! Yes please to T-shirts, but I don't see what we'd gain by going to that nightclub with flyers. The people there now won't be the same people who were there thirty years ago. They'll all be too old to go clubbing now. You'd be better off going to the local bingo hall!

Sasha Walters

Erm . . . None taken!

I'd be well up for a trip back to Newquay. I can show you where we went on the hen weekend. There was a cracking little café near the beach. It was lush. Shall I set up a Google poll to see if we can find a weekend when everyone is free? (Maybe the T-shirts should say 'Truth Seekers On Tour'??!!)

Chapter 16

Eloise

Pins and needles rushed up Eloise's neck and prickled her scalp. Holly had asked her the million-dollar question. Was she ready to admit the truth about Kit?

Was she?

The short answer was no, she wasn't, but she couldn't stand the thought that Holly knew something about him that she didn't. Or maybe she did know. She'd certainly had her suspicions. The lies about where he had been, the distant behaviour. They'd barely talked or touched in weeks. All the signs pointed to an affair, but she wasn't ready to hear the confirmation.

'Eloise,' said Holly. 'Did you hear me?'

Eloise wanted to press pause on the world. Take a moment, a breath, a break. She dabbed at the sweat on her top lip.

'Yes, I heard you,' she said. She thought it was probably too late to pretend that she had no idea what Holly was talking about. It was better to face it head-on. 'And I think I know what you're going to say.'

'You do?'

'I've had doubts, sure, what with this conference he's at

and the way he's been acting recently. I just never thought he'd be the kind of man to . . .'

She couldn't say the words 'have an affair'. It was too humiliating. 'Do you have proof?'

Holly shook her head. 'Not absolute smoking-gun proof, but yeah, I did find her handbag in your house.'

'In our . . .' Eloise put her head in her hands. 'Christ.'

'I'm so sorry,' said Holly. 'I don't know what else to say.'

'Do you . . .' began Eloise. 'I don't think I want to know the answer, but do you know her name?'

Maybe she didn't want to know who it was. A name, a face, and this would all be too real. She'd have to track the woman down, and then there was the whole issue of who she would slap first – Kit or his mistress.

Holly nodded. 'Yeah, and so do you. It's that girl whose remains they found. Elizabeth King.'

Eloise felt the floor drop away and grabbed the table's edge. 'Sorry? I didn't quite hear that.'

'Her name was Elizabeth King. That's why you were at the engine house. You suspected something, didn't you?'

Eloise's voice cracked. 'No. That's . . . I think we might be talking at cross-purposes here.' She blinked hard, but her vision was still blurred.

'I was looking in your cupboards and under beds and stuff,' said Holly. She stopped and suddenly looked at her fingernails. 'The reason for that isn't important right now.'

'I know you've been stealing from us, Holly. You're not that subtle.' Eloise wiped her eyes with the back of her hand, too overwhelmed to confront the girl over the missing items.

Holly at least had the decency to blush. 'I only took things you didn't need,' she said. 'Just some old clothes, and you had a shit-ton of old records cluttering up your attic.'

'Kit used to be a DJ,' Eloise explained. 'That collection is his pride and joy.'

Holly's eyes lit up. 'Oh, now that makes sense. Was this in Bertie's in Newquay?'

'What has that got to do with anything?' Eloise asked. 'We're talking about you stealing from us.'

Holly snorted. 'That's the least of your problems. Anyway, the point is, I found a case with Kit's name on it, and inside I found some old handbags. And in one of those bags, I found Elizabeth King's driving licence.'

Eloise tried to take a deep breath, but her whole body was shaking.

'You see what this means, don't you?' asked Holly.

Eloise put her hand over her eyes. She could hardly believe this was happening. She sat back in her chair, folded her arms and looked to the ceiling as if calling on a higher power for strength. 'And you've put two and two together and decided . . . what?'

'Isn't it obvious?' said Holly. 'Mr Ford had something to do with her death. Maybe he was the one who phoned the police. Maybe he couldn't take the guilt any more, so he had to come clean.'

Eloise shook her head. 'Oh Holly. You have no idea what you've done.' She groaned. The story was meant to lose momentum and peter out. Not be picked at and pored over.

'You stupid, stupid girl.'

Holly smoothed her hair over her shoulders. 'Hey, I've not done anything except expose a killer. I'm not going to apologise for that.'

Eloise let her hands drop to her lap and looked around the cavernous room at the people scurrying by without the faintest clue that her life was unravelling. How could she explain this to Holly without giving everything away?

'You're wrong,' she said, shaking her head. 'Just wrong. Kit isn't capable of something like that.'

'Then what—'

'Kit didn't hurt Elizabeth King. I'm certain of that, so can you just drop it?'

'But you said you suspected him.'

'I did,' Eloise groaned. 'I do. But not of . . . *that*. I thought you'd seen him in a sordid embrace or heard him on the phone declaring undying love to some woman.'

Holly grimaced. 'Shit! An affair, too? He's had us all fooled, huh? I thought he was a lovely bloke, and I don't like that many people.'

'He *is* a lovely bloke,' said Eloise. 'One of the best. Usually.'

'But he's not, is he? I'm sorry,' Holly said, leaning in closer, 'but you got off lightly. The worst thing he's done to you is sleep with someone else. Elizabeth King wasn't so lucky, was she?'

Eloise put her head in her hands. If she was going to tell anyone about Elizabeth, it wasn't meant to be her son's ex-girlfriend, but she couldn't let her think that Kit was a killer.

'He's not a . . . He isn't capable of what you're suggesting.' She glanced around to check that no one was eavesdropping.

Holly looked at her pityingly, as if she was the poor wife who was the last to know.

'Really, Holly,' Eloise said. 'You have to trust me on this one. Please let it go.'

'You tell yourself whatever you have to, to get through the day,' Holly said. 'But this is too big to keep to myself. Unless you can give me an innocent explanation for why Elizabeth King's stuff is hidden under a cabinet in your house—'

'Please,' said Eloise. 'You don't know the full story.'

'Explain it to me then. I'm part of this true-crime group and we will solve the case of Elizabeth King with or without your help. I'm doing you the courtesy of telling you first because you're Eddie's mum. You might want to get home and clear out your stuff. Leave Kit before this story hits the news. Because it is going to hit big.'

'I can't let you do that,' Eloise said. 'As well as accusing an innocent man, you'll look like a complete fool.'

'I don't have a choice. Your husband is a murderer.'

Eloise leaned across the table. 'I am one hundred per cent certain that my husband did not kill Elizabeth King,' she hissed.

'Really,' said Holly, folding her arms. 'And how can you be so sure?'

'Because . . .' Eloise took a sip of her drink, but it spilled down her chin. 'Because,' she went on, wiping her mouth, 'I'm Elizabeth King.'

Part Two

Part Two

Chapter 17

Eloise

Holly had sworn for five blue minutes, hardly drawing breath, while Eloise told her repeatedly to calm down, be quiet and stop causing a scene. Eventually Eloise suggested they drive to where it all began, and she dragged Holly away from the people listening hard to every word while pretending they weren't.

After sitting in stunned silence for a further thirty minutes, Holly asked, 'Who else knows that she's you, and you're her?'

'Kit knows I used to be called Elizabeth, but he doesn't know the whole story about why I had to change my name and start afresh. Until a couple of weeks ago, I thought I'd left that old life behind. And if you think about it, I'm not Elizabeth, not really. The person I am today is completely unrecognisable from the person I was back then. If an old school friend passed me in the street, I swear they wouldn't know me.'

'I can't bloody believe it,' said Holly. 'I mean, shit, that's mental. Whose remains were in the engine house then?'

'I don't know.'

'Why would someone say it's you if it's not?'

'No idea.'

'Who killed her?'

'Your guess is as good as mine.'

'That's so messed up,' said Holly. 'So if they're saying those remains are you ... was it *meant* to be you? Does someone out there think they killed you?'

'I ... I don't know. I'd not really considered that.'

'I bet they'll be pissed off when they realise that they killed the wrong person. Why would they want you dead? *Who* would want you dead? Damn, Mrs F, this is wild.'

Eloise shook her head. 'You're getting carried away. For a start, we don't know that woman was murdered or if it was meant to be me.'

'Of course she was murdered,' said Holly. 'And unless you have a better explanation for why an anonymous caller gave your name, they definitely thought it was you wrapped up in that carpet.'

Eloise didn't have a better explanation, but she was sure she would eventually work it out with enough thought, Post-it notes and brightly coloured pens.

'Maybe we shouldn't overthink it,' she said. 'It might be a simple mistake. They've got the remains of someone who died thirty years ago, and they remember hearing about a woman who went missing around that time. You can see how they might've arrived at the conclusion that the two events were related.'

'Nah,' said Holly, shaking her head. 'No offence, but who even remembers that you disappeared? Especially after all this time. They must have a link, or at least some knowledge of you.' She put her hand to her mouth. 'Damn. When they work out that it's not you in that engine house, will the killer come after you? Because if they wanted you dead thirty years ago . . .'

Eloise braked hard and slammed the car up a kerb. Holly had to brace herself against the dashboard. 'Holly. Could you just . . . not. Okay?'

Holly sighed. 'I'm just trying to help.'

Eloise pursed her lips. 'I'm having some difficulty getting my head around everything that has happened recently,' she said. 'If you hadn't accused my husband of being a killer, I wouldn't have told you anything about this. Don't make me regret admitting who I used to be.' But the truth was, she had regretted it as soon as the words left her mouth.

She turned off the engine and looked out the window. They were parked outside a bank of semi-detached houses. To all the world, they looked like happy family homes. A trike was lying on its side by the front steps. Rose bushes hung their heavy heads in respect above neatly trimmed flower beds. A pair of children's shoes stood pigeon-toed on a low wall. Through the open car window, Eloise could hear children playing football on a parched square of grass at the far end of the street, just as they always had.

'Where are we?' asked Holly.

'My childhood home,' said Eloise.

'Until today, I'd always thought you were Cornish.'

'I've lived in Cornwall most of my life,' said Eloise. 'But no, this is the city that raised me and made me who I am today.'

Holly raised one eyebrow. 'That's not the selling point you think it is.'

'Come on,' Eloise said. She hauled herself out of the car and pressed her hands into the base of her spine. The drive had stiffened her back, but Holly accusing Kit of murder had stiffened her neck, shoulders and resolve. Despite being annoyed with him for his recent behaviour, she still loved that man like no other, and she would do anything to protect her family. She always had and always would.

Holly got out of the car and stood by Eloise. Somewhere in a neighbouring street, an ice cream van played a familiar tune, and Eloise could almost feel scabs on her knees and pigtails streaming out behind her from a time she'd all but blocked out.

'What's that smell?'

Eloise sniffed the air. 'It's not as bad as it used to be. There's a chicken factory down the road.'

'When you say "factory" . . .?'

'Abattoir.'

'Eww.'

'There were days when the wind was blowing in the wrong direction that the stench was almost unbearable, but you get used to it after a while.'

'Okay,' said Holly. 'I'm guessing dead chickens weren't the only reason you left this place, though.'

'No. You have to remember that I haven't spoken about any of this in a long time. I never expected to hear the name Elizabeth King again. I feel like . . . like it's almost impossible to recall my childhood. It physically hurts to think about it. My heart right now . . .' Eloise put her hand on her chest.

'Don't go having a heart attack on me,' said Holly. 'Eddie won't forgive me. What was your childhood like?'

Eloise took a minute to consider her answer. It would have been too easy to say it had been traumatic, but there were happy memories too, and that was what made it so difficult.

'You'd have liked my dad,' she said after a moment. 'Everyone did. He had a story for every occasion, was always quick to laugh, and always believed he was *this* close to making his fortune. There was nothing he wouldn't do to make money, except, that is, get an actual job.' Her face softened as she thought of him.

'He was many things, my dad, but unfortunately he was mostly a small-time criminal. He was in and out of prison a lot. I hated what it said about our family, because it didn't matter how good my school grades were or how polite and kind I was, when your dad's inside, the whole family is scum. You need to work twice as hard as everyone else to get half the recognition. The worst thing was, it made Dad go after the next scheme with even more determination than before. I used to get so mad, but he said that "one of these days" he'd get away with it, and all those failed attempts would be chalked up to experience.'

'Shit,' said Holly.

'This estate was rough back then. Really rough. Not like it is now. There were few ways to escape the hand you'd been dealt, so he did what he thought he had to do. Despite what the neighbours might have said, he was a good man.'

'And your mum?' asked Holly.

'Mum? Oh, she was a grade-A bitch. A cruel, heartless, selfish woman whose bitter outlook on life poisoned her from the inside out. She died the year I left home, and I'm just sorry she didn't do it sooner.'

'Oh,' said Holly. 'If it's all right with you, I'll take back my earlier "shit" card and play it here instead.'

'Fine,' said Eloise. 'But you might want to make that card reusable.'

'And laminated?'

'Sure. Why not.'

'Are you, like, totally messed up by your childhood then?' Holly asked.

'Of course not. I'd never let the past define me,' Eloise lied. 'I suppose Dad being in prison was hard, but Mum's cruelty was worse. I shouldn't complain, because I turned out okay, considering who my role models were, and my kids have turned out better than okay. Brilliant, in fact, so . . . I guess I did it. I broke the cycle. I'm proof that you don't have to repeat your parents' mistakes. I've got my issues, sure, but it could be worse. Maybe I wouldn't be as focused on my children if I hadn't been badly treated. Who knows? Maybe my parents did me a favour.'

'Do you believe that?' asked Holly.

'Not for a second,' said Eloise. 'It was easier to forgive my dad because he was at least doing what he thought was best, even though he inevitably made things worse. Mum only did what suited her. She was a woman who should have never been allowed to raise kids. And, you know,' she continued, 'I look back on it now and shudder, but it wasn't that uncommon at the time. We weren't the only kids scared to go home at night. We never felt like we were completely alone. There was a kind of comfort in knowing that there were secrets behind every one of these doors.

'Does it freak you out being back here?'

Eloise nodded. 'More than I expected it to.' She'd thought she'd feel sad, maybe scared, but she wasn't prepared for the guilt she felt looking up at her old bedroom window. Was she wrong to have left when she did? Should she have stayed and faced the music?

Next door to her old house, a door opened, and a woman shouted, 'Oi! What do you think you're doing?'

Holly stepped forward before Eloise could speak. 'It's okay. My friend knew the family who used to live here. We're just taking a trip down memory lane.'

'Oh really?' said the woman. 'Is that right? You're all coming out of the woodwork now, aren't you? Ghouls trying to find dirt on that poor girl . . . Well, shame on you. Lizzie King died of a broken heart after what happened to those girls, and that's all I know, so bugger off.'

She slammed the door, and Holly and Eloise exchanged a look before smirking.

'Well, she's nice,' said Holly.

'She's new,' said Eloise. 'There used to be three brothers living in that house.'

Holly kept watching the closed door. 'Who's Lizzie King?' she asked.

'My mum.'

'What did she mean by "what happened to those girls"? Did someone else go missing when you did?'

Eloise shrugged. 'Who knows? Like I said, she's new. Shall we stretch our legs in the park before we get back in the car?'

They walked away from the twitching curtains and the uneasy past without saying a word, but Eloise's mind was spinning. Despite her assertions that no one would recognise her, she half expected someone to stop her in the street and say, 'You've got some nerve coming back here.'

So much felt the same as it had ever been, yet everything was different. As a kid, she'd stayed out later than the others, who'd been called in for tea and bath time. It was just her and Deborah, making mud pies in the park until they couldn't feel their fingers.

Holly jumped on the graffitied roundabout and spun around, hanging backwards off the bars with her eyes closed. Then she ran towards the swings, peppering the air behind her with dust. Eloise watched as she bounced over the bare earth. There were times when Holly seemed wise and mature beyond her years. This was not one of those times.

Despite having split from her boyfriend and finding out that Eloise had lied about her identity for years, the girl was decidedly upbeat. Perhaps it was the relief of finding out that Kit was not a killer and knowing she didn't have to take it upon herself to bring him to justice. Or perhaps she was just a kid doing what all kids do when they're in possession of gossip hot enough to burn a hole in their tongue.

No matter how Eloise looked at it, there was very little for her to feel optimistic about. Confessing her identity to Holly had come at a price, and she was struggling to separate the person she was today from her past mistakes. Now she would have to address all the questions keeping her awake at night instead of pushing them back into the darkness where they belonged.

Contrary to what the papers were saying, she hadn't gone missing under mysterious circumstances. As far as she knew, no one had looked for her day and night, wondering what had become of her. The news report said she had stolen money before leaving, but she hadn't taken anything that wasn't hers, despite what her mother might have thought. It was more likely her mum had gone to the police to report the loss of cash rather than the loss of a daughter. If there had been a missing person report, she'd never heard about it. If anything, she would have been classed as a runaway. She wouldn't have been surprised to find the police had been looking for her to interview her about what had happened that night, but not because anyone was worried about her.

Holly's question about whose remains had been found in that engine house had been the same one that had been going around Eloise's head on a loop since she had first heard the news. She wondered how long it would take for the police to realise that the bones belonged to someone else entirely. Another missing girl. Someone else's daughter.

She crossed the dusty park towards Holly on the swings, her shoes scuffing against the dry earth. She was suddenly more tired than she had ever been, but she was too wired to sleep. They would have to get a hotel now rather than push through the night to get home. She didn't care whether it was a two-star or five-star establishment as long as there was chocolate, wine, and a pillow for her heavy head.

The park was smaller than she remembered, and the sky felt oppressively close. If she'd been shown a picture of this place, she never would have recognised it. She sniffed the air. In her memories, her childhood had been lived exclusively in the winter months, and the air had always been

131

thick with the comforting smell of coal smoke. Now, it seemed lighter, and all she could smell was barbecues, sun-baked earth and only the faintest hint of abattoir.

Holly arced back and forth, the metal chains clunking every time the swing changed direction.

'Why are you so happy?' Eloise asked.

'I wouldn't say I was happy, just . . . yeah, actually, happy will do. It's a mystery solved, isn't it? "Hey, Holly, what happened to Elizabeth King?" Well, I'm glad you asked. She married, had two kids, opened an art gallery and went to yoga with her friends on Mondays. Mystery solved.'

'Okay,' Eloise said uncertainly. 'It's probably best to keep it between ourselves for now, just until we work out what's going on.'

'What happened to make you leave this place?' Holly asked. 'Got to be something really juicy for you to leg it and change your name, right?'

It was one thing for Eloise to admit to who she was, but quite another to admit to what she'd done.

'What's that quote about the past being a foreign land?' she said.

'Were the police after you? Are you on Interpol's Ten Most Wanted list? Oh my God, is there a bounty on your head? How much money could I make from turning you in?'

Eloise rubbed her eyes and mascara came off her lashes in clumps. 'I'm not a criminal mastermind, Holly. I was a kid who did some stupid things and decided to start fresh some-where else. As far as I know, the police weren't after me. There was this big party one night and I decided to treat it as a going-away party. I left shortly afterwards and never came back. It's that simple.'

'Right,' said Holly. 'I don't buy it. Someone with a link to your name turned up dead a few miles from the town where you ended up living, hundreds of miles from where you fled from. You can't tell me anything about this is simple.'

Sally Ann

Has anyone heard from Holly? She said she had a lead on Elizabeth's Cornish link but hasn't been online since. I'm starting to freak out. Sorry to ask, Patty, but can you do your magic and track her down through her Facebook profile? Does anyone know her real surname? I remember her saying that she didn't live far from the place where Elizabeth's body was found, so that gives us an area to start looking, but I don't know what else to do.

Patty Hansen

Sweet Jesus, you're right. She's not been active on here for a couple of days. Leave it with me and I'll see what I can find out. I know we've ruled out Gavin Gallagher as a suspect in Elizabeth's murder, but Holly had been communicating with him online. Could he have tracked her down to stop her talking?

Andy Pickford

I don't know how comfortable I am with this. It's one thing investigating the Welsh douche-canoe but entirely another invading the privacy of one of our own. It's only been a couple of days. It is possible that Holly – unlike you lot – has an actual life.

Sasha Walters

Honest to God, Gavin Gallagher is my nephew's football coach. I know his ex-wife from Zumba!! I'll pay him a visit and see what I can find out. OMG, this is scary but exciting, like we're real-life private investigators.

Patty Hansen

Be careful, Sasha!!! Take someone with you. If Gavin is behind this then he could be a threat.

Sally Ann

Absolutely. Don't put yourself in any danger, Sasha. I'll never forgive myself if anything has happened to Holly because of this. WE MUST FIND HER. For all we know, she could be with the killer right now!

Chapter 18

Eloise

When she'd fled from Nottingham in the middle of the night, Eloise had planned to lie low in Wales. Unfortunately, when she got there, she'd found Gavin with another girl, and she had nowhere else to go. It was a stark and sobering moment when she realised there was no one she could turn to for help. She was on her own, and no one cared if she lived or died. In the space of six months, she had become everything she hated. She was just as bad as everyone said she was. Worse.

She'd been at the coach station, wondering how long it would take to die of hypothermia, when a hen party had found her. Until that day, she'd not believed in God, but she'd thrown a weak prayer to the heavens asking for a sign. She hadn't expected it in the form of a gaggle of girls going to Cornwall. What were the chances that their friend had bailed at the last minute and there was space on the coach? And so these angels with penis-adorned deely bobbers instead of halos took her to Newquay, where she ultimately decided to stay and get a job.

She'd met Kit in a nightclub and changed her name to Eloise by deed poll, and the rest – as they say – was history. For thirty years she thought she'd escaped her past, and the repercussions that came with that. When those remains had turned up in Cornwall, and everyone started talking about Elizabeth King as if she was a much-loved and sorely missed daughter who had been killed and left in the ruins of an engine house, she'd known she would eventually have to face what she'd done.

'I'm not saying you're right . . .' began Eloise.

'God forbid,' said Holly, rolling her eyes.

'. . . but on the off chance that I was the . . . intended victim, it is important that we keep all this between ourselves. At first I only wanted to keep it quiet so that no one discovered my less-than-wholesome past, but you've got me thinking.'

'Well, think harder,' said Holly. 'Unless you can work out who those remains belong to and who put them there, you don't know who wanted you dead.'

'Maybe no one wanted me dead.'

'You want to take that risk?'

Eloise stroked the chunky chains of the vacant swing next to Holly. She used to spend hours here pursuing dragons and princesses, flying through the clouds. She sat down and pushed backwards, letting gravity bring her back again.

'How much does Kit know?' Holly asked.

'Kit? Do you mean my husband the killer?'

Holly laughed. 'God, that sounds mad now, doesn't it? Sorry about that.'

Eloise sighed. Whatever her husband's faults, he could never physically hurt someone.

'He thinks I changed my name because Elizabeth was my mum's name and I didn't want anything to do with her, and that's half true. I don't understand why parents name their children after themselves. Narcissism at its finest. Mum was always known as Lizzie, but I insisted on being called Elizabeth. Kids said I was up myself and had ideas above my station, thinking I was the Queen of England or something, and with the surname King . . . well, I was an easy target, wasn't I? Kids called me "Your Royal Highness", and I threatened to send them to the Tower and chop off their heads.'

Her swing was gathering momentum now, moving in the opposite direction to Holly. As they passed, she said, 'I became Eloise by accident. I went for a job in a nightclub, and when they asked my name, I started to say "Elizabeth" but stopped. If there was a time to reinvent myself, I thought, that was it. So I changed my mind and said "Louise" instead. The manager thought I'd said Eloise, and I went along with it. I liked the name, so I changed it officially. When Kit and I married, he said I didn't have to take his surname, but I was adamant. It was another step away from who I used to be, another step closer to safety and a normal life. He was fine about me not wanting to dwell on the past, and in my experience, honesty is rarely the best policy.'

'What does he think about these remains suddenly popping up with your old name attached?'

Eloise looked at the ground. Out of everything that had happened recently, this was the one thing that made her want to collapse and curl up into a ball. 'I don't know,' she said. 'I don't even know if he's seen the news. I was going to talk to him about it, but then . . . oh, I don't know. He lied to me about something, and instead of opening up to him, I found myself closing down.' She wiped her nose on her arm. 'He hasn't mentioned it and neither have I. I don't know if he even remembers that it used to be my name.'

'What about Eddie?' asked Holly. 'How much does he know?'

'He knows that I had an unhappy childhood. That my dad died when I was fifteen, and my mum when I was nineteen. That's about it. I made some poor decisions when I was his age that I would hate him to find out about. Though I suppose you're going to tell him, aren't you?'

Holly looked at her feet as she leaned backwards and toe-poked the sky. 'Honestly? What would I say to him? "Oh, hey, so I was nicking things from your house the other day, found the driving licence of a woman who I thought was dead and accused your dad of murdering her. So, how's your course going?"'

Eloise laughed. The situation was so ridiculous that she couldn't help herself.

'This is the kind of stuff I'd usually want to talk to him about,' Holly said. 'He's my best friend. Or he was. Now, I don't know. But I guess . . .' She swung hard again, giving herself time to think. 'Yeah, I guess I won't say anything if you don't want me to.'

Eloise looked up, surprised. She'd expected Holly to do anything she could to get between her and Edward. 'Thanks,' she said. 'I appreciate that.'

'But if he asks me a direct question, I'm not going to lie.'

She looked to the horizon, remembering what Edward had said about her constant search for perfection, meaning that the rest of them could never live up to her high standards. She felt her stomach clench. Would it be so bad if she came clean and told her family everything? She'd spent her childhood being judged for other people's actions and trying so hard to show that she wasn't like the rest of them, but when she'd gone off the rails as a teen, they'd all said it was inevitable. Though she'd clawed it back and no longer lived under that shadow, it looked like all that was about to change.

'You're right, you know,' Holly said. 'About you having produced some pretty dope kids.'

Eloise smiled. 'Thanks, but that wasn't quite how I put it.'

'Eddie's great. He's like the best boyfriend I've ever had, which means you can't be too shit as a parent.'

Eloise couldn't take all the credit for how amazing her kids were, but she'd happily accept a pat on the back for always being there for them. She'd done what she'd set out to do – create a stable home life for them. She was the safety net under the tightrope of their lives.

'What was there to do around here when you were a kid?' Holly asked.

'Nothing,' said Eloise. 'We hung out in the park. Walked for miles. I used to paint and sketch on any scrap paper I could find. I would draw mythical creatures and magical landscapes. And dragonflies in every picture I ever did. My little sister loved them. We'd sit here for hours,' she said, 'talking about where we would go when we grew up, but it was never anywhere exotic. It was silly things like searching for the Loch Ness Monster or finding Bigfoot, but the furthest we ever got was Wales the year before . . . before everything fell apart.'

She slowed the swing, nostalgia hitting her hard enough to wind her. She was sad for a life she'd never known, for the carefree existence she'd never had. It was all an illusion.

'When I was a kid, we used to stand up on these things and see how high we could go, but we didn't have this rubber matting everywhere. If you came off the swings back then, you'd crack your head open, but no one seemed to care.'

She touched the space between her top lip and nose. 'I don't know if you can see it, but I have a scar here from where I got hit in the mouth by one of these swings when my sister smashed it into my face.'

'Oh my God!' said Holly, skidding through the dirt to stop her own swing. 'Wait! No. This is amazing.'

'Me being scarred for life is amazing?'

'I can't believe I didn't say anything before. Shit. Yeah, so this Facebook group I'm part of, the one that is looking into your death … It seems weird to say that now, because you're not dead, are you? Anyway, the reason I got so involved with this case was because your niece is desperately trying to discover what happened to you. She says your sister has never recovered from losing you.'

'What?'

Holly stood up and dug her phone out of her pocket. 'Sally Ann is going to be so excited to—'

Eloise jumped off the swing and knocked the phone out of Holly's hand.

'What the hell?' Holly shouted.

Eloise grabbed her arm. 'You can't say anything.'

141

'What? I can't tell your family that you're alive?' Holly shook her arm until Eloise let go. 'It's not right to keep this from them. Do you know what it's like to wonder every day where your sister is? Because I do. They're grieving for you, Eloise. Imagine how happy they'll be when they find out you're not dead. I'd give anything for someone to tell me my sister is alive. Lisa has been missing for three months, not three decades, and I feel like I'm going out of my mind wondering what's happened to her and not knowing if I'll ever see her again. You don't understand the thoughts that go through your mind. It's torture. We can spare Sally Ann and her mum all that pain with just one message. Why wouldn't you want to do that for someone?'

Eloise ran her hands through her hair. 'I'm sorry about your sister, and I feel for you, Holly, truly I do. I hope you get some answers soon, but my situation isn't the same as yours. You haven't the first clue what's going on here.'

'Trust me. It doesn't matter what you did,' said Holly. 'Nothing will ever be so bad that you can't go home. They'll forgive you anything. All your family wants is to have you back safe.'

Eloise shook her head. 'That's not my family,' she said.

'Yeah, I get it. Family isn't just about DNA. Blah, blah, blah. They're strangers right now, but your niece wants to get to know you. And she's got a kid, which would make you a great-aunt and your sister a grandmother. You've got—'

'For Christ's sake, will you shut up and just listen to me?' snapped Eloise.

'No,' said Holly. 'Sally Ann cares about what happened to you. She's been the driving force behind the whole thing,

142

and she deserves to know the truth. I'm sorry, but there is nothing you can say to stop me from telling her you're alive.'

Eloise stepped closer to Holly and waited for the girl to look into her eyes. 'I don't know what this Sally Ann has told you, but I need you to listen to me carefully. I do not have a niece.'

'You do! I've told you, her name's Sally Ann.'

'No. I don't. And I know for a fact that I don't have a niece because my sister died before she could have children.'

More than anything, Eloise wished that everything Holly had said was true. If only Deborah was living her best life with a daughter called Sally Ann and a grandchild she doted on.

'You're wrong,' said Holly.

'I wish I was.'

'How can you know for certain?'

Eloise looked at her feet, the dirt, the stones, and tried to keep the unwelcome images of Deborah at bay. Eventually, she looked up at Holly's face. 'It was my fault she died. That was the reason I left home that night.'

Patty Hansen: Hi everybody. Okay, so I've not got far on tracking down our girl Holly. Her privacy settings are water-tight, but from what I can see, she was a student at Truro College until a few weeks ago. I've been searching for students named Holly but there are maybe a hundred of them. I've sent her profile picture over to the college admin, but they're not too chatty. They will only talk to the police and only if this is a genuine missing person case. I told them I couldn't report her as a missing person if I didn't know her surname, but they still wouldn't budge.

I might have a lead on her boyfriend, though. She's been tagged in a few photos with a nerdy-looking lad named Eddie Ford. He's just started university in Sheffield. I have sent a friend request, but as yet I haven't received a response. Do young people even use Facebook nowadays? Does anyone on here live near Sheffield and can go and track him down?

Sally Ann

Ah, okay. Thanks for trying. I don't know if we should tell the police our suspicions. What does everyone think? I just wish I knew what Holly was working on when she went silent on us. Got the feeling it's something big. Keep us posted, Patty.

Ken Marchpane

Dear all, from my forensics contact: 'We have not been able to confirm that the remains belong to Elizabeth King.' Kind regards, Ken.

Patty Hansen

Honestly, the ever-rising level of police incompetence astounds even me. How difficult is it? Those remains are the right age, there are no other leads for who they might belong to, and the police had an actual tip-off telling them the woman's name. What else do they need – a signed statement from the corpse?

Ken Marchpane

It's not that easy, I'm afraid. They need to conclusively match the DNA, and I imagine they've only managed to retrieve a small sample. She's been dead so long there will be very little tissue left. Even if they can extract DNA, they would have to exhume the bodies of her parents to get a match. Sometimes there's DNA on file in case a body is found in later years, but there seems to be some confusion about whether Elizabeth was ever listed as a missing person. She was assumed to be a runaway, and no effort was made to find her. Kind regards, Ken.

Marsha Pirolo

That's so sad that no one tried to find her. Imagine vanishing one day and no one caring enough to get answers. Heartbreaking. No wonder lost souls try to communicate with the living through me.

Patty Hansen

Uh, HELLO? They can use DNA from Sally Ann or her mother. It turns out our resident boffin isn't so smart after all, is he?

Sally Ann

Honestly, this is what we've been up against all along. There's no joined-up thinking. Don't worry, Ken, we'll take it from here. I think your contact might have their wires crossed. We've not heard anything from the police about this latest development. I suppose they might have spoken to my mum. I'll call her later and see.

And Patty, I think a trip to Cornwall is a great idea. My mum lives down south now and I keep meaning to visit. Let's do it asap. We're getting close to discovering the truth about Elizabeth. Finding Holly might be the key.

Chapter 19

Holly

Once again Holly was sitting in the passenger seat of Eloise's car. Thousands of people bumper to bumper, making the most of the remaining good weather by flocking to the sea, and Holly and Eloise sandwiched between them. Neither of them was desperate to get home, but for different reasons.

She marvelled at the randomness of life that had led to her squirming in her ex-boyfriend's mother's car, in yesterday's underwear, dumb with shock. If Lisa hadn't disappeared, she wouldn't have found the Facebook group talking about Elizabeth King and would never have known the significance of that driving licence in Eddie's house. If she hadn't got the wrong end of the stick and accused poor old Mr Ford of being a murderer, she would never have found out that Eloise was really Elizabeth, and she would never have found out about Deborah.

It was random – totally random – and yet it seemed inevitable that she was involved. She was the link. Only she knew about the Truth Seekers group and Eloise's true identity. It wasn't chance that this had all happened on her doorstep.

'How are you doing?' Eloise asked. Her voice was croaky through lack of use. They had barely spoken for the last four hours, as if conserving the little energy they had left.

'Desperate for a wee.'

'You're going to have to hold it in. We're miles from the next service station.'

Holly grabbed an empty water bottle from her bag and looked at the neck. 'Do you ever think that life would be so much easier if you had a penis?'

'Every time I see the queue for the ladies' toilets.'

She dropped the bottle and crossed her legs. 'So, I've been thinking about your sister.' She noticed the muscles in Eloise's forearm tense.

'What about her?'

'You know you didn't kill her, right?'

'It was my fault.'

'Yeah, I get that you think that, but you didn't actually . . . you know, strangle her, shoot her or whatever.'

Eloise stayed quiet.

Holly adjusted her position in the seat to reduce the pressure on her bladder. 'How did she die? If you could explain it to me, maybe I could . . .'

Eloise indicated and edged into the other lane. 'All you need to know is that she died because of something I did. I found her body and I left home that night.'

'But what about Sally Ann saying she's Deborah's daughter? Why would she say that if it's not true?'

Eloise reached for her tepid coffee in a takeaway cup in the centre console. 'I can't help you there,' she said.

Holly leaned against the window. 'Like, who is she? Who have I been talking to for the last couple of weeks? We think she's lying about being your niece, but maybe she's just got the wrong end of the stick. Could you have a half-sister you don't know about? Or a whole other family somewhere?'

'Definitely not. Some people like to put themselves in the midst of stories like these because they get off on the attention. Maybe Sally Ann's trying to get sympathy and a feeling of importance. Or maybe she's nuts.'

Holly wrinkled her nose. 'It's more than that. She's invested in this. I think she knows something about those remains. And maybe she thinks it really is you. They're practically the same age as you were when you went missing. I mean, there's no reason to think it *isn't* you.'

'Apart from the fact I'm sitting here driving the car,' said Eloise.

'Yeah, there's that. But I'm saying that maybe she made an honest mistake, or maybe she thinks people are more likely to talk to her if she tells them she's family.'

'That's a lot of maybes,' said Eloise.

'You don't go to all this trouble to solve someone's murder if you don't know them,' said Holly.

'Until yesterday, you didn't know who Elizabeth was, and yet you were still going out of your way to find out who killed her, visiting the place where the body was found, swapping theories with your friends.'

'That's different. Most of us in this group are looking for some purpose, and in my case at least have a personal interest in people who have gone missing, but Sally Ann has this whole backstory about her mum, and she knew all about your

Welsh boyfriend. Oh, by the way, I should probably tell you that I've been chatting to Gavin Gallagher over Messenger.'

'You've what?'

'Look, we thought he'd killed you, kept your body hidden in a fridge for thirty years and then dumped you in the engine house. He was a credible suspect for a while.'

'Oh dear God.'

Holly looked over at Eloise, whose cheeks were tinged pink. 'And I'll tell you something else. You're better off out of that one. Did not age well at all.'

'Right.'

'Completely bald.'

Eloise turned her head away as if she didn't want to know.

'And I don't mean bald in that sexy Jason Statham way, either,' Holly said. 'I'm talking about one of those guys who looks like a thumb with a face drawn on in biro.'

'I'm sure he'd be thrilled to hear that,' Eloise said. 'But can we leave him out of this and concentrate on Sally Ann instead?'

Holly nodded. 'If you told me why you feel responsible for your sister's death, we could work out what Sally Ann has to gain from all this. And then maybe we could work out who she is.'

Eloise's hands tightened on the steering wheel.

'I know you don't want to talk about it,' said Holly. 'But Deborah's death started this sorry chain of events. We can't get to the bottom of it all without you telling me the whole story. If you won't tell me, the least you can do is go to the police so they can confirm that the remains belong to some-one else.'

The car swerved slightly. 'No chance,' said Eloise. 'At some point the police will work out the truth, and it'll be out of my hands, but until then . . . it's not my problem.'

Holly sat up in her seat, her belt straining against her shoulder. 'But that woman deserves a name, and her family deserves to know what happened to her.'

'It won't make her family happy to know that someone probably killed her and held on to her body for thirty years. Besides, what she and her family deserve has nothing to do with me. I'm sorry if this sounds selfish, but my only concern is protecting *my* family. The more distance between me and Elizabeth King, the better.'

'Why?' Holly asked. 'What's so bad about people finding out who you are? What else are you hiding?'

'Drop it, Holly.'

'I could go to the police without you,' she said, folding her arms. 'Tell them everything I know.'

'You could. But you won't.'

'How can you be so sure?'

'Because you're in love with Edward and don't want to hurt him. You hope he'll want to get back together with you one day. Well, that's never going to happen if you're the one responsible for destroying his family. I'll make sure of it.'

Holly reared back in her seat. 'Shit, Mrs F. Look at you, getting all badass. Have you finished with that coffee cup? I think it might be the right size for my pressing need.'

Chapter 20

Eloise

At the beachside café, Eloise and Holly stood in line behind children in wet bathing suits and teens covered head to toe in black. It was sunny enough for Eloise to lament the loss of her sunglasses, though not quite hot enough to warrant the amount of flesh on display on the small rocky beach.

Everyone was clinging to the final days of summer, soaking up enough vitamin D to get them through another wet winter. Kids threw seaweed at each other and paddled in rock pools. Now and again someone shrieked at the sight of a jellyfish and sprinted from the sea as if they were in mortal danger. The whiff of sun lotion competed with the aroma of chips and ketchup, while seagulls strutted about perusing the all-inclusive buffet.

'We know that the remains don't belong to Elizabeth King,' said Holly. 'And that someone, possibly the killer, gave the police the wrong name.'

Eloise pinched the bridge of her nose. Her headache was back, and she wondered if Holly would ever stop talking.

'And we also know that Sally Ann is pretending to be your niece for reasons we don't understand.'

They shuffled closer to the ordering hatch, and Eloise wondered how Edward had put up with this girl. She was exhausting. But like it or not, she was stuck with her now, because Holly knew too much about her and she couldn't walk away without giving her clear instructions on what she was to do with this knowledge.

'Sally Ann won't be her real name,' Holly went on. 'If she's lying about being related to you, there's a good chance she's lying about everything else too. All we know about her for certain is that she is a liar. I'm so annoyed with myself that I didn't see any of this coming. You know, a teacher once told me I was as sharp as an egg. That's how stupid I am.'

Eloise frowned. 'An egg? I thought teachers were meant to nurture and encourage, not humiliate.'

'Let's just say it's been a long time since you were at school, Mrs F. It's survival of the fittest in there. Teachers are the mean girls now.'

'Well I don't think you're stupid. I've kept my identity secret for decades, and you discovered it within a few days. You've alerted me to the fact that someone could be looking for me. I think that's pretty smart.'

Holly made a scoffing sound and waved her hand to show her scepticism, in the way that people who can't take compliments often do, but the twitch at the side of her mouth suggested she was pleased and embarrassed.

'Just because other people lie and deceive doesn't make you stupid,' Eloise said. 'You take people at face value, and so you should. I would rather be trusting like you than suspicious like me. I trust a tiny group of friends and my immediate family, and that's it. And, to be honest, I'm not sure I even trust those. Kit's lying to me, Meghan isn't returning my calls, which means she's probably hiding something, and I've never come clean to my friends about my link to Elizabeth King because I think they'll reject me, so . . . I think you're doing okay, Holly.'

'Not good enough for Eddie, though?' Holly asked.

'God, no,' Eloise said, placing her palm on her chest. 'But then no one ever will be, so don't take it personally. See? Trust issues.'

'You just haven't had a chance to get to know me. I'm bloody adorable. You'll see.'

Eloise smiled. 'It's not you. For what it's worth, I'm glad you were Edward's first girlfriend. You treated him well and made him feel good about himself. You . . .' She considered her words carefully. 'You made him laugh, and you've shown him what a positive relationship looks like, so I'm grateful for that.'

'Cheers. I mean, it looked like it nearly killed you to say something nice about me, but we'll skate over that bit. Talking of relationships, though, what about you and Mr F? You said you thought he was having an affair?'

'I'm probably reading too much into his moods,' Eloise said.

'And if you're not?'

'I'll find out soon enough.'

They ordered their drinks and an ice cream for Holly and moved to the next window to wait.

'Aren't you furious with him?'

Eloise sighed. 'Of course I am. But a part of me is clinging to the hope that I'm wrong. I'm not letting myself go there because I don't want to get worked up about it without absolute proof. And I won't let myself get angry, because I don't do anger.'

'Honest to God. Some of the things you come out with,' said Holly with a shake of her head. 'You can't choose not to "do" an emotion.'

'Anger is more of a reaction than an emotion. When you've grown up around violence and seen how destructive it can be, you learn to be wary of losing control, of doing something you can't take back. If you lose your temper, you've lost your argument.'

'I'm not talking about losing your temper,' said Holly. 'It doesn't mean punching walls or people. Anger is real and necessary. And if you don't let it out, you'll explode.'

Eloise shook her head. 'I prefer to take myself out of the situation rather than lose control. Anger is . . .' she paused. 'Anger is a response to a situation, and you should be able to choose how to respond, right? It usually comes from a place of hurt or fear. I'm hurting, so I lash out. Understandable, sure, but it makes me act rashly, and so far I've always ended up in a worse situation because I've taken it to a place I can't come back from. So I *choose* to avoid anger at all costs.'

Holly nodded. 'I get it,' she said, tapping the side of her head. 'You're a control freak.'

'What makes you say—'

'The lack of control scares you. I bet you don't get properly drunk either. Or do drugs. Have you ever smoked a spliff?'

Eloise looked around her and lowered her voice. 'No, but I—'

'Control issues,' said Holly. 'Knew it from the moment I met you.'

'You hardly know me.'

'And whose fault is that?'

'I feel like you're suggesting it's mine, but it's not my responsibility to foster a relationship with my son's girlfriend.'

'Er, yeah, it is. Do you have any idea how intimidating you are?'

'Me?' asked Eloise, her voice raising to an unnaturally high pitch.

'Your perfect manners, your perfect house, your perfect life.'

'Oh yes, of course. So perfect that my husband is having an affair.'

Conversations silenced around them, and even the gulls stopped calling.

'Two cappuccinos and a Berry Breeze in a tub?'

Eloise blinked at the server. 'Yes. Thanks.'

They took their drinks and the ice cream and found a free table. They sat in awkward silence, shifting on the uncomfortable wooden benches. Eloise watched the sea as if it could wash away the last five minutes. Despite the signs, accusing Kit of an affair felt like she was betraying him. Now that half the people on the beach had heard, she would have to confront him. It was too much to hope that all of these people were holidaying here. Someone was bound to know Kit. The gossip mill would already be grinding out untruths in whispers.

'He's at a conference,' she said without looking at Holly. 'At least he says he is. He took a day off work last week and lied about where he'd been, and now this conference has come out of the blue . . . well, I don't think he's being honest with me, and I'm scared about what that means.'

'Do you want me to see if I can find out whether he really is at this conference? Then at least you'd know if you've got something to worry about.'

Eloise shook your head. 'I couldn't ask you to—'

'You didn't ask. I offered.'

'I can only deal with one thing at a time, Holly. Right now, I need to work out what Sally Ann is up to.'

They drank their coffee and Holly ate her ice cream. They watched people cautiously approach the sea. Some strode straight in, kicking white spray behind them. Others shuffled and tensed up as the water rose up their thighs.

'What do you want to do about her then?' asked Holly.

'We need to work out who she is without her getting wind of the fact that I'm still alive.'

'I took photos at the engine house when those remains were found,' said Holly. 'Patty said something about killers often returning to the scene of the crime. They like the circus. Do you want to look at the pictures and see if you recognise anyone? One of them might be Sally Ann.'

'Sure.'

Holly got out her phone and swiped through the photos. Eloise studied each one, but the group of stragglers were unfamiliar to her. Many wore hats and sunglasses, so it was difficult to tell if she'd seen them before. The last photo was of her and Joseph after the car accident. 'No,' she said. 'No one looks familiar except for Joseph, the man I ran into.'

'Do you know him?' asked Holly.

157

'He's Arthur's nephew, the man who owns the yoga studio. All I know is that he's recently arrived in Cornwall and is trying to evict Mimi so he can sell the building.'

'Nice bloke,' said Holly. 'It doesn't mean he's got anything to do with Sally Ann, but he's worth keeping an eye on for sure. I think it's too much of a coincidence that he was there where the body was found, don't you?'

'And there's something about *this* guy.' Eloise showed Holly the screen. 'Everyone else is in T-shirts, but he's in a long black coat.'

'Oh, I know him,' said Holly, taking back the phone. 'That's Ken. He knows everything about forensics. I met him that day, and he joined my Facebook group. He's a bit odd, I guess, but I can't see him being behind the Sally Ann profile.'

Eloise shrugged. 'Let's keep an open mind. This is where my distrust of everyone might come in handy.'

Truth Seekers UK

Sasha Walters

Right then, I spoke to Gavin, and he was well shifty. The good news is that his van failed its MOT, so he's been unable to drive anywhere, let alone Cornwall, to see Holly. Unless she came to Wales, she's not with him. Has anyone else heard anything?

Sally Ann

Well, I suppose that's something. I keep thinking that the key is the Cornish link that Holly was investigating.

Patty Hansen

I've got a better idea of where she's from. Looking at places she's checked into over the past few years and a couple of public posts complaining about buses, she lives in Helston. Without her surname, I can't be any more specific than that. Also, her boyfriend still hasn't accepted my friend request, which is odd because have you SEEN my profile picture? I am GORGEOUS. (It's not actually a picture of me, but Eddie Ford doesn't know that!) I think he has something to do with Holly's disappearance. It's always the boyfriend.

Andy Pickford

Someone should sue you for false advertising! Not even your picture? Then who am I thinking about in the shower?

Patty Hansen

Why haven't you been kicked out of this group yet? Who's the admin on this page?

Holly Bobs

Hey guys!!! I'm so sorry for the radio silence. I was dropping Eddie off at university. Please cancel your friend request, Patty. Eddie has nothing to do with this.

I'm up for meeting in Newquay in the next couple of weeks. I would love to find out more about you all. I'm free whenever.

Also, thanks for worrying about me when I went quiet. I really appreciate that. I was beginning to think that no one would notice if I dropped off the face of the earth. I wouldn't go as far as to say this has restored my faith in humanity, but I'm feeling slightly less hatred towards my fellow man right now, so cheers for that.

Sally Ann

Oh, thank God! For a second there . . . I must be getting paranoid. What was the Cornish link that you mentioned, hun? Did you follow it up?

Holly Bobs

Sorry, no, that was a dead end. However, there is one thing that's quite interesting. After dropping Eddie off at university, I went to see the place where Elizabeth and your mum grew up. I spoke to the neighbours. They said your grandmother died of a broken heart. Does your mum remember much about it?

Sally Ann

You're right about the broken heart. Lizzie and Grandpa Tony died within weeks of each other. I'm just sorry I never got to meet them. Elizabeth's disappearance ruined a lot of lives. Someone should be held accountable for that.

Chapter 21

Eloise

The gallery had been busy throughout the summer, with a staggering amount of passing trade and holidaymakers wanting to take a piece of Cornwall home. A watercolour of their favourite beach, a sea glass composition of the 'Nearly There' trees, postcards and birthday cards by local artists. But when September came, people didn't walk past the window, their eyes not caught by images of mermaids amongst the seaweed or brightly painted houses propping each other up on steep lanes overlooking the harbour. Fishing boats, and fishermen. Snapshots of an idyllic life.

The shop was dark now that rain clouds had smothered the sun. It was only a small space, and if a dozen people came in at once, they would bump elbows and step on toes. Stunning paintings adorned the walls. Oils, watercolours and prints. Eloise had hand-picked each one. In the centre of the room was a table that tried hard not to take up much space but was brimming with items that said, 'Treat yourself. You deserve it.' And because these objects were so much cheaper than the art on the walls, it hardly seemed like an extravagance, not when you thought about what you *could* have spent.

Through an archway at the back of the shop was a desk where Eloise did her paperwork whenever the place was quiet. It was now covered with coloured Post-its and copies of the photos that Holly had taken at the engine house. Eloise had started trying to piece together who might have wanted her dead and who the remains in the engine house belonged to, but there were still more questions than answers.

She wondered whether she might be better off closing the shop and going away somewhere. Anywhere. But when she got there, would she ever come back? It was hard to know whether there was anything worth staying for.

She watched the rain snake down the window. The gallery had been open since ten o'clock, and not one single person had ventured in. Very few people had been walking on the streets, so no one had stopped to look through the window. Over the course of the week, she hadn't sold anything – not a postcard, not one pen.

September was usually the month she spent doing her accounts, booking new artists and arranging open evenings and events. Still, this solitary time gave her too much space to think about Deborah. And when she wasn't thinking about Deborah, she was thinking about Kit.

He had arrived home on Sunday, needing a shave, and said he had nothing interesting to tell her about the three-day conference.

'That's interesting,' Eloise had said.

He said it had gone well, even though a couple of senior directors had drunk too much on the first night, and they were quietly optimistic about the company's future. He told her he was sorry about being away for so long when she must be upset about Edward. He said he'd make it up to her. Perhaps they could plan to visit their son in a week or two and take him out to a carvery. 'Talking of food,' he'd said, 'anything to eat in the house?'

'Lots,' she'd said. And under her breath, she'd muttered, 'And I hope you choke on it.'

She had ordered her usual amount of shopping, even though Edward wasn't there to eat it. She didn't know how to shop for two. If it was just her at home, she would have survived on a perfectly balanced diet of wine and cheese, but she felt she needed a fully stocked fridge in case either of the kids paid them a surprise visit and brought their friends.

She had filled Kit in on dropping Edward off at university, told him that he and Holly had split up, and it had been on the tip of her tongue to tell him how she'd gone by her old house on the way home and spent a night in a hotel by the motorway with Holly in a twin room. And how the whole weekend had blown her mind, and not in a good way, and how someone was pretending to know her and trying to find out what had happened to her after she'd left home that night thirty years ago. She'd been desperate to tell him everything and explain how she had felt like an intruder at the same time as feeling she'd left a part of herself there. But watching him sitting there, not looking her in the eye, her words dried up, and all she wanted to do was shake him and shout and demand that he tell her what he was hiding.

Kit *had* been at a conference, that much was true, but it had only lasted for two days, finishing at lunchtime on Friday. Two nights unaccounted for. Holly had called the conference centre, and they'd confirmed it. And now Holly knew three things about Eloise that no one else did. Her real name, that she was responsible for her sister's death, and that her husband was a lying, cheating bastard.

At night, when Eloise lay awake listening to him breathing and wondering about putting a pillow over his face, she would have given anything to return to how things used to be. There was too much change, and none of it was for the better. Maybe she could move past his affair – because surely that was what it was. She wondered whether it was possible to carve out a new chapter for them and fall in love all over again, but by the time morning peeked through the curtains, she was back to keeping him at arm's length.

She touched and rotated her wedding ring, then shook her head and turned the sign on the gallery door from *Open* to *Closed*. She had some artwork to drop off at the yoga studio, and she may as well do it now. The sooner it was done, the sooner she would be lying up to her hairline in bubbles with a glass of wine while listening to an audiobook and pretending that the world wasn't ending.

The ringing phone made her jump, and she looked at it on the counter. She sighed when she saw who was calling. What kind of a monster called when a text would suffice? She would pick up the phone for her kids, her husband, and the Tesco delivery guy when he called to say he was running early, but she certainly didn't plan on answering the phone to her son's ex-girlfriend.

The sensible thing to do in this situation was to let it ring out. And then Eloise could send a text saying, *Missed your call. Everything okay?* because that was what a normal person would do. She should have known better than to give Holly her phone number, but they'd just spent thirty-six hours in each other's company, bonding over Edward and sharing secrets about Elizabeth. In her highly emotional, sleep-deprived state, it had seemed like a good idea.

Well, that had backfired quickly.

She folded her arms and took a step away from the phone. Holly might have found out something interesting about Sally Ann. Still, a text would do. Or . . . or maybe she'd heard from Edward, and he was in trouble and—

'Hello?'

'Hi, Mrs F. It's Holly.'

'Hi, Holly. Is everything okay?'

'Yeah. No, not really, but it's fine. Listen, Sally Ann knows a bit about Elizabeth's family. Well, your family. Or is it? I find it weird thinking about you as Elizabeth. I looked at that photo in the article, and it looks nothing like you. Did you honestly have black hair?'

'I did, but I shaved it off when I got to Cornwall because I was worried it made me easily recognisable.'

'Imagining you with a buzz cut is melting my brain,' said Holly.

'Are you okay, Holly? You sound a bit . . .'

Eloise heard Holly sniff. 'I've just had the world's worst interview. I forgot everything I'd prepared, accidentally insulted the interviewer, and now I've lost my bus pass. I think I left it on a bench, and I swear this fucking seagull took it. I'm stuck in Truro with no idea how to get home, and there's a weird bloke who keeps staring at me, so yeah, I've had better days. But anyway, about Sally Ann—'

'Holly,' said Eloise. 'Stay there. I'm coming to get you.'

Chapter 22

Eloise

Eloise arrived at the yoga studio early, of course. Her hair was misbehaving in the rain, and her clean top turned out not to be so clean after all. Was it just her imagination, or was she wearing odd socks? But apart from that, she was completely in control.

'Could you straighten that painting?' she said, pointing to an acrylic of Kynance Cove.

Wendy sighed. 'It won't get any straighter than that. You'd need to straighten the wall, the floor and the ceiling first. There's not a straight line in this whole place.'

Eloise placed a hand on her stomach. She wasn't opposed to having a tantrum, scooping up her paintings and going home. It was funny how fear tried to give you an escape route like that. Good old anxiety always had her back. But despite the squirming discomfort, she would stay and help Mimi, save the yoga studio and go home victorious.

Wendy stepped closer to the painting. 'You did these, did you?'

'Yes. I don't sell my work any more. I only paint for . . .' Eloise lost the word she was trying to say.

'Fun?' Wendy suggested.

Eloise thought for a moment. Fun wasn't the right word. Painting was relaxing, cathartic. It made her stay in the moment and ignore the madness of the world that was raging around her. But it hadn't been fun for a long time. She wasn't an artist who experimented with colours and textures. Even as a child, she preferred to colour within the lines rather than paint with her fingers and handprints. Her art was where she made sense of the world.

She looked at Wendy's rigid face. 'You don't like them, do you?'

Wendy forced a smile. 'Who, me? No, I do. Are you okay? You're sweating buckets.'

'What if people hate them?'

'They'll do the decent thing and pretend otherwise.'

'You mean like you're doing now?'

Wendy peered closely at the brushstrokes.

'Why are you going through with this if it's stressing you so much?'

'I was just asking myself the same question,' said Eloise. 'Because Mimi needs my help, I suppose. I've watched her build this place from scratch. This is her passion, and it's sickening that she's being pushed out so that someone can make a profit. I don't have much to offer except my time and art. Mimi is like a sister to me – an exasperating, argumentative sister, but one I don't know what I'd do without. And I know you understand what I mean when I say I'd do anything for my family.'

Wendy made a strange choking sound and coughed to cover it.

'What was that?' Eloise asked.

'Sorry. I find it funny, that's all – the thought of you and the earth goddess as sisters. Do you want a coffee?'

'Please.'

As Wendy disappeared through the kitchen door, Eloise looked about her. She hoped today would be a success for Mimi, but she mostly just wanted to go back home and talk to Kit about Elizabeth and the conference. Until then, she was going to put a smile on her face and help her best friend save her studio.

Yoga classes would be free all day, though donations wouldn't be refused. Wendy had been up since five baking cakes and preparing food. She'd even told her daughter she couldn't look after her grandson today, which was unheard of because Wendy doted on that boy. She was still trying to make up for leaving the studio unlocked.

Mimi was hoping for an outpouring of love and support *EL* from the local community and an article or two in the local papers. Every person through the door would be asked to sign a petition against the planned housing development. People loved a cause, and what greater cause was there than protecting where they lived and supporting the underdog against corporate greed?

Though it had been less than a week since Eloise, Jan and Wendy had talked about putting on an open day, they'd managed to pull it off. It wasn't perfect by any means, but it was happening, and that was something. Joseph was keen to push the sale through as quickly as possible, so there was no time to lose.

It was a shame that it had been raining for the past twenty-four hours, and they wouldn't be able to make the most of the outdoor space, but at least this meant that people would be inside smelling the food and the coffee and being unable to resist. And then they'd sit a while, and that was when they'd see the art.

Eloise's art.

If she'd had a paper bag, Eloise would have been breathing or vomiting into it. At the gallery, she didn't just sell other people's work. She *championed* it. She was a great cheerleader for other artists, but never for herself; she used to sell her work at Christmas markets and craft fairs, but ever since she'd opened the gallery, she'd not sold a single piece of her own. She struggled to take herself seriously as an artist amongst the fantastic art on display. The talent, the expertise and the hours of work these artists poured onto canvas or into clay made her feel like she was doing little more than doodling on a napkin in comparison.

She took a deep breath and reminded herself that this was for Mimi. Twenty of Eloise's paintings were now hanging in the café and the two studios, each one for sale for more than she believed them to be worth. She had twenty prints of each of those twenty paintings, though she was sure she would be lucky to sell a dozen. However, Jan saw it as a marketing opportunity, and had called it the Twenty-Twenty exhibition. She had a whole speech about twenty-twenty vision. About hindsight. About how they would look back at this moment in time and either be proud they did something to stop the onslaught of the greedy developers or see how they missed their opportunity. She could see clearly how this was the tip of the iceberg, and if the developers weren't stopped now, there'd be nothing left of the land they loved. Or something like that.

Jan walked by, pushing a blinking young man in front of her. 'Not one person steps over the threshold of this café without signing the petition. Persuade them that it's in their best interest.'

'Got it,' he said, and went to stand by the open door.

Jan nudged Eloise with her elbow. 'Holly is working in the café.'

'I know.'

'I know you know. But what I don't know is why she's here. Is she trying to get to Edward through you?'

'Have you considered that she might enjoy my company?' asked Eloise.

'Seriously, though,' said Jan. 'What's the story?'

'She's looking for a job. I said she could help out here so she has something to put on her CV. She doesn't have anyone else to turn to, so . . .'

'Ah, another one of your pet projects,' said Jan. 'Figures.'

'What's that supposed to mean?' asked Eloise.

'I'm sorry. Am I being too subtle? I must be losing my touch. I'm saying that you tend to be mother hen to every waif and stray, whether they like it or not.'

'I do not.'

'Surely it's awkward, since your offspring broke her heart?'

Eloise folded her arms and lowered her voice. 'Not as awkward as the fact that Holly's sister used to work here before Wendy.'

Jan's eyes widened. 'Who?'

'Lisa.'

'No! The one with the sticky fingers?'

'Shush!' Eloise looked over at Holly, but she was taking an order from a woman with a yoga mat under her arm. 'I completely forgot about it until we pulled up here this morning. Don't say anything to Mimi. Or Holly. Holly thinks Mimi is a mean boss, and that's why her sister quit. She doesn't need to know that Mimi threatened to call the police over that missing money. And Mimi . . . well, she's got enough on her plate today without us bringing it up.'

'You do know that Mimi will kill you when she finds out, don't you? And she *will* find out.'

At that moment, Wendy hurried over with a coffee for Eloise. 'Bloody hell,' she hissed. 'It's only ten, and I'm almost out of brownies.' She shook her keys. 'I'm going to have to get another tray of them from the back of the van.'

'Here, I'll do it,' said Jan. 'You stay and work your magic.'

'It's parked up the hill. Rusty old white thing. Can't miss it.' Wendy tossed Jan the keys and then turned to Eloise. 'Isn't this great? I was worried no one would turn up. Hey, will you save me one of your prints?'

'You don't have to do that,' Eloise said.

'I do. I want the one of the high street under that colourful bunting. Let me know how much I owe you.' Wendy scuttled back behind the counter.

It might have been the lack of breakfast, but Eloise felt decidedly light-headed. People looking at her prints was one thing, but buying them? She knew that was the point, but she felt ill-prepared for the scrutiny and needed a moment to grab hold of her anxiety before it spiralled. She

172

slipped past Studio One, where a yoga class was coming to an end, past the young man on the door and out into the courtyard. Though it was spitting, the worst of the rain had passed, and the air smelled fresh and full of promise.

A man stood at the far side of the small courtyard with his back to her. Kit. Eloise recognised that coat, because she'd bought it for him. She used to smile every time she saw him unexpectedly, but now her stomach was somersaulting for a different reason. It was the wrong time and the wrong place, but she couldn't hold it in any longer; she had to say something.

She stepped towards him, gripping her coffee tightly. His words were quiet, and occasionally lost between the wind chimes, but she tilted her head and listened.

'Hang in there,' he said into the phone. 'We'll work something out.' There was a pause, then, 'No. I've not said anything to her. You're right. But I can't go on like this for much longer. She'll guess that something's up.'

Eloise would wait for him to get off the phone, and once he turned and saw her standing there, he would realise the game was up.

'What the hell is going on here?'

She spun around to find Joseph marching towards her. His fists were balled up, fury knitting his brows together.

'Are you out of your tiny mind?'

Chapter 23

Eloise

'Have you come to tell us that you've changed your mind about selling the building, or are you here for breakfast?' asked Eloise. 'I can heartily recommend the waffles.'

'What's this?' Joseph asked, peering inside the building.

'I'm sure you already know what "this" is, or you wouldn't be here. We're raising awareness of your plans to destroy a vital community space. Someone from the local radio station is already inside, and we're expecting TV cameras later. I hope you've brought a fresh shirt in case of any further accidents.' She waved her coffee at him, and he took a small step backwards.

'This is absurd. Shut it down now, or I'll shut it down for you,' he said.

Eloise hadn't noticed Kit sidle up next to her. 'Are you threatening my wife?'

'Only with legal action,' Joseph said.

'Right,' said Kit. 'It sounded like you were throwing your weight around there, buddy.'

'I've got this, Kit,' said Eloise. 'I'm handling it. Perhaps you should go back to your phone call.'

He held his hands up and backed away, but he didn't go far.

'If you're saying that I'm exploiting my uncle or that I'm after his money,' said Joseph, 'I will sue you for defamation of character.'

'Does it count as defamation if every word is true, though?' asked Eloise.

'It would be unwise to make me your enemy.'

'Again, bud,' said Kit. 'Getting close to intimidating behaviour there.'

'Kit,' said Eloise. 'Back off. I can't deal with you right now.' She caught his puzzled look, but she could only cope with one problem at a time.

She turned back to Joseph. 'You're a bully who is kicking a woman out of the business that she has been building for years to aid the physical and mental health of hundreds of local people. It's just my opinion,' she continued, 'but it seems to me that you will benefit financially from the sale of the studio, even though – from what I've heard – you haven't seen your uncle in years.'

'Money doesn't interest me. All you see is a nephew concerned about his uncle's welfare, especially as he has no other living relatives.'

'That's been the case for a long time,' said Eloise. 'Yet you only moved to Cornwall a couple of months ago. My friend looked you up online. Your last business went bankrupt, so I assume you're desperate. You're lying if you say money doesn't motivate you.

Joseph shook his head. 'I have reasons for being here that have nothing to do with my uncle and certainly nothing to do with you.'

'Where did you move from?'

'Up country,' he said.

'That hardly narrows it down,' Eloise said. 'Everywhere is up country when you're in Cornwall.'

She was almost impressed by how calm he remained despite her accusing him of being after Arthur's money and lying about it. He'd been angrier when she'd driven into the back of his car.

'What were you doing at the engine house?' she asked.

He blinked rapidly at the sudden change in questioning. 'What are you talking about?'

'When we first met. You know, where those remains were found. What were you doing there?'

'I wasn't at the engine house. I was driving along the road next to it,' he snapped.

'Where were you going?'

'Nowhere. I was just driving.'

'You stopped,' Eloise said. 'We had that accident because you stopped to look. You were interested in what was going on.'

'What accident?' asked Kit. 'You didn't tell me you'd had an—'

'Not now, Kit!'

'So?' Joseph asked. 'Who wouldn't be interested? It's not every day you see that sort of thing. I could ask you the same question. Why were you there?'

'I'm a naturally nosy person,' Eloise said. She stared into his face, wondering whether she recognised him from somewhere and whether it was a coincidence that he'd turned up when he had.

She was convinced that Sally Ann was behind it all, but who was to say that Sally Ann wasn't a front for a man like Joseph?

'Is anyone going to tell me what's going on here?' Kit asked.

Eloise heard Holly call her name and took a grateful step backwards. She was breathing rapidly, and her teeth ached from where she'd been clenching her jaw. 'Is everything okay, Holly?'

'I need to show you something,' Holly said.

'Hold on a minute!' Joseph said. '*You* were the supposed witness. Did you plan that whole thing at the engine house? What are you two up to? Are you following me? Is this a pathetic attempt to discredit me?'

'Right, that's enough,' said Kit. 'I think you should move on.'

Joseph pushed past them and stormed into the yoga studio, looking around for Mimi.

'He seems nice,' said Kit.

'I didn't need your help,' Eloise snapped.

'Didn't say you did, but I wasn't going to stand by and say nothing.'

'I've heard enough of what you have to say,' said Eloise.

Kit frowned. 'What? I don't—'

'I heard you on the phone, Kit.'

He looked at his feet and scratched the back of his head. 'Ah, that was Meghan.'

'Do you really expect me to believe that?'

'Mrs F,' said Holly.

'Sorry, Holly. What is it?'

177

'I do need to show you something. I was looking through lost property – the reason for that isn't important right now . . .'

Eloise lowered her head. 'Could you maybe not steal from my friend's business?'

Holly held up a bejewelled phone case. 'And I found this.'

'What am I looking at?' Eloise asked.

'I found this iPhone in the lost property box,' said Holly.

'Okay,' Eloise said. 'And?'

'It's my sister's.'

Truth Seekers UK

Sasha Walters

Hello, everybody!!! I've put a poll in the group. Please fill it in and let me know your availability for the Truth Seekers trip to Newquay. I am looking forward to us getting together and meeting in real life x

Patty Hansen

Done! Thanks for arranging. And I've got the final price on those T-shirts. (And hoodie for our resident hooligan Andy.) I will put up another post now with costs and pictures. Please DM me with your size and pay me via PayPal at TruthSeekerPatty@gmail.com.

Sasha Walters

Paying now. Thanks for sorting x

Holly Bobs

I know we're focusing on finding out what happened to Elizabeth, but I don't know who else to tell. My sister, Lisa, has been missing for three and a half months. She said she was going to London to stay with friends and would let me know when she was settled. I've called her phone a hundred times since then. But yesterday I found her phone at the place she used to work! The last thing she told me was that she was going to collect the wages owed to her on her way to the train station. What do I do? Do I tell the police? I'm scared her boss did something to her.

Sasha Walters

Oh babe! I had no idea. Yes. Police. Now! We're here for you. Just let us know what you need.

Patty Hansen

Oh Holly! You poor thing. Okay, first things first. Stay calm. You don't know that her phone being there means anything. This might be why she hasn't been in touch with you, nothing more sinister. If she's lost her phone, she'll have lost all her numbers. Who even remembers phone numbers nowadays? Having said that . . . You need to take action, because if something happened there and your sister was hurt, then the boss must be held accountable.

Tell me more about him. Is he a sleaze? Give me his name and I'll see what I can find out about him.

Holly Bobs

The boss is a woman called Mimi Wheaton. She's a bitch, though. She was always looking down on Lisa. She's all peace, love and condescension. I wanted to confront her when I found the phone, but my ex-boyfriend's mother dragged me away (long story). I heard them arguing, though. Mimi said she gave my sister her wages and that she never saw her again. She says that a load of money went missing at the same time, but she didn't even go to the police, so I don't believe her for a second.

Chapter 24

Holly

On the television, the police officers were always clean-shaven, but this one looked all wrong. His badger-striped beard was unkempt, and the hairs above his top lip were too long. Holly couldn't look at him without imagining food caught among the fibres.

'The phone's been sitting in the lost property box for over three months,' she said. 'I put it in a sandwich bag straight away to preserve the evidence, but you'll need to take my fingerprints to exclude them when you dust the phone for prints.'

The police officer's smile got lost in the facial hair, but his eyes crinkled at the edges. 'If this has been sitting pretty in a lost property basket, anyone could have laid their grubby little paws on it, I'm afraid.'

'What about text messages?' asked Holly. 'You've got people who can unlock phones and look through search history and stuff, right?'

The officer chuckled. 'Someone's been watching their crime dramas on the telly, haven't they? You leave the policing to us, and if it's necessary to investigate this further—'

'Excuse me,' Eloise said. 'But did you say "if it's necessary"? It's not up to you to decide whether it's necessary. Lisa Bond hasn't contacted her family in over three months. This is clearly out of character for her. She would never go this long without getting in touch with her sister. Do you understand what I'm saying? I'm telling you that it *is* necessary. The last time Holly came here to talk to someone about her concerns, you fobbed her off. We are not leaving until we make a missing persons report and we're satisfied that you are taking this seriously. You are aware, are you not, of the remains of a young woman being found a few miles from here? Lisa Bond will not be another statistic. She will not be passed over and ignored. And if you're not going to do something about this, find me someone who will.'

The bearded man was replaced by a woman who sacrificed friendliness for efficiency. They filled in forms and answered questions, and at last it felt like someone was taking Holly seriously. The detective, Terri, agreed that she was right to be concerned and Lisa's welfare was paramount. *People go missing for many reasons*, she said. *Try not to worry.* But her face had worry etched into the creases.

Everything about this day was turning out to be surreal, but Holly was relieved that she wasn't carrying this on her own any more. She wasn't sure what she'd hoped for when she'd shown Eloise the phone, but she hadn't expected her to take her side. No one, literally no one, took Holly's side any more.

Though it felt like they'd been at the station for twelve hours, it was still light when they exited the building. Once outside, they stood side by side on the pavement staring out across the traffic, fully drained and spent.

182

'Thanks for stepping in like that,' Holly said.

'No problem.'

'You didn't have to come in with me.'

'I told you, I'm here for you.'

They walked towards the car park.

'I reckon I've pissed off your friend Mimi.'

'It's easily done,' said Eloise. 'She'll get over it.'

'I accused her of killing my sister,' said Holly. 'And then you came with me to the police station instead of helping her at the yoga studio.'

'I love Mimi with all my heart,' Eloise said. 'But she's incredibly self-centred. She will have moved on to thinking about something else the moment we left. And not because she's mean – she's actually one of the most generous people I know – but she only sees what's in front of her and only if it's relevant to her somehow. I know you don't think much of her because of how she treated your sister, but I'm sure she didn't hurt her. She has a way of making you feel small and stupid, but I've never known her raise a hand to anyone. She wouldn't even discipline her son. Refused to say no to him or set a bedtime. She might not go about things in the way I would, but at heart she's a good person.'

'Maybe,' said Holly. 'I suppose it is difficult to imagine a murderer called Mimi. It's more of a pole dancer's name.'

Eloise smiled for the first time that afternoon. 'You should tell her that.'

They got in the car, but Eloise just stared through the windscreen and chewed the inside of her cheek. 'I need to say something,' she said eventually.

Holly blinked slowly. 'Okay.'

183

'Sitting in the station talking about your sister made me . . .' Eloise shook her head. 'Let me start again. You told me that Lisa was missing the day we dropped Edward off in Sheffield, and I didn't ask you anything about her. I didn't ask you when it had happened or how or why. I didn't ask whether the police were involved. Nothing. I was completely focused on my own problems. But I know what it's like to be all alone, and I know what it's like to worry about a sister. I should have been more sympathetic, because trust me, I do understand a little of what you're going through.'

'Don't worry about it,' Holly said. 'It was quite a day, and honestly, I didn't expect you to act as if you were bothered.'

'Well, you should have done. It was unforgivable, and I'm sorry. I know from personal experience that people can vanish and not be in any danger, but just because that's what happened with me, it doesn't mean we can assume that your sister is okay. You must be terrified, wondering what has happened and where she is right now. I should have been more supportive.'

Holly looked down at her lap. 'Don't be too hard on yourself. If you'd offered to help me out at the time, I'd have told you to piss off, so . . .'

'Charming.'

'Don't act all hurt. You didn't like me any more than I liked you.'

'It wasn't personal,' said Eloise.

'It never is, but I appreciate you stepping up now. If my mum was still alive, she wouldn't have rested until she found out where Lisa was, but then if Mum had still been alive, Lisa would never have left.'

184

'How did your mum . . .'

'Cancer.'

'I'm sorry.'

'I feel like I've let her down by not doing anything to find Lisa. She'd be so disapp—'

'No. Don't say that,' said Eloise. 'She'd be proud of you.'

'Yeah? And how do you know that?' asked Holly.

'Didn't you know? We have a secret club, and I'm the spokesperson for all absent mums. Look, I might never have met her, but I know you and I know what it's like to be a parent. She would have seen that you were doing your best and would have been in awe of everything you do. What about your dad?'

'Never on the scene,' said Holly. 'I live with my stepdad, but he's . . . I mean, he was great until Mum died, and then I guess we were too much for him. He rowed with Lisa two days before she disappeared and, you know, I worry that maybe he . . .'

'Do you think he hurt her?'

'No. Not really. But he's a heavy drinker, and I've wondered whether he might have, well, you know . . .'

'Are you in danger, Holly?' asked Eloise.

Holly shrugged. It wasn't like she hadn't considered that herself, but she still found it hard to believe. 'Probably not, but I've got the offer of a room in a shared house if I can get a job, so I just need to keep Liam sweet until then.'

'Move in with us. Edward's room is empty.'

'Oh my God, no. That would be too weird.'

'But if you aren't safe . . .'

'I am. I shouldn't have said anything. He's good, really. He just lost it when Mum died. If I leave now, he'll have no one, and I don't want to torpedo our relationship when he might be the only family I have left.'

'You just said he was a heavy drinker who argued with your sister and could be behind her disappearance. This might not be a relationship worth saving.'

'Says you,' said Holly.

'What do you mean?'

'Your husband is keeping something from you – probably an affair – and yet you still haven't confronted him about it. Why's that?'

Eloise blinked rapidly. 'It's not that simple. I've got a lot going on.'

'Yeah, or you don't want to face up to the truth and risk being alone. People put up with a lot because they think they won't make it on their own. They kid themselves that if they can just hold on for a little bit longer, it will go back to how it was before. But it never does.'

'Then why are you insisting on staying with Liam?'

'I've lost everyone. Mum, Lisa, Eddie . . . I don't want to face the fact that I've lost Liam too. Not yet. And yeah, I still have hope it'll all work out somehow. A bit like you and Mr F, I guess.'

Eloise was silent for a while. 'You've had a lot to deal with. I don't want you to think you're on your own, though. No one should have to deal with everything you're going through alone. It's a wonder you've got on with your life and passed your A levels when you could have gone down a far different path.'

'What, like stealing stuff from my boyfriend's family?'

'Pah! That's small fry,' said Eloise. 'When I was your age, I was dealing drugs.'

Chapter 25

Eloise

Holly gasped. 'Shut up! You were not!'

Eloise sank in her seat. Why did she keep telling Holly things that she really should keep to herself?

'It was how I was going to get me and Debs off that estate. I was going to make a better life for us.'

'Couldn't you get a paper round?'

'Obviously it doesn't make much sense now, but I only planned to do it for a year, two at most. I was working at a club in Nottingham, so I met quite a few . . . *clients* that way. I never did drugs myself, but I needed the money, and I met this guy who offered me the opportunity to make cash quickly. It also messed up my life, so I wouldn't recommend it.'

Holly looked at Eloise like she'd never seen her before. 'Nah. I can't picture it. You're, like, the most strait-laced person I've ever met.'

Eloise considered this for a moment and found she was strangely offended. 'I've barely put a foot wrong since then. I've been a model citizen, partly because life is so much easier this way, but mostly to make amends for things I did back then.'

'This isn't like offsetting your carbon footprint,' said Holly. 'Sell drugs, plant a tree. Cycle to work to make up for poisoning the water supply. Stolen someone's wallet? No problem, just recycle your milk bottles.'

'For the record, I've never stolen anything,' said Eloise.

'Unlike me?'

She sighed. 'That wasn't a dig at you. You took things we weren't using so you could buy clothes for an interview. You were just being . . .'

'Resourceful?' Holly offered.

'Resourceful,' agreed Eloise. 'I'm not proud of my past. That's why I've lied about it. I don't want to admit to being that person. When we were in the police station, it made me think about what I must have put my mum through. I doubt I was easy to live with. We didn't get on, but I would have liked to get to know her as an adult. Maybe we could have learned something from each other. I wonder whether she sat in a police station like that one to report me missing. Maybe they fobbed her off too, because I was a kid from a bad family who had every reason to run away. We weren't the kind of people the police bothered with. There wouldn't have been anyone there to help her. I might've been too hard on her all these years. I was a nightmare. To be fair, so was she, but I wasn't a good daughter.'

'It's hard to be a good daughter when you have to be the parent,' Holly said.

'I guess. I've tried to be a decent mother and not make the same mistakes as my mum. Never absent, never missing a carol concert, sports match or play. I've set boundaries, shown them love and tried to build their self-confidence.

And do you know what I've got to show for it? Absolutely nothing. Meghan won't return my calls. Edward does, but I can tell he's trying to get me off the phone because he's on his way out or in the middle of something more important. We were so close when they were little, but now they've flown the nest, none of the work I put into our relationship counts for anything.'

'They'll be back,' said Holly.

'I hope you're right,' said Eloise. 'It had to be hard on my mum to lose Deborah and me at the same time. The only difference was that I could have come back if I'd wanted to, only I never did because I was too scared that I would get the blame for Debs's death.'

'You still haven't told me what happened with your sister,' Holly said.

Eloise shifted in her seat so she couldn't see Holly's face. If she was going to tell her the truth, she didn't want to see her shock and disgust at what she'd done.

'Debs was eighteen months younger than me,' she began. 'She was my responsibility. She always had been, but more so after Dad died. We used to be close. God, she thought she knew it all. She was argumentative and opinionated, and I loved her to bits. We'd drifted apart, but I always thought we'd find our way back to each other. Everything I was doing, I was doing for her, whether she appreciated it or not.'

She paused, wondering if there was any way she could tell this story that wouldn't make Holly ashamed of her. 'There was a big party on the estate, and I told her not to go, but when I turned up, she was already there with her

189

girlfriend, Mel, who by the way I never approved of. This girl was scarily intense. Scars up her arms and thighs. She was passionate one minute, desolate the next, and God, she was volatile. You never knew where you stood with her. The police could never prove it, but everyone said she was the one who'd set fire to the school, after she'd been excluded. I thought she wasn't good enough for Debs, but they had this "us against the world" thing going on. If you thought our home life was messed up, you should have seen Mel's. She was in a similar boat to me in that she had a younger sister she looked after, but her parents made ours look like saints. The girls were left to fend for themselves all the time. The mum would go out partying for days on end. Weeks. I think the dad was sporadically on the scene, but I never met either of them. Anyway, that night felt different somehow. Or maybe I'm just imagining it because of what came next. But Debs was manic. Something was going on with her. Maybe I should have taken her home, but I didn't because I thought I had better things to do with my night. If I'd dragged her out of there . . .'

'Rubbish,' said Holly. 'As if any self-respecting girl will listen to her older sister. I wouldn't have left a party if my sister had told me to. I would've stayed and partied harder.'

Eloise looked down at her balled-up fists. 'That's kind of what happened. She was drunk, and we had a huge fight. I didn't have a leg to stand on, but I wanted so much better for her. Debs was furious with me for treating her like a child, and she stormed out of the party saying I'd humiliated her. Later that night, I discovered that she'd stolen my drugs from the hole in my mattress, so I went after her. You can't just take that stuff from someone. There were people I had to pay, and I was going to make her see sense. I was going to . . .' She fell silent. Eventually she cleared her throat.

'When I got to her girlfriend's house, the door was unlocked. It was the rougher end of the estate, if that was possible. Nearer the abattoir. I walked through the house screaming Debs's name. Shouted that I was going to kill her. Nothing I hadn't said a hundred times before, for using my hairbrush, my eyeliner. But when I got upstairs . . .' She took a deep breath, and it juddered in her chest. 'The two of them were lying on the bed. They weren't breathing. I don't know whether it was an accident, or if they'd made a pact to do it together, but they'd overdosed. I suppose I'll never know the truth. All I know is that if I hadn't been dealing, and she hadn't been angry with me . . .'

'I'm so sorry,' said Holly. 'That must have been horrendous.'

'I didn't go for help, I didn't call an ambulance, I just froze. I remember sitting on the floor, watching them. I willed Debs to make a noise. Breathe. I was hoping that I would see her chest rise and fall. Something. I don't know how long I sat there, but eventually I crawled over to her and checked for a pulse – something I should have done when I first found her. She was cold. I . . . I just left. I left her there. The streets were empty. I went home, packed my bag and hitchhiked out of there without telling a soul, and until today, I've never told anyone the reason why.'

Truth Seekers UK

Holly Bobs

Hey guys. Thanks for all your support. Appreciate it. I have officially reported my sister as missing. The police are talking to my stepdad and the Missing Persons Unit. At least something is happening. Obviously I'm not going to leave it all up to them. I will be following up on my own leads. It feels pretty shit to finally admit she's missing. I can't stop crying, but I know that I need answers. I owe it to Lisa – and myself – because not knowing what has happened to her is torture.

Patty Hansen

That sucks, but I'm glad they're taking this seriously. I'm relieved you're not leaving it all to the police. As we all know, they have their own agenda. I know we're coming to Cornwall to see if we can learn more about Elizabeth, but why don't we also get our heads together and look at leads to find your sister? Nothing that says we can't investigate two cases at the same time, is there? What's your step-dad's name? We need to investigate him (sorry, but step-parents are often involved. It's no coincidence that the stepmothers in fairy tales are evil). Was Lisa seeing anyone at the time of her disappearance? Are there any ex-boyfriends we should be aware of?

Andy Pickford

I know that your ex was a twat, Patty, but why do you always assume it's a fella who did it? Maybe it was a woman. In my experience, women can be nastier. Perhaps not as overtly violent, but they can hold a grudge like nobody's business. My money's on the boss, who was the last to see her. Where there's money involved, there's motivation for murder. Not that I'm saying your sister is dead, Holly. I'm trying to keep an open mind here.

I hope that didn't sound insensitive. I've been told I can be a bit of a dickhead at times.

Patty Hansen

Statistically speaking, it's unusual for a woman to kill another woman. But yes, I concede we shouldn't be too hasty to rule out Mimi-the-Boss. I'll put her on the list of suspects.

Andy Pickford

Did anyone else see that? I think Patty just agreed with me. Fuck me, that felt good!

Sally Ann

Oh Holly, sweetie. I'm sorry to hear about your sister. Of course we will do anything and everything we can to help. I just wanted to check what Elizabeth's Cornish link was. DM me. Let's not lose sight of the need to find out what happened to her.

Andy Pickford

And people call ME insensitive??? There's a chance that her sister is still alive – whereas your aunt is nothing but a big bag of bones.

Sasha Walters

I'm thinking of you, Holly. It breaks my heart. I swear we'll get to the bottom of this.

So far, we've got me, Marsha, Patty, Ken and Holly for the Newquay meet-up this weekend. Any more takers? Sally Ann? Andy? Are you sure we can't tempt you?

Sally Ann

I would love to, hun, but I don't know if my mum is up to having my little boy for the weekend, so put me down as a maybe. I know this is all happening because of my aunt, so I really appreciate you doing it. I know I need to be there, but I've got to put my family first.

Andy Pickford

I'll probably regret this, but if I can find someone to have the dogs for the weekend, I'll be there.

Ken Marchpane

Dear all, you might want to know that there has been an update. It's not hit the papers yet, but according to my source, the police have found a second set of remains in another engine house. Kind regards, Ken.

News article from *The Beacon*

HORROR AT THE ENGINE HOUSE

In what police are describing as a worrying development, a second set of human remains have been found in a Cornish engine house. The discovery was made by a group of astronomers at the accredited Dark Sky Discovery site at Wheal Tremaine.

Ren Williams said, 'We thought that someone was dossing in a sleeping bag or something. You see it quite a lot nowadays, people sleeping rough on the coastal paths, but when they hadn't moved by the time we were all set up, we took a closer look and found it was a rolled-up rug tied with ropes. We thought someone had tipped rubbish down there, so we were going to drag it up top to dispose of it properly when someone remembered those remains that had been found wrapped in carpet in another engine house a few weeks ago, and that's when we called the police.'

A police spokesperson said it was too early to tell whether these remains are linked to the ones found last month. The area is still sealed off this morning while investigations are concluded at the site. As it is an area that is popular with dog walkers and ramblers, the police are hopeful that someone will have seen something.

Despite early reports that the first set of remains were those of Elizabeth King, the police have been unable to confirm this. A spokesperson said, 'Any speculation about who these remains belong to is unhelpful at this time. But if anyone saw anything suspicious, we would like to hear from them.'

Anyone who has any information related to either case is encouraged to call our hotline.

Chapter 26

Holly

Holly snuggled into Eloise's pale blue sofa and pulled the soft cream blanket around her. She wasn't even cold, but blankets were for comfort as much as for warmth, and what Holly needed more than anything was a hug.

When she'd heard the news about the second set of remains, she had gone straight to Eloise's house. She'd been sitting on the doorstep in the rain when Eloise returned from the gallery. Eloise looked like she was going to pass out when Holly told her about another engine house, another body, another woman, and what everyone was saying about it being linked to the first set of remains, but she soon recovered her composure and started preparing dinner as if it was a typical day.

'Can I help?' Holly asked.

Eloise looked at her blankly, as if she'd forgotten she was there. 'Perhaps you could set the table. I'm assuming you're staying for dinner?'

Holly got to her feet, but before she could answer, Eloise said, 'Could we not talk about any of this in front of Kit? I haven't had a chance to speak to him properly. Somehow he seems to be pissed off with *me*.'

'How come?'

'He thought I was unreasonable at the yoga studio. He thinks I'm accusing him of something.'

'Well, you are.'

'Yes, but he doesn't have the right to be annoyed about it. He's the one acting suspiciously, yet he's giving me the silent treatment.'

Holly stretched, and her back cracked. 'I can't believe you've sat on this for so long,' she said. 'I would've had it out with him a dozen times already.'

Eloise continued finely slicing an onion. 'I know. And usually I would. I don't normally bite my tongue, but every time I think about what I'm going to say, I tie myself up in knots about whether to confront him over his sneaky behaviour or start with confessing all about Elizabeth King. And now there's a second body . . . It's overwhelming.'

'It'll get worse the longer you wait,' Holly said, leaning on the counter between them.

'I know. I'll do it tonight after dinner.' Eloise lifted her arm to wipe her forehead, the large kitchen knife still in her hand.

'Shit!' said Holly. 'You're bleeding.'

'Am I?' Eloise looked at the blood snaking down her thumb. 'Oh. I don't know how . . . I didn't feel . . .' The knife clattered to the floor as she stepped backwards.

'Here,' Holly tore off a couple of sheets of kitchen roll and pressed them to Eloise's thumb. 'Hold it up for me. A bit higher. That's it.'

Eloise turned her face away and heaved into the sink. 'Sorry. I'm a firm believer that blood belongs on the inside of a body.'

197

'Amen to that,' said Holly. 'Sit at the table for a minute. Where do you keep your plasters?'

'In the cupboard above the microwave.' Eloise sank into a chair, elbow on the table, keeping her thumb elevated as if she were hitching a lift.

Holly sat beside her with a Tupperware box full of plasters and bandages. 'We might need to give it a minute to stop bleeding.'

'Okay,' Eloise said meekly.

Holly peeled back the kitchen roll and grimaced. 'You might need stitches. We should probably get you up to the Minor Injuries Unit before they close.'

'Perfect,' said Eloise. 'Just perfect.'

'What's going on in your head?' Holly asked.

'That my thumb is probably going to get infected, and then I'll have to have it amputated, and I'll never paint again.'

'I mean about the second set of remains,' said Holly. 'I'm guessing that's why you were preoccupied enough to slice through your thumb.'

Eloise shrugged. 'I'm not sure I'm thinking anything coherent. I'm just stunned.'

'Yeah.' Holly nodded. 'Same. Do you have any idea – any idea at all – who those second set of remains are?'

'I don't even know who the first set belong to.'

'Is there anyone from your Elizabeth King days who you pissed off?'

'Plenty,' Eloise said. 'But no one who would still hold a grudge thirty years later.'

'I think you're wrong,' said Holly. 'You're the key. Not many people knew you were missing, and no one was

198

talking about your disappearance any more. The fact that someone identified those first remains as yours means they knew you hadn't been heard from in thirty years. There's got to be a limited number of people who remember you even existed. No offence.'

'None taken. It's how I wanted it. I hoped if I left the past alone, it'd forget about me.'

'You say your family are all dead. What about aunts and cousins? Old boyfriends? First loves?'

'Literally no one. If I had any extended family, I never met them. I didn't have a close set of friends who would have wondered what happened to me. I had acquaintances who bought drugs from me, but they'd keep their distance unless we were at a party. And there are no ex-boyfriends still holding a flame. You've spoken to Gavin. I wasn't the kind of girl that boys pined over. But I suppose . . . No.' Eloise shook her head.

'Go on.'

'It's probably nothing, but when I was, you know, dealing, I was selling on behalf of a guy called Mack. I took my cut, but he had to make a profit too. It wasn't a lot, but he'll have noticed I never paid him the money I owed him.'

'It's as good a theory as any,' Holly said. 'Someone could be after you to pay your debts, realise you're still alive, plant a body with your name all over it and wait for you to come out of hiding. And when you still don't come forward, they plant another one. Genius, really.'

Eloise rolled her eyes. 'Firstly, people don't have a chest freezer full of dead bodies for occasions such as this, and secondly, it was only a few hundred pounds. That's not enough for him to worry about all these years later.'

'Imagine the interest on a thirty-year debt,' Holly said. She whistled. 'It could be thousands by now.'

'I doubt very much that Mack is still a dealer.'

'It's a funny word, that. Dealer. You make a deal. You deal cards. Surely you *sell* drugs.'

'Taking drugs is a game of chance,' said Eloise. 'Just like cards. You don't know how you'll react. You don't know how clean the drugs are. You don't know if they'll mix badly with other medication you're on and whether that will lead to an accidental overdose. My sister shouldn't have died that night. I have no idea what caused it. I mean, yes, she took the drugs, but she should have got high, not dead.'

Holly's phone buzzed. 'Oh, hold on,' she said.

'Everything okay?' asked Eloise.

'Sally Ann is asking again what I meant when I said there might be a Cornish link to Elizabeth's disappearance. She's like a dog with a bone. She says that even if it's a non-starter, it tells her where not to look. It's got to be her behind all this, right?'

'Got to be.'

'Some of the Truth Seekers group are coming down to Cornwall next weekend. Sally Ann is on the fence, presumably because it will blow her cover, but I think I might have an idea to bring her – or him – out of hiding. Are you up for it?'

'This might be the blood loss talking,' Eloise said. 'But sure. I'm getting sick of waiting for their next move. What have we got to lose?'

Truth Seekers UK

Holly Bobs

Hey everyone, okay, so this is BIG. I don't want to hijack the trip to Bertie's, BUT . . . I don't think there's any point in going to that nightclub to look for clues about what happened to Elizabeth. Sorry, Sasha. I know you were looking forward to visiting your old haunts, but I have an even better idea.

Seeing as the aim of this group has always been to seek out the truth (#TruthSeekers), I suggest that we widen the remit of this weekend. We need to raise awareness about ALL the missing people, not just Elizabeth King and my sister. There's another set of remains now – another missing girl – and I think it would be better if we shone a spotlight on the whole issue. What do you think?

I don't know everyone's story here – maybe you're just curious, or perhaps you've lost someone too – but I know that we all feel pain at the thought of these unsolved disappearances, and I want to do something more significant than just going around handing out leaflets in a nightclub.

The simple fact is we need to identify the remains so that families can get closure and those women get the burials they deserve. It's not even about getting justice for them at this point, though that's the ultimate goal, obviously.

Here's my plan. This Saturday, I want to gather people in Cornwall for a vigil. We need to get country-wide attention for these cases. So far, only the local news has reported the story. We need the nationals to come on board. Someone must know who these girls are.

Sasha Walters
Oh my God, I LOVE this idea. Yes! I'll get the old hen party back together. I can feel another coach trip coming on.

Patty Hansen
I'll order Truth Seekers badges to hand out at the vigil and I'll get the info on the local Facebook pages I'm on. I made a few friends when talking about coming down to Bertie's, and I know they'll be up for it. The problem is going to be getting them out from behind their computers. I'm on other missing person pages, too – I'll see who I can drum up. As soon as you decide when and where, let me know.

Holly Bobs
Ah guys, you're the best.
Since you started us on this path, Sally Ann, I really hope you can make it. I have a feeling that we're going to get some answers this weekend.

Sally Ann
Oh, I'm sure of it.

Chapter 27

Holly

Holly woke up feeling refreshed and energised. She'd run, showered, dressed and hung laundry on the line, all before nine o'clock. If she didn't achieve another thing all day, it would still be her most productive day in months. The only thing that dampened her mood was a note from her step-dad propped up on the kettle asking if they could grab dinner together later.

It wasn't that the thought of dinner with Liam was particularly bad; it was that her heart had lifted at the thought. She was annoyed at how pathetically pleased she was that he wanted to see her, but then she'd realised that he would probably tell her she had to move out, and Holly needed to buy a little more time. The job at the council hadn't come through – no surprise there – but she had an interview for a receptionist job at the hotel and spa in town on Saturday morning. This time she'd be prepared. She scribbled a response to Liam. *Sorry. Already got plans. Maybe Sunday?*

She had contacted Patty directly to ask for her help tracking down some information about Sally Ann, though she dressed it up as looking for further information about

Elizabeth. It was one of the reasons she had been so productive this morning. She had to keep busy because the waiting was driving her mad.

She was on the bus on the way to meet Eloise so they could visit the site where the second set of remains had been found when she finally got a response from Patty.

I've found the death certificate you wanted. Liz King senior died the year after junior Liz went missing. No cause of death was given, as far as I can see. She was only in her forties. No age at all. I guess what they say about a broken heart is true. However, I also looked for the dad's death certificate while I was there, but there's nothing for Tony or Anthony King from that year. I guess Sally Ann might be confused about dates, because it all happened before she was born.

Holly had spoken with Eloise about it while they were waiting for a nurse to do her stitches, and it turned out that Sally Ann was wrong about the dad's name. It was Bill, not Tony, and he'd died when Eloise was fifteen, so Holly responded with *Thanks, Patty. That stacks with what we know about Liz's death. Sally Ann is wrong about her grandfather, though. I think he was called Bill or William King and died around 1990/1991.*

The bus stopped, and several people climbed aboard. Holly placed her bag on the empty seat next to her and avoided meeting anyone's eye. Her phone chimed and she looked down to find a response from Patty already.

Bingo! William (Bill) King died of a heart attack in June 1990 in Nottinghamshire – a big news article about him. A bit of a wheeler-dealer, it seems. He was survived by a wife, Lizzie, and two daughters, Elizabeth and Deborah. Curiouser and curiouser. This is Elizabeth King's dad, then, not 'Tony' like Sally Ann said? I'm sending you the link to the article and obituary. Now are you going to tell me why you're asking all these questions behind Sally Ann's back?

Holly smiled. Sally Ann should have done her research before playing this game.

Thanks, Patty. You're a star. I didn't want to ask Sally Ann a load of intrusive questions when she was dealing with such a lot right now, but something in her story seemed a bit off. Did you find out anything about Eloise's sister?

Holly was aware of a woman behind her shifting in her seat and breathing heavily. She lowered her phone screen to make sure she couldn't read it over her shoulder.

A reply popped up from Patty. *Who's Eloise?*

Holly cringed. Shit. Her phone almost slid from her sweaty hand.

I meant to say Elizabeth. Duh. I don't know why I said Eloise. Is that even a real name? The more I say it, the less it sounds real. I meant Elizabeth, obviously.

She flapped her hand at her face. She couldn't make mistakes like that.

Okay. Well, her sister, Deborah, was born a couple of years after her.

What about Deborah's death certificate? Holly responded. She watched as the cursor showed that Patty was replying.

No death certificate. Still alive as far as I can tell.

Holly frowned and shook her head. *Are you sure? She died in February 1994, if that helps?*

It was a couple of minutes before Patty responded. *Nope. Nothing. But that's Sally Ann's mum, right? So we already know she's alive. Colour me intrigued. What aren't you telling me?*

Holly chewed her lip. That couldn't be right. Eloise had said that Deborah died the night she left Nottingham in February 1994. Patty must be mistaken.

Or Eloise had made the whole thing up.

She felt a wave of nausea wash over her and looked out of the window, trying to spot the horizon. She took three deep breaths before typing out a response to Patty. *Yeah. Sorry. You're right. I don't know what I was thinking.*

She tapped the phone against her mouth. Sally Ann had been wrong about her grandfather being called Tony and was wrong about when he died, but could Eloise be lying about her sister's death? And if Deborah didn't die in 1994, then that wasn't the reason that Eloise had fled into the night. Holly searched in her bag for a bottle of water. No, not her bag, Elizabeth King's bag. Eloise had seemed genuinely devastated about her sister's death, but was there a chance that Deborah was still alive and had a daughter called Sally Ann?

She didn't know what to believe any more. Was she really that gullible? She'd felt like she'd grown close to Eloise. She'd thought Eloise liked her, respected her opinion, but perhaps she'd been manipulating her all this time. She touched her phone screen and pulled up Sally Ann's last message asking about Elizabeth's Cornish connection. Maybe she should tell her everything. After all, she didn't owe Eloise her loyalty if she wasn't being straight with her.

The more she thought about it, the angrier she became. She was furious with Eloise for lying to her and angry with herself for falling for it. She was sick of everyone treating her as if she was stupid. It was time for the truth.

Hi, Sally Ann, sorry about the delay in getting back to you. Been hectic here with reporting my sister missing and everything. The Cornish link is this – I found Elizabeth King's old handbag. In fact, I have it here with me now. Those aren't her remains in the engine house – because she's not dead. She lives in Cornwall and calls herself Eloise Ford.

She sat back in her seat, her thumb hovering over the 'send' button, anger rolling in her stomach. She thought about what Eloise had said about 'not doing' anger, and wondered if that was even possible. All she had to do was press send, and Eloise would be exposed for who she really was.

But . . .

Eloise had explained that anger was an emotional response to hurt, and Holly was certainly feeling hurt right now. The idea that someone she trusted had lied to her wasn't easy to sweep aside. Still her thumb hovered.

It wasn't Sally Ann she needed to talk to, it was Eloise. She had to at least give her a chance to explain herself.

Her phone chimed as another message came in, and her heart hammered as if she'd been caught out. She swiped the message symbol on her phone and saw it was Patty again.

All righty. I got curious and delved a little deeper into our friend Sally Ann. For one thing, her Facebook account is fake. I did a reverse search on her profile picture, and it came back to a French woman living in Turkey. It's not uncommon – I 'borrowed' my photo too – but she hasn't posted anywhere online except our Facebook group, so it seems like she only created an account to track down Elizabeth King. Also – though again it's not that uncommon – I can't find anything about her mum. There is no marriage certificate for Deborah King and no sign of her having children. Hey, it happens – some people have no digital footprint – but Sally Ann isn't who she says she is. Some people, huh?

As the bus lurched, so did Holly's stomach. She was sweating, but relieved she hadn't sent that message to Sally Ann. Eloise might not have been entirely honest with her, but Sally Ann was the one who had misled her from the start. Maybe Eloise was right about anger being a response you could choose to have.

She brought up the message that she'd almost sent to Sally Ann so she could delete it. The bus slowed, and she looked up to see it was her stop. She grabbed her bag and jumped to her feet.

And that was when she heard the unmistakable sound of a message being sent.

Chapter 28

Eloise

The weather had turned a page, and summer was a distant memory. The sky, the sea and the mood were sombre. The Atlantic surged and spat as Holly adjusted her hood. Eloise wiped her hair out of her eyes, but it didn't make anything clearer.

The engine house squatted beneath them, built into the side of the cliff. Unseen were the tunnels stretching out under the sea. Flooded now. The building looked sturdy, the chimney tall and proud. But for lack of a roof, it was easy to imagine miners searching for rich seams of tin a hundred years before. They would have recognised the landscape, little having changed, but not the small white tent giving scant shelter to those piecing together the evidence and the remains. A police officer in a high-visibility jacket stood by the engine house to stop anyone from coming any closer, but Holly and Eloise had seen all they were going to see.

'Are you feeling okay?' asked Eloise.

Holly's face was the same grey as the sky, and she'd barely said a word.

'Yeah. I think maybe I'm coming down with something.'

Eloise took a step away from her.

A man walked behind them with his big shaggy dog on a lead. 'Afternoon,' he said as the dog sniffed Eloise's hand.

'Afternoon,' they said in unison.

After he had walked on, Eloise said, 'Any news on your sister?'

'Not yet.'

'Have you checked if any of her friends have heard from her?'

'Despite what you think of me, I'm not completely stupid,' Holly said. 'It was the first thing I did.'

'I didn't mean to imply . . .' Eloise turned away. She had the feeling that she was somehow responsible for Holly's bad mood. 'You've not told me much about Lisa,' she said. 'What's she like?'

Holly folded her arms and stared straight ahead. Eloise thought she was going to tell her to mind her own business, but eventually she said, 'She's a lot of fun. Opinionated. Loud. She got even louder after Mum died. Like she couldn't have a quiet moment in case the sadness came crashing in. She's sensitive, though, and easily hurt, so she drops anyone who upsets her, says the wrong thing or forgets her birthday. On the flip side, she makes friends quickly. She can sit next to someone on the train, and by the time she gets off again she knows their life story and has arranged to meet them at the pub that night. I couldn't tell you who her friends were at the time she disappeared. Same with boyfriends. They were the love of her life for maybe a month and then . . . dead to her. I gave up remembering their names. I've messaged everyone I can think of asking them to get in touch if they see or hear from her, but most of them say the same thing – that they haven't heard from her since Mum's funeral. She started hanging with a new crowd after that. People who didn't ask how she was feeling or treat her like she was made of glass.'

'I hope I get to meet her one day,' Eloise said.

'We both know that's unlikely. Can we not talk about her for now?'

The rain was keeping the gawkers away. Dog walkers and ramblers stopped to point but soon moved on. They didn't have the same fascination as Holly and Eloise did. Eloise watched Holly wipe under her eyes but couldn't tell if she was crying. Maybe she was thinking that one day she could be standing by an old ruin as the police recovered her sister's body.

'By the way,' said Holly, 'I keep meaning to ask you about the paintings you had for sale at the yoga studio.'

'What about them?'

'I noticed that you painted engine houses. Have you done this one?' She nodded down the hill.

Eloise's whole body tensed. 'I was wondering whether anyone would spot that. Yes, I've been trying to work out if it's a coincidence or not.'

'Did you paint the one where the first remains were found too?'

Eloise nodded. 'Yes, but lots of people do. I used to sell prints of engine houses at craft fairs. They were some of my most popular pieces. I suppose I can't ignore the fact that two sets of human remains have been found in engine houses that I've painted and that my old name was given to the police. It's beginning to feel like more than a coincidence now.'

'Beginning?' said Holly. 'Now?'

Eloise shrugged. Some things were easier to ignore than acknowledge.

'How many engine houses did you paint?' asked Holly.

'Three. I used to sell them as a set.'

'Oh my God. Do you think there's a body in the third one too?'

Eloise's eyes widened. 'Not until you just brought it up.' She turned her face to the drizzle. 'Please God don't let there be another body.'

'But if there is,' said Holly slowly. 'If there is, then it means that the killer knows that Eloise Ford and Elizabeth King are the same person. So, you know, we could plaster it all over social media if we wanted and it wouldn't matter.'

'It would matter to me,' said Eloise.

'Have you spoken to Kit yet?'

Eloise adjusted her hood. 'He was asleep – or pretending to be – when I got home from the hospital, so I didn't get the chance. Have you managed to find out anything else about Sally Ann?'

Holly took her phone out of her pocket and checked the display. 'Ken's late,' she said.

'That's okay. What about Sally Ann? Any progress?'

'Sorry, what was that?'

'I asked if you knew anything else about Sally Ann.'

'Oh, not much. We might see her this weekend at the vigil after all. I know she's lying about some things, but she's not the only one.'

'What do you mean?' asked Eloise.

Holly shook her head. 'Nothing.'

She hadn't looked Eloise in the eye all morning.

'No, come on,' said Eloise. 'Say what's on your mind.'

'We all show a certain side of ourselves, don't we? That's so much easier online. We can be whoever we want to be. Taller. Braver. We use filters to make ourselves look younger, thinner, or use AI-generated images that show us as superheroes or Viking warriors. We only share the things that paint us in the best light. It's hard to know what's real. For all we know, Sally Ann could be a sixty-five-year-old man living in his mother's basement or someone you see at yoga every week.'

A man was walking towards them down the coastal path. He was wearing a long black coat and was hunched over against the weather. His hands were shoved deep into his pockets. As he got closer, he looked up and waved.

'Is this Ken?' asked Eloise.

'Yep.'

He didn't quicken his pace or seem in any hurry, so the silence between Holly and Eloise lasted long enough to become uncomfortable.

'Good afternoon,' he said as he reached them. 'Excuse my tardiness. I took several wrong turns, unfamiliar as I am with this part of Cornwall. I hope I haven't kept you waiting long.'

'Ages,' Holly said. 'But only because we were ridiculously early, thanks to this one.' She poked her thumb in Eloise's direction. 'This is Eloise, by the way.'

'Pleased to meet you,' he said, pushing his rain-splattered glasses up over the bridge of his nose.

Eloise held out a hand, but Ken looked at her bandaged thumb and shook his head. 'I don't do handshakes,' he said. 'I hope that doesn't offend.'

213

Eloise dropped her hand. 'Of course. No, that's fine. Nice to meet you anyway.'

'So,' said Ken.

'So,' said Eloise.

They all looked towards the white tent.

'I've told Eloise about your contacts and forensic knowledge,' said Holly. 'She's interested in finding out more about these remains. So am I, obviously. This is mad, isn't it? I can't get my head around there being another discovery like this.'

'Yes. It is rather confusing,' said Ken. 'I did not expect this in the least. Our . . . I hesitate to say "killer", because we do not know that these are murder victims, but the person who moved the remains here took quite the risk. If their crime has been hidden for decades, it seems an odd choice to move them to a place where they could be found. I would love to see a personality profile.' He looked at Eloise over the top of his glasses. 'Holly tells me that you have information about the first discovery?'

Eloise crossed her arms. 'I don't know.'

Holly scowled. 'If he's going to help us, we have to give him something in return.'

'I know, but how do we know he has anything else to tell us? He might just be getting his information off the internet like the rest of us.' Eloise turned to Ken. 'Sorry, I don't mean to be rude, but I have no way of knowing that you're not just, well, making stuff up.'

Ken took a raggedy old tissue out of his pocket and blew his nose. 'I have a contact in the police who gives me information before it is made public in return for me not leaking information about him to his employers. It is a mutually

214

beneficial relationship. So no, I am not "making stuff up", as you so eloquently put it.'

Holly gave Eloise a nudge. 'If you don't tell him, I will.'

Eloise narrowed her eyes and shook her head ever so slightly. 'I just think that the fewer people who know . . .'

'Why can't everyone just be open and honest? It would save us all a lot of trouble.'

'Fine,' said Eloise. 'Ken, I have a link to the first set of remains. I just don't know exactly what it is yet. I'm hoping you can tell us more about this one, because if we can discover who these remains belong to, then I might be able to work out why this is all happening.'

Ken took off his glasses and wiped them with the same tissue he'd used to blow his nose. 'Please do go on,' he said.

'The anonymous tip-off was incorrect,' said Eloise. 'The police have already said that the DNA was inconclusive, and everyone is now backtracking on claiming it's Elizabeth, but I knew from the day the news broke that it wasn't her. You see, Elizabeth King didn't die thirty years ago. She ran away from home, just as the reports are suggesting, but she is still very much alive.'

Ken's eyebrows shot up under his hood. 'Is that right? That *is* interesting.'

'For me, the question has never been what happened to Elizabeth, it has always been why someone would say that it was her body.'

'Remains,' Ken said.

'I beg your pardon?'

'Remains. You said "body". There is no body as such. We only have remains.'

Eloise took a deep breath, and Holly gave her a look that was both a warning and a message to play nice.

'Fine then. Remains. But I don't like how impersonal that sounds. These girls had names and lives. They were more than their bones.'

Ken's eyes grew larger behind his thick lenses. 'Of course. Yes. Can I ask how you are so sure Elizabeth is still alive?'

Holly and Eloise exchanged glances. 'I've met her,' Eloise said. 'And if it becomes necessary, she is willing to talk to the police and tell them that they're looking in the wrong place. But not yet. She prefers to let this play out. Now it's your turn. Why are you so involved in this? Isn't it a bit strange for you to be hanging around sites where human remains are found?'

Ken twisted around to gaze down on the engine house. 'I'm looking for someone who went missing twelve years ago in Cornwall. Every time a body is found, I can't help but wonder if it's her. And if I can't find her, I can at least help someone else get answers so they're not going through the worry that I am going through every day. It could be said that with each case I'm involved in I learn a little bit more, and hope that one day it will lead me to solve the mystery of what happened to her. It is both that simple and that complicated.'

Eloise nodded. It was hard to argue with that.

'I told you,' Holly said to her. 'Many people in this Facebook group are looking for someone, so they're invested in these cases. Others on there are cyber-sleuths and tragedy pimps, but, you know, we all have our place.'

Eloise said. 'I'm sorry for your . . . for what you're going through. I didn't mean to imply that you were suspicious or anything.'

'I think you did,' said Ken. 'But that's all right. You are not the first person to question my motives. I spend far too much of my time looking at missing persons cases and pictures of dead bodies. It can be off-putting for people who do not understand my motivation.'

Ken had an unnerving way of staring too long into people's eyes, as if he'd once been told to hold eye contact and now treated it as a sport. Awkward and socially uncomfortable, he was an intense man.

'Is there anything you can tell us about what they've found in this engine house?' Eloise asked. 'I'd appreciate any information that hasn't already been released.'

Ken sniffed. 'Yes, of course. On initial inspection, these remains . . . sorry, this *person* has many similarities to the first victim. They appear to have died at around the same time. The coverings are the same. It's the same type of carpet and tarpaulin. The bungee cords used to, um, keep everything together are new, but otherwise it is identical to what we saw before. The remains were likely left here around the same time as the first set. It is too soon to say how old the victim was at the time of death, but preliminary reports suggest a young woman again. The difference this time is that this one has a healed break in her femur and has some personal items with her. Jewellery. Rings and a distinctive necklace. The police will release pictures in due course to see if anyone recognises the personal effects, but my contact hasn't seen them, so I am unable to share the information with you at this time.'

Eloise nodded. She still couldn't work out what this had to do with her. A necklace was unlikely to jog her memory, and she didn't think she knew anyone who'd ever broken their leg.

'There's a database of bodies, of remains, spanning decades,' Ken said. 'People can check to see if someone they know is on it. People who are looking for answers or closure. Sometimes there are pictures of the clothes they were found in, or descriptions of tattoos and personal items. Information about when and where they were found. You'd be surprised by how many people die in this country without anyone noticing. Victims of crimes, suicide or even natural causes. I find it one of the saddest things to read stories of bodies found at the bottom of cliffs or hanging from trees. Here's a person who felt that no one cared if they lived or died, only to be proved right when no one comes forward to claim their body and give them a decent burial.'

Holly spoke without emotion. 'I check those websites every couple of days.'

Ken looked at her kindly. 'It does not make for happy reading. Those people. Those poor unnamed people. It's a strange feeling when you don't find the one you're looking for. You are both relieved and disappointed at the same time. You don't want to know the worst, but it's another day in limbo. I hope that the families of these girls, whoever they are, don't have to wait much longer for closure.' He looked at Eloise. 'And if you can work out how these remains are linked to you, you could be the one to give them answers.'

Truth Seekers UK

Ken Marchpane

Dear all, an update on the second set of remains. Police have confirmed that it is the same carpet and the same plastic wrapping. It's extremely unlikely this is a copycat.
Kind regards, Ken.

Patty Hansen

OMFG, we have ourselves a serial killer!

Ken Marchpane

Technically speaking, there would need to be more than two victims for this to be a serial killer. Also, can I stress that there is no evidence of foul play. We do not know that these two young women were murdered. Kind regards, Ken.

Patty Hansen

Ken, honey, 'technically speaking' young women don't tend to die of natural causes and then wrap themselves up in a rug before hiding away for thirty years. And they certainly don't then get up, shuffle to the nearest mine shaft and throw themselves down it. Say what you want, but these women were murdered, and they were murdered by someone who was known to them. Just because we're only aware of two victims doesn't mean there aren't more.

Sasha Walters

God, it makes me sick. It could have been any one of us on the hen trip. There are some disgusting people around. Also, will send link to local hotels for our Newquay trip. Patty will bring T-shirts for everyone who can make it. Sally Ann and Holly, we WILL find out what happened to your loved ones.

Holly Bobs

The sad truth is that thousands of people go missing every year. Some loved ones are never found, and some bodies are never named. These women need justice. And not just these women – every missing person. And I know this might sound selfish, but the FAMILIES need closure. We're the ones living this nightmare every single day.

Chapter 29

Holly

By the time they got back to Eloise's gallery, Holly had a message from Sally Ann asking for more information. It was hard to tell the tone from a sentence or two, but Holly didn't get the impression that Sally Ann was surprised. If it had been her and someone knew where Lisa was, she would have been messaging them every minute of every day until they told her everything. She would be beating down their door. Begging them. Threatening them.

She told Sally Ann she would introduce her to Eloise at the upcoming vigil. One way or another it was all going to be out in the open. Now, she just had to confront Eloise about lying about her sister's death and confess to accidentally revealing Elizabeth's new name.

Eloise handed Holly a letter that she'd just opened.

'What's this?' Holly asked.

'Eviction notice. My landlord's selling up.'

'Oh crap. Sorry.'

'It looks like the company that wants the yoga studio is buying up several of the buildings in this part of town. Luckily, I've got far more important things to worry about,' Eloise said.

Holly and Eloise were drinking instant hot chocolate, hoping it would warm their bones, but theirs wasn't the kind of chill that could be thawed with a hot beverage. Eloise had brought back the unsold prints from the yoga studio's open day. The originals would remain hanging until Mimi had to move on or until she raised enough money to buy the studio from Arthur.

Eloise had only sold half of her paintings and a third of the prints, so the required money wasn't likely to come from her endeavours. Holly found it hard to feel sorry for Mimi. She still didn't know what to believe. All she knew was that Mimi was the last confirmed person to have seen Lisa.

'I need to understand why someone would choose the ruins in my paintings to dispose of human remains when they've been hanging on to them for decades. Why now, why there and why me?' Eloise shuffled closer to the prints, peering at them like she was looking at them for the first time. 'It must be someone who has seen these paintings. I can tell you without false modesty that I haven't sold many full sets of these. They've been popular, but I've only sold maybe fifty of them. Why would someone look at these paintings and think, "Oh, now I know where to dispose of those skulls I've got cluttering up my cellar. And while we're at it, let's say that one of them is Elizabeth King"? I don't understand.'

They'd propped up the three engine house prints side by side against the counter and knelt on the scrubbed wooden floor to admire them. Two had been painted in the summertime, when the gorse erupted in yellows and purples and blue skies waved the wispy white clouds along. But the last one was set against the backdrop of a storm. Angry grey waves arced, reaching for the building, desperate to drag it into the sea. Holly wouldn't have hung them on her bedroom wall, but she could admire the skill that had gone into them. She leaned forward until her elbows were on the floor.

'You don't sign the paintings,' she said. 'There's just a squiggle that starts with an E, but it looks more like it says ... Elora? Emma? How would anyone know that Elizabeth King painted these? You did them long after you'd stopped being known as Elizabeth, right?'

'Right. It makes absolutely no sense.'

'I don't see the dragonfly in this one,' Holly said.

Eloise leaned closer too. 'It's there somewhere.' She tilted her head one way and then another. 'There!' she said. 'On that bush.'

'It's a bit on the skinny side,' Holly said. 'Looks more like a stick insect.'

'They're not meant to stand out. It was a secret sign between me and my sister.'

'Okay. But she's dead, right? So why do you still do it?'

'To honour her memory, I suppose. One of the many downsides of not being open about my past,' said Eloise, 'is that I don't get to talk about her.'

Holly got to her feet and placed her cup on the table by the pot of paintbrushes. 'We've got to go to that third engine house,' she said.

'Terrible idea,' said Eloise. 'There could be more remains, or a murderer lurking in the shadows.'

'That's exactly why we should go,' said Holly. 'Sometimes I don't think you're serious about finding out who's behind this. We owe it to these women to name them and find out who did this to them. I still think the first step is you coming clean about being Elizabeth King.'

'You know I can't do that, Holly.'

'You're being incredibly selfish, you know. You're thinking about yourself and your cosy little life instead of getting justice for these girls.'

Eloise rocked backwards as if Holly had slapped her. 'It's a bit more than that.'

'Then what is it?'

'We keep asking what this has to do with me.'

Holly nodded. 'As I say, you're the key.'

'And on the face of it, we can't see anything. The Truth Seekers group, and Sally Ann in particular, are trying to trace the last movements of Elizabeth King so they can find her killer and get justice, right?'

'Right.'

'But what if that's not true? We already know that Sally Ann is lying about who she is. What if she discovered I'm still alive from these paintings?'

'Do you think she could have recognised the stick insects?'

'Dragonflies.'

'Whatever.'

'She must know that I can't escape the local media coverage of the discovery of those remains, given that my old name is all over the news. She's not trying to find Elizabeth's killer. She's trying to find Elizabeth. And she's not doing it because she's a long-lost niece wanting to reconnect, is she? She's trying to flush me out.'

'Okay,' Holly said. 'I hear you. And if she does know your new identity, this is *definitely* how she found out about it, not someone blabbing to her, but . . .'

'But?'

She looked at Eloise closely. There was never going to be a better time than this to bring up Deborah's death. 'There's something I'm not telling you,' she said. 'Actually, there's something you're not telling me. So really, if we're being honest, you started it.'

'Started what?' Eloise asked.

'Right. So what I'm saying is . . .' Holly blew out her cheeks and scratched the back of her head. This was more difficult than she'd expected. She didn't want to address the fact that Eloise was lying to her. She didn't want to address the fact that she'd told Sally Ann about Eloise. She didn't want this all to come crashing down around them when Eloise was the closest thing she had to a parental figure in her life right now.

'I don't suppose you want to make this easier for me by coming out and saying it, do you?' she asked. 'Tell me the truth about what happened. You know. Clean slate and all.'

Eloise blinked and shook her head. 'Come again?'

Holly sank to the floor to sit cross-legged opposite her. 'I trusted you,' she said. 'I believed every word you said, but when I asked Patty to look into your mum's death, I also asked her to find Deborah's death certificate.'

Eloise narrowed her eyes. 'Okay. And?'

Holly studied Eloise's face, but she didn't look like a woman worried about being found out.

'And . . . nothing,' she said. 'There's no record of Deborah's death. I couldn't find any mention in the local papers about two teens overdosing, and no mention of the tragic story of Elizabeth King's younger sister, even though that's the kind of stuff a journalist would be all over.'

'What? I . . . I don't . . . What are you saying, Holly?'

'When we went back to your old house, the neighbour said that people had been sniffing around trying to find out more about Lizzie King. You said that everyone knew everyone else's business on that estate, so why has no one mentioned your sister dying on the night you disappeared?'

'I don't understand.'

'No death certificate. No news reports. No loose-lipped neighbours. In fact, that woman we saw at your old house mentioned something happening to those girls *plural*. Deborah and her girlfriend *didn't* die that night, did they? They just did the same as you did and disappeared. You wanted me to feel sorry for you. You know my sister is probably dead. We're skating around it, but that's what we're both thinking. Did you think I was more likely to keep your secret about being Elizabeth if we'd bonded over something as tragic as the death of our sisters?'

Eloise got shakily to her feet and backed away. 'How can you think I'd lie about something like this? I saw my sister's dead body in that house. I . . . I swear on my children's lives, Holly, and you know I wouldn't do that lightly.' She put her hand to her lips. 'She was dead. I'm sure of it. I checked for a pulse.'

'And her girlfriend?'

She shook her head. 'I . . . She looked dead. And I only really cared about Debs.'

'Then why is there no record of her death?'

Eloise rested her forehead on the wall and closed her eyes. 'If I hadn't seen her body, I wouldn't have left. I wouldn't have been hiding from my past for thirty years. I know what I saw.'

Holly stood up and went to her. If she was still lying, she deserved an Oscar.

'Your sister survived, didn't she? Ran away the same night you did.'

Eloise shook her head. 'No. I . . . don't think so. I was so sure that . . . But I suppose it's possible.'

'And you really didn't know?'

'I swear, Holly.'

'Listen,' said Holly. 'We need to consider that she is alive and looking for you. Sally Ann said that her mum had recently moved down south, but if she's behind all this, my guess is that she's pretty pissed off that you left her for dead, and right now, she's not looking for a happy family reunion.'

Chapter 30

Eloise

The sun was setting by the time Eloise and Holly got to the third engine house. Eloise had always thought of herself as a sunrise person – all about the new day and the new start – but as she stood and watched the setting sun turning the sea into molten gold, she was astounded by its beauty. There was a very real sense that something was coming to an end, but that a new dawn was on its way.

'Is this the place?' asked Holly.

Eloise nodded, but hung back, not keen to go any further.

'Imagine working here. Do you know what they mined for?'

'Copper, but it closed in the 1840s. There's not much to it any more. There are several tunnels set into the cliffs from the beach, but they're all blocked up, and the shafts have been capped.'

'If there's another set of remains here, where would they be?' Holly asked.

Eloise pointed up the hill. 'That's the bit I painted, so I guess we should start there. Maybe we should call the police.'

Holly shook her head. 'If there's anything here, we need to see it first.'

They climbed the dusty path to the engine house. A sign on a wooden fence warned them to go no further, so they checked that no one was looking and climbed over anyway.

The windows and doors were long gone, as were the roof and the floor. The place was in three distinct sections. On one side, the walls were little more than waist height and there was a space where a door used to be. To the left, the chimney itself. Grey bricks at the bottom, red at the top. The narrow building attached to it looked like someone had begun renovating it a few years back. There were several converted engine houses around the county now being used as family homes or Airbnbs. Kit had always fancied living in one, but Eloise was no longer keen.

'Are you ready?' asked Holly.

'No,' said Eloise.

Holly slipped behind a wall. Eloise could see her hair through the space that used to be a window. Though she was in no rush to find out what was in there, she was seized by a sudden concern for the girl. 'Holly, wait!'

She climbed through the window and waited a moment for her eyes to adjust. Though the engine house didn't have a roof, it was still dark inside, so Holly turned on her phone torch.

'Be careful,' said Eloise. There's a hole in the centre.'

'Got it,' Holly said. 'Do you think that's where . . .?' They both edged forward, sliding their feet over the dirty ground. Holly swept the torch beam about the space. They both exhaled with relief as they saw it was empty. The ground dropped away, showing a shelf, and then darkness.

229

'Could there be something hidden down there? In a tunnel or something?' asked Holly.

'It's all blocked up,' said Eloise. 'And the other two women were clearly visible from above. If there was something here, we'd see it.'

'I don't understand what I'm looking at,' Holly said peering into the darkness. 'Is this the start of the mine?'

'The mines are below here, and there would have been a beam over the shaft. They would have been pumping water out of the lower levels from here.'

'Cool,' Holly said. 'And they were steam-powered, yeah?'

'Yep. That's what the tall chimney is for.'

'So that drop . . .'

'It's been filled in, but this is where the engine would have been.'

'But no dead bodies,' said Holly. 'So that's good.'

'Yeah,' said Eloise. 'So good.'

'Great.'

Eloise sighed. 'Is there something wrong with me? I actually feel a little disappointed. I'd prepared myself for another carpet roll of remains. I thought we'd been so clever figuring it all out.'

'I know,' said Holly. 'Are we meant to assume that those two sets of remains found at the other two engine houses were just a coincidence then?'

'And the mention of my name just a mistake?'

'And the fact that we can't find a death certificate for your sister . . .'

'Okay,' Eloise said. 'This is what we know so far. My sister may or may not have survived the overdose. I may or may not have been responsible for that overdose.'

'Yep.'

'And regardless of whether or not she survived, there is little doubt that I should have stuck around to call an ambulance and deal with the fallout – whatever that might have been.'

'For the record,' said Holly, 'I think it's perfectly understandable that you would do a runner. If you thought you could have helped, you would have done. You only ran because you thought there was nothing else to do and nothing to stay for.'

Eloise almost smiled. Holly was a lot nicer to her than she deserved.

'Bless you, Holly.'

'What? It's true.'

'And we also know that the two sets of remains that have been found are young women who were around my age when I left home, and they died around thirty years ago. They are somehow linked to me because my name was mentioned to the police and the bodies left at locations in my paintings.'

Holly nudged Eloise with her elbow. 'I bet you're wishing you hadn't painted those dragonflies now, aren't you? I mean, it has to be your sister, right? Who else but Deborah would have noticed those skinny insects.'

Eloise deflated. 'I know what you're saying makes sense, but I can't unsee my sister dead in that bedroom.'

'I'm just going to come out and say it,' Holly said. 'If your sister is behind this, just to track you down and make you pay or whatever, then she is also behind the deaths of these two women. And I don't care how upset someone is that their sister did a runner and left them for dead, you don't go around killing people, you know?'

She put her hands on the warm brick wall and peered into the darkness. 'The way I see it, we have two problems. One is that you have a murderous sister on the rampage, and the other is that there are two women who never got the burial they deserved and their families who never found out the truth. I hope that in thirty years I'm not still wondering what happened to my sister.'

'You will find out what happened to Lisa,' Eloise said. 'And as long as my sister doesn't kill me and dump my body in an engine house, then I promise I'll help you get answers.'

She looked around the space, imagining the people who had passed through here and wondering why, of the three engine houses, this one had been overlooked.

'Do you still think I was lying to you about believing my sister was dead?' she asked.

'No,' Holly said.

'What changed your mind?'

'I decided that I wanted to believe you. So I did. Even though part of me is screaming out that I'm too gullible and I should be cautious. Sod it, I'm all in anyway. You had every chance to push me down that bloody great hole and make me the third body in an engine house, but you didn't, so I guess you've passed the test.'

'That's a high-risk strategy, Holly. Please don't do that again.'

'I reckon everyone tells fibs, but at least I understand why you changed your name and lied about where you came from, so I can trust that lie.'

Eloise nodded. That was the kind of logic she could get behind.

'Hey, listen,' said Holly. 'I've had a thought. Why don't we let your sister know we're on to her, by holding the vigil here?'

'I'm not against the idea,' said Eloise. 'But we don't know that Deborah is behind this for sure.'

Holly snorted. 'Now who's being gullible?'

Chapter 31

Eloise

Eloise arrived at the wine bar early. She poured two glasses of white from the bottle she'd ordered and waited. She'd been feeling good about herself when she'd left the gallery in the early-evening sunshine. The stress of the past few weeks had slimmed her hips and eradicated that thigh chafe that had been bothering her. She couldn't remember the last time she'd felt confident enough to wear this dress, but it used to be her favourite. Flattering, quirky and with much-needed pockets. But now, with her hair a mess and surrounded by the chic and the beautiful, she felt drab and frumpy.

Asking Kit to meet her here, at their favourite little wine bar, was a coward's move. She knew they should be discussing this at home, in private, but she needed the public setting to make sure they both kept their voices down and didn't cause a scene.

She was in the corner, with her back to the wall, where she could see everyone who came in through the door. She'd ignored two of Mimi's EGM demands; it was more important to have this out with Kit. It wasn't that she didn't have sympathy for what Mimi was going through, but it was hard to care about her losing her yoga studio when

234

Eloise feared she was about to lose her husband, her family and her carefully curated life.

These minutes before Kit turned up were necessary for her to gather her thoughts and rehearse what she would say. She'd always had a desperate need to be early. Tardiness suggested either a lack of care for the person you were meeting, as if their time wasn't as important as yours, or an inability to be organised or to tell the time. Arriving late meant that everyone else could gather ahead of you and gossip about the weight you'd put on or the skinny jeans you'd worn to that fundraiser that were at least two years out of fashion and two sizes too small. They could bring to life your biggest fear that your husband had been spotted at a McDonald's drive-through with a mystery blonde and a McFlurry, and by the time you arrived, not even fifteen minutes late, no one would meet your eye and the social humiliation would be complete.

Eloise would panic so much at the thought of being late that she was almost invariably early for doctor's appointments, trains and nights out, already covered in a sheen of anxiety sweat, her clothes bunched up under her armpits. That one morning when she was late for yoga with Mimi was an anomaly. And look how it had turned out. If she hadn't been late and trying to fill time, maybe she wouldn't have seen that tiny news article, barely a headline, with her old name in it. Maybe her life wouldn't have imploded. Perhaps she would still be living in a blissful state of ignorance. No, for Eloise, being late was not an option. She could not think of one situation where it had ever been beneficial. But now she was waiting for Kit to arrive, she was desperate for him to get there soon so she could get this over with.

She would start by telling him her real name and about the bodies in the engine houses, and when he inevitably accused her of betraying him, she would counter with the bombshell that she knew all about his little affair.

She took a sip of wine and resisted the urge to down it in one. She felt sick and hot and would have welcomed a meteorite landing on the wine bar to save her from this conversation. She'd only ever wanted a peaceful life.

Peace. She scoffed at the thought. She hadn't had a moment of peace since those remains had been found. Just as Holly had said, there was no record of Deborah's death. She'd found her mother's and father's death certificates and ordered copies for no apparent reason. It felt like she was claiming them as hers. Acknowledging that, despite their faults, they had made her. But they'd also made Deborah, and who knew what she was capable of.

In Eloise's mind, Deborah was still seventeen years old. Angry and skinny, all knees and elbows and chewing gum. It didn't seem possible that she could have been alive when Eloise fled. She'd searched for marriage certificates, birth certificates, anything that could have hinted at Deborah having lived a decent life these past years, but there was no trace. She was a ghost.

The idea that she might have survived didn't make Eloise as happy as it should have done. She'd been certain that Deborah and Mel were dead. She'd never seen a dead body before, but she'd known that what she was looking at was no longer her sister.

Had she been wrong?

Had she walked out on Deborah, leaving her all alone? Or maybe not alone, but with their mother, which was far worse. But then when Lizzie had died, who'd been looking out for her then? Had Debs ever wondered what had happened to her older sister? Did she miss her? Had she assumed that Elizabeth was dead too? Did she feel betrayed when she found out that she was alive and living as Eloise with her neat little house, her husband and two kids?

Eloise would have done.

There was no easy end to this. She couldn't envisage a tearful happy reunion with her sister. For a start, there were the remains of at least two unnamed dead women in engine houses around the county. That wasn't the kind of thing you found in a garage sale. That Debs had gone to this much trouble to flush her out did not bode well or speak kindly to her sister's state of mind.

The door opened, and Kit paused at the threshold. He forced his face into a smile and waved.

'This is nice,' he said. 'And on a school night too.' He leaned in to kiss her. A chaste peck on the cheek, which barely made contact with her skin.

'We've hardly seen each other recently,' Eloise said as he took his seat opposite her. 'I thought we needed . . . something. And we probably need to clear the air.'

Kit took a sip of his wine and smacked his lips together. 'That's nice,' he said. He eased the bottle from the ice bucket, read the label and nodded appreciatively.

'Are we getting food while we're here?' he asked picking up the menu. 'I do like their Mediterranean platter.'

'Sure. But can we wait a few minutes before we order? There are a couple of things that—'

'That's new,' he said. 'They do a Spanish one now. Decisions, decisions.'

'Kit, I'm trying to talk to you about something important.'

'More important than chorizo?'

Eloise put her hand on the top of the menu and pulled it down until it was flat on the table and Kit's eyes were on her.

'Go on then,' he said. 'Let's hear it.'

'There are some things I need to get off my chest,' she said.

She reached for his hand and noticed him flinch, but he recovered quickly. She rubbed his knuckles with her thumb. 'These past few weeks, everything has been changing. Things have caught up with me and I can't ignore it any more.'

She closed her eyes. She mustn't lose sight of why she'd brought him here. She took a sip of wine to steady her nerves, but her shaking hand betrayed her. She lifted her chin and focused on Kit. If she left it any longer, she'd never do it.

'So here it is . . .' She took a deep breath. 'The truth is . . . the thing I need to tell you is . . . yeah, so I'm being evicted from the art gallery.'

'What?'

She grimaced at her own weakness. This wouldn't get any easier if she kept putting it off.

'The landlord's selling the building to developers. But there's more. There's something else.'

'Sorry to hear that. Are you looking at other premises?'

'No, but . . . that's not what I was going to say. I'm trying to tell you the main reason I brought you here this evening.'

She nodded to herself. It was now or never. 'There was an article in the local newspaper,' she said. 'Just a small thing that I could have easily missed.'

She didn't notice the door opening or the harassed-looking woman striding towards her.

'It caught my eye because it mentioned the case of a young woman who went missing thirty years ago. At first the police thought they'd found—'

'There you are,' said Mimi. 'Bloody hell, I've been trying to reach you all afternoon.' She sat down heavily.

'What are you doing here?' Eloise asked, startled.

'I saw you through the window. God, I love this place. Why don't we come here more often?'

'Actually, we were just having a quiet—' began Eloise.

'Oh, sorry. Do you want me to leave?'

'Don't be daft,' said Kit. 'I'll get you a glass.' He stood and hitched up his trousers.

'Good man,' said Mimi. She turned to Eloise. 'You won't believe what's happened. They've shut down the yoga studio because it doesn't meet some ridiculous fire regulations that I swear they made up on the spot. Joseph is behind this, I'm sure. Honestly, when I get hold of him . . . And if that wasn't bad enough, I've had Holly and Lisa's stepdad at the studio today. He said he was retracing Lisa's last movements, but it was obvious he was trying to track Holly down. He says she's rarely home any more. I hope you don't mind, but I told him to check with you at the gallery. That's one headache I don't need.'

Eloise watched Kit at the bar. He looked more relaxed now that Mimi was here. Almost as if he'd planned it.

Truth Seekers UK

Patty Hansen

Really looking forward to seeing everyone who can make it this weekend. I have the T-shirts and badges. Holly made me think about the number of people who go missing and the families who never get closure. We could help so many people with our skills in this group.

Andy Pickford

When did I ever say I wanted to help other people? When?

Patty Hansen

Why are you such an asshole?

Andy Pickford

Must've been starved of affection when I was a child.

Sasha Walters

I'm packed and ready to go! Is it wrong to be this excited when we're only going because of such sad reasons? It's just amazing that we get to do something to help. Especially as I feel so guilty about what happened to Elizabeth. This is my way to right the wrongs of thirty years ago. Women should look out for other women, not just leave them to fend for themselves in dingy nightclubs.

Marsha Pirolo

I must admit I'm quite nervous about meeting you all. It feels significant that this is moving from an online to a face-to-face group – like a dream coming to life. I'm convinced that we're being guided by a higher power to do good.

Andy Pickford

Jesus. I just gave myself a hernia from cringing so hard.

Chapter 32

Eloise

Eloise stood in front of the gallery and looked again at the damage. The site of impact was an inch or two below centre, but the reinforced glass had held firm. She touched the bullseye, almost as if to confirm it was real. Someone had thrown a brick at her window.

The damage would likely only cost hundreds to repair instead of thousands, and the artwork beyond was thankfully untouched, so she should probably be happy about that. She didn't think this was an attempt to steal anything, because there were easier and quieter ways to gain entrance. This felt . . . personal.

Mimi had told Holly's stepdad where to find her. Could this be a coincidence? Was he annoyed that she was spending so much time with Holly? Was he furious that she was putting ideas in her head about going to the police or leaving home? Did he know what had happened to Lisa? It crossed Eloise's mind that this could be Deborah making her presence known, but how would she know where to find her? Her imagination was in overdrive. This was ridiculous. Whatever it was, whoever was behind it, it felt like a warning.

She looked at her phone, hoping the answer was in there somewhere, but all she saw was one missed call and a text message from Kit saying, *Call me when you get a chance.*

She was losing control, if she'd ever had it. It had been a long time since she'd felt this isolated and desperate.

She had been ready to have it out with Kit at the wine bar until Mimi had turned up, and it had been too late to broach the subject of Elizabeth or Kit's affair when they got home, so her head and heart had raced all night long. Every time she fell asleep, she was jolted awake again by a feeling of dread and anxiety and a writhing in her stomach, knowing they'd have to talk about it in the morning and rehearsing what she was going to say. When she got out of bed at 5.45, ready to talk, she was surprised to find that Kit had already left the house. His cup and crumb-dusted plate in the sink were the only signs he'd been there at all. There was no note to say good morning or explain why he'd left so early, so she'd come straight to the gallery, only to find that her morning was going from bad to worse.

Her neighbours had offered tea, words of support and the number of someone who could come and fix that broken window straight away. The subtext was that broken or boarded-up windows made the street look unsavoury, and it would hurt their businesses if she didn't act soon. The CCTV at the pharmacy across the road hadn't been working for months, and no one had seen or heard a thing. Eloise had cameras trained on the interior of the shop, but none of them had picked up anything through the window.

The police had already been and gone, but seeing as nothing had been taken, there wasn't much they could do.

Eloise had called someone to come and board up the window, but she wasn't sure it was worth replacing now she was being evicted.

'Bastards. Am I right?' Wendy appeared around the corner with a takeaway coffee and something sweet in a paper bag. 'Her highness asked me to bring these to you.' She whistled as she looked at the window. 'Bored kids, I bet. The little turds. This is what happens when they have nothing to keep them busy.'

'Thanks, Wendy.' Eloise took a sip of the coffee. 'Oat milk?' she asked.

'She insisted,' Wendy said.

Eloise smiled. At least some things would never change.

'You've got to ask where their parents are while they're up to no good at all hours, haven't you?' asked Wendy. 'My mum had a slipper she wasn't afraid to use on us when we stepped out of line. And when she ran off with her boyfriend, my sister took over slipper duty. There might have been burned-out cars on the estate, but we never had a speck of dirt on our faces. Standards, see?'

EL

'Standards,' agreed Eloise. 'How's Mimi today?'

'Hungover. Angry about the universe turning on her. There's a lot of hand-wringing and bracelet-jingling. We're stripping the kitchen today and taking anything that's not bolted down. Do you think she'll let me keep those knives?'

Eloise shrugged. 'Do you have another job lined up?'

'Nah. End of season, isn't it? I doubt I'll find anything now. I'm thinking of setting up my own business doing cupcakes for birthdays and stuff until I find something better. So if you hear of anything . . .'

'I'll let you know.'

'You don't need help here, do you?'

'Sorry, no. I'm closing everything down. It's time for a new start. Who knows what the future holds?'

'That's not like you. You're the one who always has a plan.'

Eloise shook her head. 'Not this time.'

'Anyway, I'd best get back before the earth goddess accuses me of bunking off. I can't risk annoying her any more than I already have.'

'Huh?' Eloise had spotted something on the door frame that she hadn't noticed earlier. She tilted her head to see it clearly.

'I said, I'd best be off.'

'Okay. Sure. Thanks for the coffee and cake,' said Eloise.

'No problem. It's left over from yesterday, so it might be a bit stale. See you later.'

Eloise didn't watch Wendy walk away because she couldn't take her eyes away from the paintwork above the door. She didn't even realise that she'd dropped her cup of coffee until she felt it splash up her legs.

'Shit!'

She looked over her shoulder, half expecting to see some-one watching her, but the street was quiet. She turned back to the door frame and stepped closer, reaching up to touch the top.

It was a small but perfectly drawn dragonfly.

In the world's longest game of hide-and-seek, she'd been found.

Part Three

Chapter 33

Eloise

Eloise had been driving for five minutes before she registered that her car was making odd chirruping sounds. It was another two before she realised it was trying to tell her that she wasn't wearing her seat belt. She tugged the belt across her body and crunched the gears.

She barely slowed for the roundabout, causing another driver to sound their horn at her. By the time she was at the top of the hill, waiting for the traffic lights to change, she was frantically searching her mind for somewhere she could go where she would feel safe and away from danger. The car in front of her pulled away, and she stalled the engine.

'Come on!' she said as she restarted the car and lurched for the lights, but they were already changing back to red. 'You've got to be kidding me.'

She tried to picture Deborah as she would look now. Would she still have that dimple in her chin? Would she be blonde or brunette? Heavy or slim? She didn't know if she dared believe that Deborah was behind the dragonfly and the broken window, but it had to be someone from that time in her life. If they'd just wanted to say hello, there would have been no need for bricks through windows and

249

human remains in engine houses. If they'd wanted to get her attention, they'd succeeded.

Eloise spotted Holly standing outside the school, just where she'd said she'd be, but she wasn't alone. She had her back to the road and was talking to Arthur's nephew, Joseph.

Eloise pulled into the car park and revved her engine. Holly said something to Joseph before jogging over and jumping in the passenger seat. 'All right, Mrs F?'

'What did he want?' asked Eloise.

'He recognised me from the café and wanted to apologise for being short with me. He's got a daughter at the school,' said Holly. 'Single dad. And judging by the fact that he's been called in at midday, I think she might be trouble. He looks like he's barely slept.'

'He lives locally, then?' asked Eloise. She wondered whether he was local enough to smash the gallery window.

'I guess.'

'I bet he doesn't even have a kid. And if he does, there's probably a harassed wife chained to the kitchen sink. He's playing you, Holly. He's even managed to get the yoga studio closed earlier than planned because apparently it doesn't meet fire regulations.'

'Good,' said Holly. 'My sister told Mimi she wasn't meeting the basic requirements months ago. They had a big row about it, and Mimi told her to stick to making the coffee. Lisa used to say that she would end up dying in that place.' Her voice trailed off, and she went quiet for a moment.

'Anyway,' she said, giving herself a shake. 'What's all this about a brick through the window and dragonfly drawings in the gallery?'

'The brick only cracked the window, and it was only the one dragonfly. I can't be sure the two things are related, but I think I would have noticed the dragonfly if it had been there before. I don't know. I'm starting to doubt my own sanity. Mimi said your stepdad had been asking after you at the yoga studio.'

'Liam? Why?'

'He wanted to know what happened when Mimi last saw Lisa. He was worried because he'd not seen much of you.'

'Oh, okay. He could have just messaged like a normal person, but sure.'

'She told him to talk to me at the gallery, so I was wondering . . . Not that I'm accusing him of anything, but do you think he might have broken the window?'

Holly shook her head. 'Why would he?'

'I don't know. I'd just rather it was him than my dead sister.'

Eloise drove them away from the school and headed towards the road above the beach, where they could sit and talk.

'Current suspects include Deborah back-from-the-dead, or your stepdad who might be behind your sister's disappearance, or your friend Joseph who took a dislike to me when I crashed into his car, or—'

'Or maybe it's Mr F's fancy woman, taking it out on you because you're the wife he won't leave.'

'I don't believe I asked for your suggestions. The point is, there's more than one person who might want to throw a brick through my window.'

'But,' said Holly, 'there's only one who knows about the dragonflies.'

'Yeah,' sighed Eloise. She stopped the car on a quiet road by the park where the sea glistened through the trees.

'Why are you smiling?' she asked.

'Because you called me.'

'And?'

'You called *me*. You could have called anyone. Mimi, Jan, Kit, Meghan, Eddie ... but when the brown stuff hit the fan, you called me. You can't help it. You like me. I told you I was bloody adorable. I just don't know why it took you so long to see it.'

'Let's not get carried away,' said Eloise. 'Mimi and Jan wouldn't understand any of this. As you pointed out, Kit's possibly having an affair. Meghan won't return my calls, and as for Eddie . . .'

Holly put her fingers in her ears. 'La, la, la, la. Not listening,' she said. 'I will not have you ruin this moment with your ridiculous obsession with facts and evidence.'

Eloise rubbed her tired eyes. A few short weeks ago, calling Holly wouldn't have crossed her mind, but she had to admit it was good to talk openly with someone. She almost wished she'd done it sooner.

'Do we agree that Deborah is behind the brick and the dragonfly doodle?' Holly asked.

Eloise squirmed in her seat. 'I think we have to consider that it's a possibility. You're the only other person who knows about the significance of the dragonflies. But how did she know where my gallery was? I can understand someone tracking those paintings to Cornwall, but there are hundreds of galleries down here. I don't sell my own work any more, and there's nothing to link those pictures to the gallery or me. That time at the yoga studio was a one-off, and God knows, not many people purchased a print that morning.'

Holly was silent as she chewed on her nail.

'Thoughts?' Eloise said. 'You've normally got something to say.'

'Now listen,' said Holly. 'Promise me you won't lose your shit.'

'What have you done?'

'Me? Nothing. Well, not exactly nothing, but you know how I found out that there was no death certificate for Deborah? And how I thought you were lying to get me to keep quiet about your shady past?'

'Oh God, Holly.'

'I was hurt and thought you were a big old liar, so I was going to message Sally Ann to tell her you were alive and living in Cornwall.'

'What?'

'But then I changed my mind.'

'Good.'

'But then . . .'

Eloise laid her forehead on the steering wheel. 'Just tell me.'

'I accidentally pressed send.'

Eloise took a deep breath. 'Okay. That's . . . that's okay. She already knew I was in Cornwall because that's why she put the human remains in those engine houses, right? So that's fine. It doesn't explain how she found my gallery, though. Unless you gave her my name?'

'I might have done,' said Holly.

'Holly!'

'It was an accident.'

'How do you accidentally tell someone my name?'

'Long story involving a speedy exit from a bus, but there's no point dwelling on the past. What are we going to do about it?'

Eloise closed her eyes.

'Sorry,' said Holly. 'Are you, like, really pissed off?'

Eloise lifted her head slowly. 'Remember how you told me I should express my anger more often . . .'

'Let's not be too hasty,' said Holly. 'There's a lot of merit in sweeping everything under the rug.'

Eloise slumped down in her seat. 'I honestly don't have the energy to be angry with you. It had to come out eventually, but you should have told me. You've not just put me in danger, but my entire family.'

'You're right, and I'm very sorry. I should have said something at the time.'

'These little displays show me that she knows where I am and is watching me, letting me know she can reveal my identity at any point. But I will expose her before she gets the chance.' Eloise sat up straight and started the engine.

'I have to come clean about everything to Kit today, and maybe he'll do me the courtesy of reciprocating. After this weekend, nothing will be the same again.'

Chapter 34

Eloise

On the drive home to what was almost certainly the end of her marriage, Eloise gave way to everyone – pedestrians, cars nudging out from side roads, and cats on their last lives. She only overtook slow bicycles on steep hills when she could no longer bear the weight of the annoyance from the drivers behind her. Their stares bored into her via the rear-view mirror as she looked straight ahead, pretending that she hadn't noticed their frustration. She'd have whistled a jaunty tune if she'd known how.

She didn't see the point of rushing head-first into something simply because it was inevitable. She had never been the kind of person to quickly rip off a plaster or dive straight into the ocean. She preferred to get mentally and physically acclimatised before doing anything remotely tricky. She only wished the drive home was longer.

She wasn't sure what she dreaded most – her confession or Kit's. They'd both been dishonest and it was hard to say whose lies were greater. He might not know why she had changed her name, but he was at least aware that she'd done it. She couldn't be held responsible for his lack of curiosity. Though she'd not spoken in detail about her past, she wasn't the first person who'd ever pretended to have no skeletons in their closet. Everyone tweaked their memories and eradicated the less salubrious ones to make them sound better, kinder, better educated, less promiscuous. Or maybe they omitted those events because it was the only way they could look themselves in the mirror. Shame and regret were heavy weights to carry.

Eloise had not revealed every facet of her life to her husband, but the parts that she'd given freely were entirely his. She'd committed herself to her family, friends and the local community. She hoped that her failure to tell them about the first nineteen years of her life wouldn't lead them to disregard the following thirty, where she had been nothing but loyal and supportive. She'd fought hard to build a life she could be proud of, and she trusted they could see that.

Kit, on the other hand . . . How hard was it to not have an affair? She'd managed twenty-five years of marriage without accidentally falling into someone else's bed or finding another man's tongue lodged in her mouth. Not that she hadn't had offers either. In the right light, after a couple of glasses of wine, she was quite the looker.

If Kit dared to tell her that he didn't know who she was any more, she might scream. She would have bet her life that he would never be unfaithful to her, so if anyone was hiding their true self, it was him. She nodded to herself. Yes, that was the counter-argument she would offer if he tried to make out that this was her fault.

Her anger, which had been steadily building, was immediately extinguished, and the fight deserted her. How would she explain any of this to the children? What an embarrassing cliché she was. She'd held the marriage together until the children left home, not a minute longer. And now someone was trying to expose who she was. She had tried so hard to break free from her past, but it had always been there like her shadow.

Holly's idea about the vigil was brilliant and terrifying at the same time. This way, the focus was on more than just Elizabeth King. It was about all runaways, the taken and the missing. It was about every single body that had been found and never given a name. That this weekend would also confirm once and for all whether Eloise's sister was still alive was almost secondary. Would she get to hold Deborah in her arms again? It hardly seemed possible.

She hadn't yet come to terms with her sister being behind all of this, looking for revenge, planting dead bodies in significant places. Deborah had never been this theatrical. She'd even refused to take part in the school nativity play as a child. Said she wouldn't get out of the manger for any part less than a wise man. She was given the role of third sheep. Theatrical, no, but ideas of grandeur, yes. She'd thought the universe had made a grave mistake not casting her as the older sister.

Eloise tried to picture herself explaining everything, laughing about the huge misunderstanding and making up for lost time. In these fantasies, she glossed over the two sets of human remains wrapped in carpet. She was happier when she had been able to refer to her tormentor as Sally Ann – faceless, neutral, someone she would happily push off a cliff if it came to it. But her own sister? She wasn't sure how to deal with that.

She had been determined to keep her identity secret so her family wouldn't find out she'd been lying to them for years, and so she couldn't be held accountable for Deborah's death, as well as selling drugs and petty theft, but that was irrelevant now. Besides, if Deborah wasn't dead, that was one less thing she was responsible for. Eloise had hidden away for too long. She had hidden from her past, from confrontation, from being let down, but that was no longer an option.

First she had to deal with the breakdown of her immediate family unit and hope there was a way to salvage some of those relationships, because she wasn't sure what her life would look like without Kit. There was no getting around the fact that she had the habit of losing everyone she'd ever loved. Her father, her sister and, in a lesser way, Meghan and Edward. Could she call Mimi and Jan her friends if they didn't really know her? Kit was getting ready to desert her too. All she was left with was Holly. Though she wasn't nearly as upset about that as she'd expected to be. She had underestimated the younger woman, that was for sure. She now understood what Edward had seen in her and was glad to have her by her side. She wouldn't be able to get through the vigil without her.

As she pulled up outside her three-storey terraced house with its steeply slanted garden, she noticed a white removal van parked on the road. Her stomach clenched. How had it come to this? She should have spoken to Kit instead of freezing him out. Maybe this could have all been avoided, or at the very least delayed until after the vigil, where she planned to unmask a killer and hoped to avoid becoming her sister's next victim.

She took a deep breath and got out of the car. She walked slowly as she climbed the path, but the front door opened before she reached it.

'There you are,' Kit said. 'I was getting worried. Here, let me take your jacket.'

'I can manage,' Eloise said. She couldn't cast him as the villain if he was going to act so unnecessarily reasonably.

She looked behind him, expecting to see packed bags and boxes. Perhaps he was waiting for her so they could divide up their life, or maybe everything was already in the van. He must have somewhere to go. A secret flat, a hidden woman.

She noticed him glance towards the lounge. It was quick and subtle, and she felt her anger rise again. 'You have got to be kidding me,' she said. 'She's not here, is she?'

She felt a rage building. How dare he do this to her? How dare he leave her? How dare he bring his mistress to their house? She might not have been a perfect wife, but she'd thought they had something special – or, if not special, something pretty bloody decent, and that had been more than enough for her.

She flung open the door so forcefully that it smacked off the wall and bounced back into her shoulder, causing her to stagger slightly. But when she saw who was sitting on her sofa, she staggered some more.

'It's you,' she said.

Ken Marchpane

The police are about to release pictures of the jewellery found with the second set of remains. There are no matches on any databases so far. I am hopeful that the additional coverage this weekend will put pressure on them to implement forensic facial reconstruction on the two women. My contact will let me have the press release before it's made public, so I will share it with you all then. Kind regards, Ken.

Marsha Pirolo

We already know that the first one is Elizabeth King, and I can sense that she has finally found peace. They only need to do a reconstruction of the second girl.

By the way, I'm already at the hotel. I had to change rooms because the one they put me in had a malevolent presence in it. Is anyone else here yet?

Andy Pickford

I'm driving down early tomorrow morning. I'm happy to pick up anyone along the way.

Sasha Walters

Me and the girls will get in around nine o'clock tonight. I've managed to rustle up ten ladies in total. Got to warn you, though, they're already on the cans of wine. It might get messy. Quick trip to Bertie's with us old birds, Marsha?

Patty Hansen

I'm in the hotel bar wearing my Truth Seekers T-shirt and sitting by the window with my laptop and a pint. You can't miss me. I'm a vision!

I cannot wait for this. I have two hundred badges and flyers to hand out, so you'll all have to collect a bunch from me to distribute on the day. Heads up though, guys, I'm deaf. I have a cochlear implant, but if you overenunciate your words or speak slowly and loudly, I will end you.

Holly Bobs

This is mad! I can't believe I'm going to meet you all tomorrow. I'm feeling super emotional that we're coming together like this. I've only got the radio confirmed so far. My mum had a freelance journalist friend who said she'd show her face. I don't know how much coverage we'll get, so I'd like us all to bring our phones and flood social media – Instagram reels, TikTok, live streams, whatever you can think of. We'll make our own news if we have to.

Chapter 35

Eloise

'Is it really you?' Eloise said.

A pretty young woman was squeezed into the corner of the sofa. A familiar woman. A woman who, despite everything, it was a joy to see.

'Hey, Mum.'

Eloise glanced behind her at Kit, who was smiling a little sheepishly, and then back at her daughter. She looked like a child who'd been caught doing something she shouldn't – small and meek, hiding behind a curtain of blonde hair. She was wearing what some people called loungewear – a cross between gym kit and pyjamas.

'I can't believe it's you,' Eloise said.

'Oh my God, Mum. Of course it's me. Do you need your eyes checked?'

She felt Kit nudge her in the back, pushing her forward into the room. 'What are you doing here? I mean, this is a lovely surprise. Is everything okay?'

'Why don't you sit down,' said Kit. 'The kettle has just boiled.'

Eloise threw her arms around her daughter as Kit left the room, but their hug was awkward, and they couldn't work out whose arms went where. Meghan felt so small that Eloise didn't want to squeeze too hard.

'God, it's lovely to see you,' she said. She pressed the side of her face into her daughter's hair. Her shampoo smelled different – coconut instead of apples. 'Have you lost weight?' she said. 'Here. Let me look at you.' She took Meghan by the shoulders and looked into her eyes. 'What's happened?' she asked.

'What makes you think—'

'You've not returned my calls in weeks, haven't been home in months, and now here you are sitting on the sofa on a Friday. This seems out of character for someone who refuses to take the annual leave allotted to her. Something must have happened.'

Meghan lowered her eyes, which was at least preferable to rolling them. 'It's no big deal, but Charlie and I split up.'

'Oh no, I'm so sorry to hear that.'

'No you're not. Anyway, don't make a fuss.'

Eloise shrugged and let her shoulders drop. 'Ah well, I tried. Which one was Charlie?'

The side of Meghan's mouth twitched.

'Is this a good time to tell you I never liked him?' Eloise said, leaning forward conspiratorially. 'There was something off about his ears. You know that one of them was lower than the other, right? It's a sure sign of psychopathy.'

'Mum,' Meghan said. 'Don't.'

'Fine. I won't say a word. Not a single word. But I can have an eight-page report on your desk by Monday morning detailing all the ways you're better off without him. It's no bother.'

Meghan folded her legs underneath herself, making herself smaller still. 'Is it okay if I stay here while I sort some things out?'

'Of course it is, but you don't have to ask. Is Charlie still in the flat, then? We could force him to move out, you know. Not that I don't want you here. I do. I really, *really* do, but I don't like the idea of him lording it about in that marshmallow you call home.'

Meghan shook her head. 'We gave notice three weeks ago when we decided to call it a day. All my worldly belongings are currently in a van outside.'

'Oh sweetheart, why didn't you say something sooner?'

'How could I? You gave me that whole speech about keeping my independence and how moving in so quickly with Charlie was a monumental mistake.'

'Did I really say that?'

'You did. You also said that a single toilet wasn't practical. You said that separate bathrooms were essential for a happy relationship.'

'And I still stand by that wisdom,' Eloise said.

'But mostly I didn't want to give you the chance to say I told you so.'

'I'd never do that.'

'Wouldn't you?' said Meghan. 'My bad. I must've mixed you up with someone else who gave birth to me.'

'Well . . .' Eloise said. 'I admit that it brings me a certain amount of joy to know that I'm right. Gives me faith in my own judgement somewhat. But I'd never beat you over the head with my superhuman ability to be correct all the time. So what if it didn't work out between you and whatshisname?

At least you went for it. I will always be risk-averse when it comes to you and your brother, and myself for that matter, but that doesn't mean you have to be. I want you to follow your heart while I shadow you from a respectable distance, picking up the pieces. I call that teamwork.'

Meghan didn't look convinced. 'I call it stalking.'

'Look, I'm sorry you couldn't tell me what you were going through. But rest assured, there is no judgement or disappointment here. I will never be anything but supportive of you. Can you work from home, or are you taking some leave?'

Meghan looked towards the door. 'Maybe I should help Dad with the tea.'

'He knows how to make tea. Does he know about you and Charlie?'

'Yeah. He's been helping me look for flats, and this morning he loaded everything into the van and said he was bringing me home.'

Eloise nodded. 'He's known for a while, then?'

EL

Meghan shrugged and pulled the arms of her sweatshirt over her hands. 'Yeah. Don't be hurt. I asked him not to tell you. I didn't want you rushing in and taking over.'

Eloise opened her mouth to say that she would never do that, but Meghan had a point. The calls, the secrecy. The whole time, Kit really had been talking to their daughter. Not an affair, yet Eloise still felt betrayed.

'I can be a bit much at times, can't I?' she said.

'No. No, it's not that. It's just . . .' Meghan threw herself back into the soft cushions and groaned. 'I'm embarrassed by how I went to pieces. I never thought I'd be *that* girl, you know? I hate disappointing you. Dad . . . well, he has no expectations, which is frustrating in an entirely different way, but he was what I needed at the time. And I can never lie to you, so that's why I've been avoiding your calls. You'd have marched right around and chopped off Charlie's balls.'

'And I would've used rusty scissors,' said Eloise. 'When you say your dad's been helping . . .'

Meghan sniffed. 'Charlie called him because he was worried about me. I didn't take the break-up particularly well. And then, a week later, Dad came for the weekend on his way back from that conference. He took me out for dinner to make sure I was eating properly, stayed a couple of nights on the sofa, and took me to look at some flats. He wanted to tell you, but I begged him to wait a week or two until I got myself a new place. Except now there's no way I can afford anything because . . .' She sighed. 'See, that's the other thing I need to tell you. I've lost my job. My life has turned into a complete and utter shit show, and I'm back to square one. Sorry, Mum.'

Eloise put her arm around Meghan's shoulders and pulled her close. 'What have you got to apologise for? If anyone's sorry, it's me. I'm sorry that this has happened to you, but I'm also sorry that I've not made it easy for you to come to me about it.'

'You're not angry?' asked Meghan.

'Oh, I'm furious . . . but not with you.'

A noise behind her made Eloise turn around. Kit was standing there with a cup in each hand. 'You all caught up?' he asked.

'Barely scratched the surface. But I've had the headlines, at least.' She took a cup from him. 'I can't believe you kept this from me.'

'I know. I know. And you wouldn't believe how hard it's been. I thought you knew,' he said.

'How could I?'

'You heard me on the phone at the yoga studio and then you kept trying to have serious talks. I knew if you asked me outright I'd have to tell you. I've done everything I can to avoid you so I wouldn't break my promise to Meghan.'

'You should have told me when you first found out.'

Kit glanced at Meghan before looking back at Eloise. 'I was just glad that she was talking to one of us about it, so yes, I kept her confidence. I didn't enjoy hiding it from you, but it was more important that Meghan knew she could trust me. I thought you'd guessed something was up when I said I'd taken the day off to be with Mum. I could tell you didn't believe me.'

'You were with Meghan then?'

'Charlie called me at work, so I drove straight up there.'

Eloise had been so sure she was going to be coming home to an admission of adultery that she hadn't had time to shed her annoyance towards him. She should have been relieved and grateful, but at that moment, she found herself unreasonably cross.

No, he wasn't having an affair, but she couldn't be thankful for that. He'd kept it from her that her daughter was in pain, though that still wasn't what annoyed her. He was the one that both their children went to when they needed

267

something because he was less likely to panic, more laid-back and calm.

With a jolt, she realised she was jealous. She envied Kit's relationship with their kids. He'd always been whatever they'd needed him to be, but never less than himself, while she'd always kept part of herself hidden, seeing danger at every turn. She'd pushed them to be the best versions of themselves because she had realised far too late in her own life just how necessary that was. But because she hadn't been open and honest with them, they were only following her lead.

'Talking of hiding things,' she said, 'I have something important to tell you both, and much as I'd like to, I can't put it off any longer.'

Chapter 36

Holly

Another interview, another disaster. Holly got off the bus knowing that once again she'd failed, and she didn't even have the energy to be disappointed.

It wasn't as if she'd wanted the stupid job as a receptionist at the gym. She'd been so consumed with thoughts of the vigil that she hadn't done any preparation, and she could easily pinpoint the moment the woman made up her mind that she wasn't right for the job. She'd asked how Holly would deal with a problematic client, and Holly had said, 'I don't suppose I can slap her?' Though she had laughed to show she was joking, the interviewer did not share her sense of humour, and after that, it was all downhill.

She'd been interviewed for three jobs now, none of which she wanted. Of course, she would have accepted any of them if offered. She needed the money. She wanted something that paid enough to rent a room in a shared house and was interesting enough that she wouldn't dread getting out of bed every morning. She had one more interview lined up, for a job helping arrange events at the local National Trust property. This one she desperately wanted, but it was hard to get excited about anything other than the vigil. She'd had a lot of thinking time recently and decided that her dream job would be event management. This vigil was an event of sorts. She wondered whether she could talk about it at her interview next week. She'd ask Eloise. Ideally, she wanted to set up and run summer events at National Trust properties – theatre at Trelissick, dancing at Lanhydrock and opera at Godolphin.

She opened the wonky wooden gate, rotten with age and battered by the wind and rain, and slipped around the side of the house. Opening the door, she froze. Liam was standing with his back to her in the kitchen. She almost slipped away again, but it was too late.

'All right there, Hols?' he said.

She'd managed to largely avoid her stepdad for weeks. He worked shifts, so he was usually asleep when she got up, and already out when she got home. When Eddie had still been in Cornwall, she'd spent most of her time around his house. She and Liam hadn't sat and chatted over coffee in months. He looked the same, but something about him was different. It took Holly a minute to realise that he was clean-shaven and wearing a shirt.

'Looks like we both scrubbed up well today,' he said, nodding at her outfit.

'Interview,' she said. 'You?'

'Yeah, me too. How did it go?'

Holly shrugged. 'They said I'd hear by the end of next week, but the only way I've got that job is if they're desperate and no other candidates turn up. Thankfully, I have an interview on Wednesday for something I really want. What about yours?' She stayed by the door, unsettled by this uncharacteristic friendliness.

'Ah,' said Liam. 'You got me. Actually, it's a date.' He cringed and shrugged his shoulders. 'A lunch date. I think she'd rather meet in daylight in case I'm a serial killer.'

'It happens,' Holly said, though she wasn't sure if she was referring to the lunch date as standard or the prevalence of serial killers. They both looked around the kitchen, at the clock and the stained linoleum – anywhere but at each other.

'So, I should probably . . .' Holly began.

'It's weird, isn't it?' Liam said. 'I can tell you're uncomfortable. I am, too, to be honest. And if you don't like it . . . if you think it's too soon after your mum, I'll cancel the whole thing. I don't know why I even went on the app. I was curious, I guess, and I wanted to see if—'

'I don't mind,' Holly said quickly. 'It's been almost a year. I'm surprised you've not dated sooner. Besides, it's nothing to do with me, is it?'

'Of course it is,' Liam said. 'I promised your mum that I'd look after you girls, and I've done a shit job of it so far.'

Holly knew she should probably say, 'Not at all! You're the best,' but instead, she dropped her bag on the floor, folded her arms and said, 'Yeah, now you come to mention it, shockingly bad. Atrocious. You turned into an absolute prat when we needed you most.'

Liam ran his hands over his face and lifted his chin. Holly could see dried blood in the crease of his neck where he'd cut himself shaving. 'I wish I could disagree with you,' he said. 'I don't know where this past year has gone. It's been a

271

haze, to be honest. God knows how I've kept my job. I miss her so much, and I know that's no excuse. You girls . . . you were her world, and I should've done more to be there for you.'

'Yeah, you should've.'

'When I spoke to the police the other day,' he said, 'well, I got a real wake-up call. I can't believe I didn't even know Lisa was missing.' He shook his head. 'I thought she'd gone quiet because she was pissed off with me, and I'd not tried to contact her because I was embarrassed by my behaviour, wasn't I? I wish you'd told me you'd not heard from her either. Not that I'm saying it's your responsibility. It's not. That's all on me, and Christ, man, it's unforgivable. I should have been calling her, checking up on her. I should never have let her leave. I should have treated her better so she didn't feel like she had to go.'

Holly's heart raced, and she didn't trust herself to speak.

'I was angry with her for no other reason than she reminded me of your mum,' he went on. 'Same eyes, same stubbornness. It was a constant reminder that your mum wasn't here. And the drinking . . . I don't know whether you've noticed, but I've not touched a drop since Lisa left. It doesn't make up for anything, but what I'm saying is I mean it when I say I'm sorry. I'll do whatever I can to make it up to you. We both know that if your mum was here, she'd kill me.'

Holly rarely spoke about her mum. She thought about her all the time but didn't have anyone to talk to about how it felt that she was no longer here. She had no one to share recollections with. She wanted to be reminded what perfume her mum wore and what her first car was. She wanted to say, 'Hey, do you remember when we went to Majorca on holiday and Mum monopolised the karaoke mic until the bar owner pulled the plug?' She wanted to laugh about how bad her mum's cooking was but how good her hugs were. She wanted to know that someone else remembered the sound of her laugh. Hearing Liam talk about her now released something in Holly's heart.

'I miss her so much,' she whispered. 'Both of them. And I'm angry with them for leaving. I'm terrified that something has happened to Lisa and she's never coming back.'

'I know, love. I know. But Lisa's always been a law unto herself. You can't let yourself think the worst, you just can't. I was expecting to have heard about her bank account by now. I'll chase that up today, I promise. And if there's anything I can do to make it up to you . . .'

Holly shook her head. 'I'm holding a vigil later with some friends, and it's going to highlight the number of missing women everywhere. I want to get Lisa's name out there, and maybe if someone has seen her—'

'The body in the engine house!' said Liam suddenly. 'I heard about it on the radio yesterday. Is that you organising the vigil? That's amazing, that is, Hols.'

Holly blushed. 'Well, you know, it's not just me . . .'

'Still, it's huge. Can I come? Or is it a women-only thing?'

'No, it's for everyone. So yeah, if you could . . . I mean, I'd appreciate a lift, to be honest. I was going to go with Eloise, but she's got some family stuff she's dealing with, and you can help hand out flyers if you like. This one woman, Patty, has flyers and badges and T-shirts printed and thinks if we

273

can solve the case of the women in the engine houses, we can help other people too.'

'Bloody hell, I know I've dropped the ball over the last few months, but it feels like I've blinked and you've gone from being a lanky kid to this powerhouse of a woman bossing everything.'

'Well, I don't know if I'd say "bossing" . . .'

'Sign me up. Whatever you need. Maybe I can bring my date? Show her what a great stepdad I am.'

'That might be pushing it,' said Holly.

Liam laughed. It seemed to Holly like she hadn't heard that laugh for such a long time. It struck her then, quite to her surprise, that she'd missed him. He was the only dad she'd ever known, and it felt like she'd lost him at the same time as she'd lost her mum. She wasn't ready to forgive him for retreating into himself as if he was the only one grieving. She might never forgive him for pushing Lisa away, but maybe she was willing to let him back into her life – just a little bit.

His phone rang. 'What do you reckon?' he said. 'I bet this is her calling to cancel the date.' He looked at the display and frowned before lifting the phone to his ear.

'Hello?' he said. 'Yes. This is Liam speaking.'

Holly bent down and picked up her bag, planning to go to her room. As she straightened up, she heard Liam gasp.

'Are you sure it's Lisa?'

Chapter 37

Eloise

Meghan was home. She was home and in her old room, and yes, the walls were thin enough for Eloise to hear her crying, but she was here where Eloise could keep an eye on her from a respectful, non-suffocating distance.

After checking that all the doors and windows were still locked and peering out of the window to make sure no one shady was hanging around outside, Eloise tiptoed around the house, unloading the dishwasher without making a sound and carefully opening the fridge and noticing for the first time that the door squeaked. She wanted Meghan to wake around noon feeling like she'd had the best sleep of her life and never want to leave home again.

God, what was wrong with her? Her daughter was broken-hearted, jobless and desperate, and here she was gleefully plotting to keep her in the house for ever. She sighed. Maybe this was why Edward and Meghan kept her at arm's length. But she wasn't going to apologise for the fact that she loved them so much that it drove her a little crazy at times. She was, however, willing to concede that if she wanted a closer relationship with them, she had to give them space, as counter-intuitive as that seemed.

Kit and Meghan had listened while she explained her background and why she'd changed her name from Elizabeth to Eloise. Neither of them had heard about the human remains being found or how one set was said to be Elizabeth King. It was hard to imagine that something that had consumed Eloise's every waking moment had passed by the rest of her family as if it were inconsequential.

If she tried hard to see the silver lining, she supposed this had given her the opportunity to come clean to her family and let them get close to her in a way she had never been able to do before. More importantly, it also gave her the chance to protect herself and her family. She just wished she knew what she was protecting them from.

She had tentatively told Kit and Meghan about how there was a chance her sister was still alive, but when Meghan got excited about family reunions and the existence of cousins, Eloise explained that if Deborah *was* alive and behind all of this, there was a possibility that she was responsible for the deaths of these two women.

Meghan had asked if she could come to the vigil. Eloise had said she would rather she didn't, in case it was dangerous, but Meghan had insisted, and that was that. They'd all gone to bed early to process this recent turn of events, but whether any of them had any sleep was an entirely different matter.

Eloise and Kit had spoken at length this morning. He was in a far better mood now that he didn't have to keep anything from her, but he was still hurt that she'd kept so much from him. They'd agreed that in the future, there'd be no more secrets between them. Though Eloise had to keep just one more: she must never let him know that she'd suspected him of having an affair. Knowing now that the messages, the calls, the missing days had all been spent looking after their daughter, she felt guilty for even considering it.

She heard her phone ringing and hunted frantically for it before it woke Meghan. She found it lodged between oranges and a softening banana in the fruit bowl.

'Hello?'

Edward's face filled the screen. 'Morning!' he said.

'Morning, my love. It's so nice to see your gorgeous smile. How are you?'

'Great,' he said. 'I stayed in last night, did some work on my assignment and had a decent night's sleep. What's wrong with me? Is this what being old feels like?'

'Why ask me?' said Eloise. 'I'm still in my prime.'

'Are you missing me, or have you already turned my room into a yoga studio?'

'Only on Tuesdays and Thursdays.'

'Lovely.'

'How are things with you, darling? How's the course going?'

'Good. Really good. It's a lot more work than I expected. You should see the reading list. It's probably optional, like lectures, but . . .'

'It is not optional. None of this is optional.'

'. . . yeah, I'm loving it. The lads on my floor are solid. And I've joined a sports team like you told me to.'

'Yeah?'

'Darts.'

'I see.'

'And the social life is pretty good,' he said.

'Are you eating properly?'

'Of course I am. Wait. By "properly", you mean Pot Noodles and pizza, right?'

Eloise smiled. She missed him so much. 'By the way,' she said, 'your sister's home.'

'For the weekend?' he asked, before yawning loudly.

'A bit longer than that. She split up with Charlie and lost her job. I'm not sure I've got the whole story about why either of these things came to such an abrupt end, but apparently I don't need to know every detail about my children's lives. Every day's a school day.'

'She okay?'

'You could call her and ask,' Eloise said.

'Mum,' he said with a sad shake of his head. 'I call you for the highlights so I don't have to talk to anyone else in the family.'

Eloise looked behind her and saw Meghan leaning against the door frame in her pyjamas, her hair piled up in a messy bun. She was wearing dark-framed glasses, which made her look older than she was. Eloise smiled at her. With everything else going on, she wasn't sure she should feel this happy.

'Speak of the devil,' she said.

Meghan walked over, put her hand on Eloise's shoulder and peered into the phone screen. 'All right, shit stain?' she said. 'Woken up in a pool of your own vomit yet?'

'On the daily,' Edward said. 'Mum told me about you and Charlie. Need me to spark him out for you?'

'Jesus. Look how puny your arms are! You don't even have the strength to write him a strongly worded email.'

'Email? Gee, Grandma, nowadays us kids use text messages. We unleash hell through the power of emojis.'

'Has Mum told you her big news yet?' Meghan said. 'About her coming from a gangland family and how we have a murdery aunt intent on getting revenge? And how your ex-girlfriend is helping Mum throw a party to, like, I don't know . . . expose a killer or something.'

'Mother?' said Edward, leaning closer to the phone screen. 'What is your least favourite child talking about?'

Eloise nudged Meghan with her hip. 'Make us some coffee while I explain everything to your brother.'

Meghan grinned and went to grab a couple of mugs from the cupboard, leaving Eloise squeezing her phone hard enough to make her fingers cramp.

'Right, so . . .' She sighed. 'Quite a lot has happened since I last saw you.' She began walking towards the sofa. 'I'm going to need to sit down for this, and I suggest you do the same.'

Truth Seekers UK

Patty Hansen

Truth Seekers assemble! Bring your placards and be in your T-shirts in reception in thirty minutes. Wear comfortable shoes. It's looking to turn a bit chilly this evening, so bring a jacket too.

Andy Pickford

I bet you're all jealous of my hoodie now, aren't you?

Could we get some other branded merch ordered, Patty? I was thinking beanies, baseball caps . . . anything we can put a logo on. We could sell them through the website and fund any expenses from our investigations. Or not. Doesn't bother me either way.

Marsha Pirolo

Since when do we have a website? If you like, I could offer readings and see if I can connect people with their loved ones who have passed.

Andy Pickford

I couldn't sleep last night so I designed a logo and set up a site where people can report sightings, anonymous info, that sort of thing. The problem with the Facebook group is that people need an account and profile. I thought a website would encourage people to give information more freely. I've put links to missing person databases, and news reports. I'm still working on the features. Thought we could chat about it over a coffee and see what ideas people have.

Patty Hansen

That's such a great idea. I love this. You're a dark horse, Andy.

Andy Pickford

Hung like one too.

Patty Hansen

. . . and he's back.

Sally Ann

I can't believe you've achieved this much and managed to arrange a whole event in such a short time. It feels like it's snowballed a little from our first aim of trying to piece together Elizabeth's last-known movements, but never mind.

I've been delayed, so I will have to join you at the engine house later.

Patty Hansen

Is your mum coming with you, Sally Ann?

Sally Ann

No, it's just me. But don't worry, I'm more than capable of pushing for answers to questions we've had for thirty years. I look forward to seeing everyone later.

Ken Marchpane

I'm already at the engine house. It seems we were meant to get permission for a protest. The police are already threatening to shut us down and it hasn't even started yet. I've been trying to get hold of Holly, but she isn't answering my calls. Kind regards, Ken.

Patty Hansen

Ken, this isn't a protest – but even if it was, protest is a human right protected in the UK by Article 11 of the Human Rights Act. New attempts by the government to reduce protest rights are in breach of international human rights law. (Or so I read on the internet.) We're holding a vigil, which will include forty-five minutes of silence after a speech from a local MP. We don't need permission from the police, but they've already been informed.

I can't reach Holly either. I guess we'll just do what we can without her. I hope she's all right.

Chapter 38

Holly

'He said not to get our hopes up,' said Liam.

'I know.' Holly stuffed some clothes into her rucksack.

'The cash card hasn't been used for a couple of weeks, so she might have already moved on,' Liam continued.

'Even more reason for me to go now, while she might still be in the area. I have a two-hour wait at Gatwick for my connecting flight, but I should be in Larnaca by the early hours of tomorrow morning.'

She rushed into the bathroom and grabbed her toothbrush.

'It might not be her,' Liam shouted after her. 'Someone could have stolen her card.'

'I know,' Holly said, thundering down the stairs with Liam close behind her. 'But I also know that if I don't go, I might never know the truth. If she's all right and just living it up in Cyprus, why hasn't she called or sent a postcard? I need to know she's okay, and I need to bring her home. And if she's not . . . if it's not her, then I need to find the bastard who stole her card and find out what they've done to my sister.'

'I don't know, Hols, it doesn't feel right you rushing out there on your own. Maybe if you give it a few days I'll be able to take some time off work and—'

'You said you need to make it up to me, and this is your chance. Get me to Newquay airport in time for my flight.'

She pushed her feet into her trainers and picked up her phone.

'You don't have anywhere to stay,' said Liam, grabbing his car keys and opening the door for her.

'Then book me somewhere near to where she last used that card and text me the address.'

Ten minutes later, they were in the car and heading towards the airport – the opposite direction from the vigil that was already getting under way without her.

Chapter 39

Eloise

Now that she was at the engine house, Eloise didn't have the first idea of what she was meant to do. Though she'd worked with Holly on getting everything organised, the younger woman had been the driving force behind it all.

The badger-bearded police officer she'd met with Holly was standing with a young woman in uniform. They looked nervous, which wasn't helping Eloise's anxiety at all.

There wasn't nearly enough parking or room for everyone to sit or stand. When Holly had suggested holding a vigil, they'd only hoped that they could cobble together enough people for a decent photo. Eloise had tried counting heads, but people wouldn't stand still, and every time she got to a hundred, she became distracted thinking she'd seen Deborah and had to start all over again.

Kit swore he wouldn't let Meghan out of his sight, but Eloise would've been happier if they hadn't come at all. There were too many people, and if Deborah was here, she would blend into the crowd far too easily. Eloise was searching for a familiar face, but would she recognise her sister after so long? Would Deborah resemble their mother or their father? Or a mix of the two?

Everywhere she looked, there was someone taking a selfie or videoing themselves. She knew this was all part of Holly's plan, but she couldn't feel pleased about it. The MP – God, what was her name? – was talking to someone. A journalist, perhaps? They seemed too young to be reporting for anything except the school paper, but it was a sign of Eloise's age that everyone looked like they were just out of nappies.

She heard someone shout her name, and she automatically ducked.

'El! Eloise! Coo-ee!'

For a moment she couldn't tell which direction the call was coming from. But then she saw Mimi and Jan pushing through the crowd with Wendy at their heels like a faithful dog, jumping up and down to see over the crowds. All three of them were wearing Truth Seekers T-shirts over their clothes. It seemed comical to see Mimi in anything as conventional as a black-and-white T-shirt.

'I didn't expect you to come,' said Eloise as Jan pulled her in for a hug.

'Well, that's a nice welcome,' said Mimi.

'Of course we came,' said Wendy. 'You couldn't keep us away. Though if the studio hadn't been closed . . .'

'Yes, thank you, Wendy,' said Mimi. 'I feel just awful about Holly's sister. I do hope she's okay. Lisa was a terrible worker, but I'd hate to imagine that . . . well, you know. And to think I might have been the last person to see her . . . It seemed like the least we could do.'

'Well, I'm glad you're here. Have you seen Holly anywhere?'

'No, but we were accosted by some people giving out these T-shirts at the entrance, and I assume it's the group that Holly's part of.'

Kit ambled over. 'Ladies,' he said.

Jan squealed when she saw Meghan standing just behind him. 'You're home!' she said. 'Oh look at you!'

Jan and Mimi had known Meghan and Edward since the day they were born. They all loved each other's children like they were part of one big extended family. While the two of them questioned Meghan about what she'd been up to since they'd last seen her, Eloise slipped away and headed towards a huddle of people wearing the same black T-shirts as her friends.

'Hello,' she said. 'Do you know where Holly is? She's not answering her phone.'

'Gone AWOL,' a woman said. 'I hope she turns up soon, though. Hey, you're not Eloise, are you?'

'Yep. That's me.'

'Great. I'm Patty. Get this T-shirt on you.'

Patty was a striking woman – fully six feet tall and strong and elegant.

'This is Marsha, and the fella is Andy.'

Marsha had bleached white-blonde hair teased into a beehive, tinted cat's-eye glasses, and a frayed denim jacket over her Truth Seekers T-shirt. Andy was baby-faced and sweet-looking and almost a foot shorter than Patty.

'Sasha will be here soon,' Patty said. She's coming on a minibus with a hen party from thirty-odd years ago, but they're having trouble negotiating the narrow roads and they've already broken down once.'

287

Eloise nodded and tried to smile. She wondered if they would recognise her after so long.

'Can I ask,' she began, 'is there someone here called Sally Ann? I gather she's the reason that all this . . . kicked off.'

Andy and Patty looked at each other and raised their eyebrows in unison.

'What is it?' Eloise asked.

'She's here,' said Patty. 'She took her T-shirt and went off to get changed about ten minutes ago.'

'Okay, that's good, so why the weird faces?'

'No faces,' said Andy. 'No, it's great she's here. Just great.'

'But?'

'Well,' said Patty. 'She's pissed off with Holly for hijacking the Truth Seekers group and making it about all the women, not just Elizabeth. But if you ask me, there's something odd going on with her. She was frantic. Eyes darting around all over the place like she was jacked up on something.'

'What does she look like?' asked Eloise. 'Can you point her out to me?'

'Well, that's the other thing,' said Andy. 'She looks nothing like her profile picture.' He glanced up at Patty. 'Which is fine. Whatever. I mean, we all choose photos that flatter, or in Patty's case, someone else's picture entirely, which, can I just say, makes no sense because Patty's better-looking than her catfishing photo. Anyway . . .' He cleared his throat, and Patty rolled her eyes. 'Sally Ann's profile picture was of a youngish woman, right?' he went on. 'But *our* Sally Ann is, like, fifty. Her mother can't be Elizabeth King's younger sister unless she's about twenty years younger than her appearance suggests.'

Eloise looked around her, thinking she might spot someone looking suspiciously straight at her, but no one stood out.

'Apart from being fifty and pissed off, how will I recognise her?' she asked.

'I couldn't tell you anything about her, and I was talking to her for ten minutes,' Andy said.

'Are all women over a certain age invisible to you?' asked Patty. Turning to Eloise, she said, 'She's a bit shorter than you. She has wavy brown hair that is going grey. She has deep brown eyes that are almost black. She wears no makeup but has eyebrows to die for. She's a strong-looking woman with plenty of self-confidence, and she will now be wearing one of our T-shirts.'

Andy sniffed. 'Yeah, like I said.'

'One of the perks about being deaf is you make more use of visual clues,' Patty said.

'There's a lot of negative energy about her,' said Marsha. 'She had dark spots in her aura.'

'Okay,' said Eloise, unsure what to do with that information. 'Thank you. If you see Holly or Sally Ann, will you give me a shout? It looks like things are about to get under way.'

Chapter 40

Holly

'Sorry about your date,' Holly said.

'Family first,' said Liam. 'She'll understand. And if she doesn't, then she's not girlfriend material.'

Holly looked at the nine missed calls and twenty-two unopened texts on her phone and switched it off. She felt bad about leaving Eloise to manage the vigil on her own, but she would explain it all to her later, and hope she understood.

She was fizzing with nervous energy. Lisa's bank records showed that she'd cancelled all her direct debits and standing orders in the days after she'd left Cornwall. That wasn't the kind of thing a scammer or thief would do. There'd been no payments going in, but she'd cleared all the money from her account over the past few months. The last transaction came two weeks ago from Ayia Napa.

'Look, Hols, I want you to think carefully about this,' Liam said. 'You don't know where to start looking. You're not just going to be able to walk into a bar and find her sitting there with a cocktail. I know why you want to get out there, but why don't we wait and talk to the police again on Monday to see if they can get the Cypriot police to put out some feelers, eh? All you know is the area the cash was taken out from.'

Holly knew he was right, but she had to do something. She needed to find her sister.

'Can't Eddie go with you?' Liam asked. 'I'd be happier if you weren't on your own.'

'We broke up.'

Out of the corner of her eye, she could see Liam looking at her, but she refused to meet his gaze.

'When did that happen?'

'The day he left for university.'

'I'm sorry, Hols, he was a decent lad. I liked him,' said Liam.

'Yeah, me too.'

They drove in silence for a little longer. The closer they got to the airport, the more Holly's stomach squirmed. After another fifteen minutes, Liam pulled into the car park and switched off the engine.

Before she could get out of the car, he put his hand on her arm.

'Right,' he said. 'This is the last I'm going to say on the matter, and if you still want to get on that plane, I fully support you. I'll book you a hotel, put cash in your account, take some time off work and come out and join you in a few days' time. But hear me out first.'

Holly turned to look at him. 'Make it quick.'

'I love your sister,' he said.

'I know.'

'But she's always been a bit . . . maybe a bit too focused on herself. I know you're terrified something bad has

291

happened to her, right? And I guess we still can't be sure it hasn't, but it sounds like she's gone to one of the party hotspots of the Med and . . . I don't know. Maybe she's having the time of her life. And if that's the case, Hols, she hasn't even had the decency to give us a call to let us know that she's doing okay. And you . . . you're a great kid. You think the best of everyone, and I don't want you to change that, but I worry about you getting into trouble over there. I worry you won't find her, or you will find her and won't like what you see. But the other thing is that you've worked hard on getting this vigil together, and you've got an interview lined up next week, and . . . I'm just saying, when are you gonna put yourself first, Hols? Don't put your life on hold chasing after other people. You deserve better than that.'

Chapter 41

Eloise

It didn't look like Holly was coming. She had been so invested in this vigil that it was surprising – and worrying – that she wasn't there to see it all come together. Eloise knew something must have happened to keep her away, but she had no way of knowing what that was unless Holly returned her calls. She was wondering about leaving the vigil to drive to Holly's house when she saw the hen party turn up.

She lowered her head. She didn't think they would know who she was, but still, she didn't meet their eyes in case there was a spark of recognition. This was too dangerous. She wanted to leave, and if Holly had been here, she would have done, but one of them had to be here to see it through to the end. Deborah was mingling in the crowd somewhere, and, oh my dear God, even Gavin Gallagher, Elizabeth's ex-boyfriend from Wales, had turned up. Eloise ducked behind the nearest stranger.

She jumped when Patty touched her shoulder. 'Oh, hi. Has Holly turned up?'

Patty shook her head. 'Nope. I was talking to the MP, Mariella. She needs someone to say a few words about why

293

we're all gathered here and then introduce her on stage. It was meant to be Holly, but I was hoping you could do it instead.'

'Me? Oh no, I don't think that's a good . . . I mean, what would I say? Can't you do it? You know as much about this as I do.'

Patty looked her straight in the eye. 'We both know that's not true.'

'I'm sorry?'

'Holly told me that you were . . . are, you know, *her*.'

'Did she?' Eloise folded her arms and looked around to see if anyone was listening.

'To be fair,' said Patty, 'I forced her into it. She was asking all these questions and getting me to look up death certificates for Sally Ann's mum and grandparents, and I knew she was hiding something. She accidentally referred to Elizabeth as Eloise, and . . . well, I'm not stupid.'

'Obviously.'

'Don't worry. I haven't told the others.'

Eloise nodded, but she didn't feel soothed by that news.

'So?' Patty asked. 'Will you say a few words?'

Eloise looked at the crowd. 'I'd really rather not.'

'Yeah, well, we all have to do things we'd rather not, so . . .' Patty put her hands on Eloise's shoulders and turned her towards the engine house and the makeshift stage. 'You're up, kiddo.'

They made their way down the slope to where the MP was talking to the bearded police officer.

'This is Eloise,' Patty said to the MP. 'She'll chat for five minutes, then introduce you.'

294

Eloise looked around her, desperately hoping that Holly would turn up and rescue her, but before she knew it, she was being ushered onto a wooden box and handed a megaphone. People stopped talking and shuffled closer, and her throat seemed to close. She never spoke in public apart from introducing artists to a select group of patrons – twenty or thirty people at most. But this was an entirely different and terrifying proposition, for which she was ill-equipped. At least from here it would be easier to spot Deborah in the crowd.

'Hello, everyone. Thanks for coming here today to . . .' A smattering of applause stopped her from finishing her sentence. She took a deep breath and looked around. Kit glanced up, surprised to see her there, but Meghan gave her a thumbs-up. Eloise scanned the crowd, looking for Truth Seekers T-shirts, searching for her sister.

'Um. I'm sure you all know why we're here. The remains of two young women have been abandoned in engine houses not far from here. Their families have been denied answers, and they're not the only ones. These women have been denied a proper burial. And more than that, they were denied the full and promising lives that should have been ahead of them.'

She paused and noticed the nodding heads. People were linking arms. Some held their phones aloft, filming her speech. She'd always been so careful to keep her image off social media, yet here she was for all to see. She knew she looked nothing like the black-haired teen who'd arrived in Cornwall a lifetime ago, but she still worried that someone would recognise her. She spotted Gavin Gallagher in the crowd, but he looked at her as if she was a stranger. Too many people already knew who she used to be. Kit, Meghan, Patty, Holly – wherever she was – and somewhere in the crowd, her sister, watching her, hating her, waiting for her moment.

'Most people who are reported missing turn up again,' she went on. 'They come home or are found within a couple of days. But what about those who aren't?' She thought about Lisa, and she thought about herself. 'We hope they're out there somewhere living new lives, happy. That all they've done is take themselves away from a situation they couldn't cope with.' She looked directly at Kit. 'Maybe they've made a perfect life with people they love. Maybe they don't always show how grateful they are for that because they still carry the weight of the past.'

Kit blew her a kiss, and she felt that maybe, just maybe, they were going to get through this.

She noticed a couple of people in the crowd looking confused. 'But sometimes,' she continued, 'they are found deceased, with no obvious way of identifying them, like the women who have brought us together today.'

She glanced to her side and was surprised to see Arthur's nephew, Joseph, holding the hand of a young girl. They were wearing Truth Seekers badges.

She thought she heard someone say the name Elizabeth King, and took a deep breath. 'The first remains were thought to be Elizabeth, but we now know that to be incorrect. We're here today to highlight that there are two women here without names, but this is just the start. There are hundreds of other people whose bodies have been left unclaimed. Hundreds of families who don't know what happened to their loved ones. They all deserve answers. They deserve closure.'

As she looked at the mass of faces, all listening to every word she said, she noticed someone pushing through the bodies to get to the front. Taking a step back, she found the edge of the box and flung her arm out to steady herself, but as the woman got closer, she realised that it was Holly.

Relief flooded through her. Holly was okay, and she was here. Thank God. She returned her attention to the expectant crowd. Seeing Holly there smiling up at her, seeing Kit and Meghan looking proud of her, something inside of Eloise seemed to click and she knew exactly what she had to do. She cleared her throat.

'DNA tests haven't been able to identify that first set of remains. And while there is so much misinformation out there, we will struggle to get the answers that we, and the families of these women, are desperate to hear.'

She walked from one side of the makeshift stage to the other. 'I myself was once among the numbers of the many missing people. I ran away from home, and my family never knew what had become of me. I had my reasons.' She looked down at the ground. 'But the fact is, I had nowhere to turn.' She looked up again. 'When we become isolated, we become vulnerable. We must make sure that no one feels alone. These women in the engine houses . . .' she pointed across the horizon, 'they were failed. We don't know how, and we don't know why, but we will find out what happened to them. All we know for certain is that neither of them is Elizabeth King.' She locked eyes with Holly. 'And we know that because I . . . *I* am Elizabeth King.'

Chapter 42

Holly

The candlelight softly illuminated the walls of the engine house. It was more beautiful than Holly could have imagined. She wondered how many of the people here had their own stories of loss. When Eloise had talked about the remains of the two women yet to be identified, explaining why linking the first set to the name Elizabeth King was a mistake, there had been audible gasps.

'*I* am Elizabeth King,' she had said. 'And it's not right that one of these young women has been wrongly named. Join me in declaring that we will not rest until they are identified and their families are given closure.'

Mariella, the MP, somehow managed to link people going missing to the housing crisis in Cornwall. Apart from her thinly veiled attempt to canvass for votes, she'd given an impassioned speech about the need for answers for the families, for justice, and to ensure this never happened again. How she intended to do that was anyone's guess, but it roused everyone and united them in their desire for action.

Andy, Marsha and Sasha weaved in and out of the crowd handing out flyers about what the Truth Seekers hoped to achieve. If people were motivated to check out the website, where they could see more about the missing – to read about them as people, not statistics – then it might lead to answers. And yes, Holly was aware that there was a lot of 'could' and 'if' and 'might', but it had to be worth a shot.

'I was so worried about you,' whispered Eloise, enveloping her in a hug. 'What happened?'

'We got a lead on Lisa.'

'That's amazing!?'

'Sort of.' Holly led Eloise and Patty away from the crowd, who were standing in silence now, thinking of those who were missing.

'What's happened?' asked Patty.

'Someone took money out of Lisa's bank account in Cyprus. We're still waiting for confirmation that her passport was used to leave the country, but it looks like she's in Ayia Napa.'

'That's great,' said Eloise. 'You must be so relieved.'

'Forget about me,' said Holly. 'What about you? I leave you alone for a minute and you tell everyone that you're Elizabeth. What the hell? That's amazing.'

'I know. I was standing there looking for Deborah, and I just thought, sod it, I call the shots, not her. The most important people already know who I am, and when I saw you there, I felt strong enough to come clean. You've known the truth about me for weeks and you haven't run screaming for the hills yet.'

'Well, I thought you were great,' Patty said.

'And what about Deborah?' asked Holly. 'Have you seen her?'

'No, but Patty says that the person calling herself Sally Ann is here. From the description, I can't be sure it's Debs, but who else can it be? Maybe I've watched too many films, but all through my speech, I kept expecting to see someone pull a gun from their waistband.'

'That reminds me,' said Holly taking her phone out of her pocket. She'd missed several calls that she was planning to ignore, but Ken had sent her a text telling her to listen to her voicemail. She couldn't see him anywhere, so she put the phone to her ear and played his message. Eloise and Patty walked to the lower path and looked out over the sea while Holly put her finger to her ear so she could listen. At the end of the message, she played it again.

She looked over her shoulder at the quiet gathering. There was something powerful about a large group of people bonded in silence. She almost couldn't believe that she had made this happen. But there was no time to bask in the glory; she had to tell Eloise what Ken had found.

She made her way down to where the two women were standing. 'I had a voicemail from Ken,' she said.

Eloise looked at her expectantly.

'Is it just me who thinks he's a bit odd?' asked Patty.

'He's sent me pictures of the jewellery found on the second set of remains. I can't download them on this weak-ass 3G signal, but he did describe them to me.'

'Why do I get the feeling that I'm not going to like this?' asked Eloise.

Holly wrinkled her nose. 'There was a silver ankle brace-let and three silver rings.'

Eloise shook her head. 'That doesn't ring any bells.'

300

'She was also wearing a necklace.'

Eloise shrugged.

'It had a dragonfly pendant on it.

She put her hand to her chest and opened her mouth as if she couldn't breathe.

'Are you okay?' asked Holly. 'Does this mean . . .?'

Eloise sank to the ground as if she didn't have the energy to hold herself upright any more.

'Bloody hell,' said Patty. 'You alright? Breathe, yeah? Breathe for me. You've gone a funny colour.'

Holly crouched in front of her. 'This means something to you, doesn't it?'

'It means,' said Eloise, 'that I know who the killer is.'

'That's brilliant,' said Patty. 'Right?'

Eloise groaned and clutched the front of her T-shirt, balling it up in her hands. 'We got it all wrong,' she said. 'So wrong.'

'I don't understand,' said Patty. 'What's going on?'

Eloise knotted her fingers in her hair. 'It means Deborah's not a killer. She's not behind any of this.'

'That's a good thing, right?' said Patty. 'But if it's not your sister, then who is it?'

Eloise sat back on her heels and looked at the sky, tears snaking past her ears. 'It's me,' she said. 'I killed them both.'

Chapter 43

Eloise

Ken skidded down the path and came to a halt where Eloise was huddled on the ground. 'I came as soon as I got your message,' he said. 'I assume the jewellery has jogged a memory.'

'You could say that,' said Patty. 'She thinks she's responsible for the deaths of the women in the engine houses, and I don't know what to think any more because when this all started, she *was* one of the women in the engine houses, and now she killed them? My head's going to spin clean off in a minute.'

'She's not,' said Holly.

'Not what?' asked Patty. 'Not sane?'

'Not responsible for their deaths.'

'I am,' said Eloise.

Ken crouched down so he was at eye level with her. 'How exactly are you responsible?'

'The remains.' She closed her eyes and shook her head vigorously. 'God, I can't call them remains. They were girls. They *are* girls.'

'If you tell us what's on your mind, perhaps we can assist,' said Ken.

She took a deep breath and looked directly at Holly. Holly had tears in her eyes too. She'd already guessed what this meant.

'I bought Deborah that dragonfly necklace for her birthday,' said Eloise. 'A month later, she gave it to her girlfriend. I was furious with her. I'd saved up for weeks, and she gave it to a girl I was convinced wouldn't be her girlfriend for much longer. They overdosed on drugs they took from me. So if we're asking who was responsible for their deaths, it was me.'

'Hold up,' said Patty. 'There's a lot to unpick there. Deborah is the girl whose death certificate you asked me to find, right?'

Holly nodded. 'She was Eloise's sister, not Sally Ann's mum. We thought that Sally Ann and Deborah were the same person for a while.'

'That's why you couldn't find a death certificate for her,' Eloise said. 'It wasn't because she was still alive; it's because no one reported her death. They just held on to her body.'

'For thirty years?' said Patty.

'For thirty years.'

'That's some sick shit. Why would anyone in their right mind do that?'

Ken scratched the back of his head as he stood up. 'Have we done it then? Have we identified the remains? It's Deborah King and her girlfriend?'

'I think so,' said Holly. 'We'll need to prove it with DNA, I suppose, but yeah, it looks like we've finally got our answer.'

'Remember when we were at my old house?' Eloise said. 'The neighbour said that "what happened to those girls"

303

broke Lizzie's heart. *Girls* plural. I thought she was referring to Debs and Mel dying, but as far as my mum knew, we both disappeared that night. She must have thought we'd run away together.'

'She never knew the truth,' said Holly. 'I know she didn't treat you well, but that's so sad.'

'The police weren't looking for me in relation to Deborah's death because I was the only one who knew she was even dead.'

'You and whoever held on to the bodies,' said Ken. 'At least we know who they are and we can close this case. It's over.'

'Is it, though?' said Patty. 'Why don't I feel like you're right about that?'

'It does feel somewhat of an anticlimax, I admit,' said Ken. 'Though death is never something to celebrate, I suppose.'

'It's not over for me,' whispered Eloise.

'We're still not sure who is behind all of this and what they want with Eloise,' said Holly.

'Yes, of course. I, um . . . yes, I see,' stammered Ken. 'But my mission is to identify the remains, which we've done. Personal vendettas are not my area of expertise.'

'Bollocks to that,' said Patty. 'You're a Truth Seeker, and we want the truth about all deaths and disappearances. We still don't know who prevented the burial of these two women or why they moved them here. You have a job to do, Ken. I'm not letting you off that easily, matey.'

Ken lowered his gaze. 'I'm sorry. Yes, I am sure you are right. My apologies. How can I help?'

'That's more like it,' said Holly.

Patty said, 'Sorry if I'm being thick, but don't we already know that Sally Ann is behind it?'

'But we don't know who Sally Ann really is,' said Holly. 'Or whether she's working with someone else. More to the point, we don't know what she hopes to gain from all this.'

'Right, this is ridiculous,' said Eloise, getting to her feet and wiping the dirt off her legs. 'Enough.'

She pulled herself up straight and lifted her chin.

'We've been looking for Deborah, but we were looking for someone who doesn't exist. Sally Ann knows about me, my sister and my paintings. She came to Cornwall specifically to find me, and she's somewhere at this vigil, watching me and knowing that I haven't the first clue about what's going on. Ken, didn't you say that the carpets had traces of coal dust on them?'

'That's right,' he said.

'Right. We had coal bunkers by the side of our houses when I was growing up, but no one used them once they had electric fires put in. Most people on our estate got rid of them, but some kept them and used them for storage. When the bodies were moved, they weren't moved far. My guess is that they were put in the coal bunker behind the house they were found in, which backed on to some scrubland. And seeing as there were some pretty ripe smells from the abattoir, no one would have questioned the stench.'

'Does this mean you know who's behind this?' asked Holly.

'You asked who else knew about the dragonflies, and truly, I couldn't think of anyone. But Mel had a younger sister. As far as I know, she was the only other person in the house. She must have come across those bodies after hearing me storm through the house screaming their names. And she must've just . . . kept them.'

'What was her name?' asked Holly.

Eloise sighed and shook her head. 'I don't know. It was a long time ago, and I don't think I ever asked. She was maybe four or five years younger than me. I think we can assume that she's in her mid forties, recently moved to Cornwall, knows all about me and is here today. That's all I've got to go on.'

'I'll let my contact know that we have positive identification on those remains,' said Ken.

'I'll come with you,' Patty said. 'The others need to know about the latest developments. I've not seen Sally Ann since she picked up the T-shirt, but I'll find her if she's still here. Leave it with me.'

Holly and Eloise watched them go. 'Are you okay?' asked Holly. 'Sorry. Stupid question. Of course you're not. What I mean is, how are you feeling?'

'Angry,' said Eloise.

'That's my girl,' smiled Holly.

'Up until ten minutes ago, I thought I was going to see my sister again, and I was scared but there was also a part of me that was excited. Now, not only is Deborah dead, but this . . . this . . .'

'It's okay to call her a bitch,' said Holly.

'This *bitch* kept hold of my sister's body for thirty years. No burial, no headstone, no pot of ashes on a mantelpiece. Mum thought we'd both run away, and she didn't know why. Sure, she wasn't a great mother, but she deserved better. She didn't know that the reason I fled was because Deborah was dead. She would have thought the two of us had just had enough of her crap and left her. There must have been a part of her that loved us. That neighbour said she died of a broken heart not long after we went missing. Maybe that's true. Maybe losing us was the final straw.'

Eloise looked out over the sea, thinking about the woman she'd hated for most of her life. She had been determined to be everything her mother wasn't, and had done her utmost to prove that she was nothing like her. She never lost her temper and never let her children think for one second of any day that she didn't love them. She never left them home alone, never made them scared of her. She never put her needs before theirs, because she wanted them to know that their lives were more important than hers and she would do anything for them. But maybe, just maybe, she could have shown her mother a little more sympathy.

Without realising it, she had married a law-abiding version of her father. The fun one, the laid-back one, the one for whom consequences didn't matter. Had being married to Eloise's dad caused Mum to always have to be the sensible one, fighting for money, jobs and food? Swearing and cursing at the neighbours for looking down on them and spitting at them in the streets because their dad was in prison again. She had taken tough love too far and her parenting style had been cruel and loveless, but was she doing what she had to do to survive?

'I'm trying to get my head around these new feelings of sympathy for my mum, even though I know I can never forgive her.'

'I know it's not the same,' Holly said, 'but it's a bit like that with me and Liam. Understandably, he went to pieces when my mum died, but I guess he's still my dad. I only started referring to him as my stepdad this year. It's difficult to balance my hurt with the fact that deep down I love the idiot. So I get what's eating you. People we love and trust let us down. They always will. And yeah, it fucking hurts, but it's okay to forgive them if that's what's best for us.'

'Is it?'

'Yeah. It is. Except for this Sally Ann bitch who's been playing us, of course. She doesn't deserve any sympathy at all. We need to find her and bring her down.'

Chapter 44

Eloise

People were starting to leave, but Eloise stayed where she was. Kit had hugged her and told her he loved her, reassuring her that she'd done the right thing by revealing she used to be Elizabeth King. And then he'd comforted her over losing her sister all over again.

Holly posed for photographs while holding a candle in front of the ruined engine house, looking solemn. The picture was to accompany the journalist's article about how the Truth Seekers had solved the mystery of the bodies in the other engine houses. She said she would give them an exclusive interview but there was one more loose end to tie up first.

The Truth Seekers surrounded Eloise as she gathered her belongings, numb from the day's events and tired from trying to process everything.

'Got to say,' said Andy, 'you're looking pretty good for a bird who's been dead for thirty years.'

'Give it a rest,' said Patty. 'Is there anyone, alive or dead, who you'd draw the line at flirting with?'

'It's called making conversation,' said Andy.

'It's called making a fool of yourself.'

Andy shook his head, but he was smiling. 'Can't believe that all this time you weren't even dead. And Sally Ann knew you weren't dead because she was using us to get to you. Never saw that one coming at all. Got to admire her balls.' He pointed at Patty. 'Didn't I say that a woman was behind this? Blokes don't hold a grudge for thirty years. They don't have the energy.'

'This is mental, this is,' said Sasha. 'The girls totally lost their minds when you said who you were. I wouldn't have recognised you. Well, I didn't, did I? I'm chuffed you're okay, though. Gavin is well pissed off and has stormed back to his car. Says people have been accusing him of murdering you and you didn't even have the decency to be dead.'

'I'm sorry I made you think that something bad had happened to me,' said Eloise. 'I didn't expect this to snowball like it did.'

'Oh my God, you've got nothing to apologise for. We should never have left the nightclub without checking on you.'

'We've looked everywhere,' said Marsha, moving Sasha aside. 'Sally Ann isn't here.'

'She did what she came to do,' said Eloise. 'She let me know she was watching me. Scare tactics.'

'Did it work?' Marsha asked.

'Absolutely.'

'I don't get it,' said Andy. 'Why go to all that trouble?'

Eloise saw Ken talking to the police officer and his colleague. She knew she'd have to give a formal statement, explain who she was and tell them why she was so sure she knew the identities of the girls in the engine houses, but not now.

'Sally Ann wanted to find Eloise because she blames her for her sister's death,' Patty said. 'She wanted to expose her, but Eloise didn't give her the chance.' She turned to Eloise. 'Ballsy move, by the way.'

'Thanks.'

'What we don't know is what she will do next. I thought she'd do something today while we were all filming and taking photos. I would have.'

'Like you say,' said Andy, 'she wanted to expose her. But Eloise came out and admitted who she was in front of the police, so there's nothing more for Sally Ann to do, is there? Job done.'

'You really don't understand women, do you?' said Patty. 'She's held on to her dead sister's body for longer than you've been alive. She's not going to go home satisfied just because the world knows what happened to Elizabeth King. She's playing the long game here. You've heard the phrase "Revenge is a dish best served cold"? Well, after thirty years, baby, this dish is frozen. We've got to get into her head.'

EL

Eloise tried to imagine what Sally Ann was thinking. She hoped she had a heart full of forgiveness, though she knew that wasn't possible. If Eloise was in her position . . .

She rose up onto her tiptoes to look for Kit and Meghan.

'What is it?' asked Patty.

'I'm just thinking what I would do to the person who hurt my sister. How I might go after someone they loved.'

She searched about her frantically until she spotted Kit standing alone in a clearing. She ran towards him. 'Where is she?' she shouted. 'Where's Meghan?'

Kit blinked uncertainly at her.

311

'Jesus Christ, Kit, I asked you to stay by her side all day.'

'She's fine,' he said. 'Don't worry. Wendy gave her a lift home about an hour ago. Meghan was tired, and Wendy said she'd had enough too. I said I'd wait to drive you back when you'd finished.'

Eloise sighed. 'Oh, okay. Thank God for—' She felt for a moment like she'd stopped breathing as everything froze.

'You okay?' Kit asked.

'Oh my God,' said Eloise. 'Where are Mimi and Jan?'

'They've gone too. Why?'

'Why didn't I see it before? It's Wendy. She's Mel's younger sister.'

Chapter 45

Eloise

Holly was in the back seat of the car, Kit in the passenger seat, and Eloise was driving like Meghan's life depended on it. The minibus behind them was trying to keep up and failing.

'Watch the—' Kit said as another car hurtled towards them. Eloise squeezed their vehicle against the hedge, causing the paintwork to screech against the brambles. Kit had one hand on the grab handle above the door and the other braced against the dashboard.

'Wendy talked about having a daughter called Melanie, but really that was her sister's name,' said Eloise. 'She talks about Melanie and her grandson all the time, but she's never brought them into the studio or shown us photos on her phone. She moved down here from the Midlands at the beginning of summer in her van, which can, you know, transport human remains and stuff. She's about the right age, lives on her own and is secretive. She fits the profile.'

'She seems sweet, though,' said Holly. 'I don't know if she looks like the kind of woman who stores dead bodies in her shed.'

'Try Meghan's phone again,' said Eloise.

313

'Voicemail,' Kit said.

'Shit.'

Eloise hardly slowed for the junction, and cornered so quickly that for a moment it felt like the car lifted up on two wheels.

'Where are we going?' Holly asked.

'I don't know,' said Eloise. 'Keep trying Mimi and Jan.'

'Their phones are switched off,' said Holly.

'Or they're in an area without coverage. Try them again.'

'Just got a message from Ken,' Holly said. 'Patty is trying to find out where Wendy lives, but no joy. She's liaising with Ken's police contact and seeing if they can get a number plate for her dodgy van.'

'Her van,' said Eloise, momentarily lifting both hands off the steering wheel. 'I always tell Meghan not to get into white panel vans.'

'Now's not the time for another "I told you so",' said Kit. 'Is there any chance you're overreacting? Could Wendy just be dropping Meghan off at home like she said?'

'That's what I do, right? Overreact?' snapped Eloise. 'I would love for this to be me just overreacting, Kit, but there's a woman who has been waiting thirty years for the chance to make me pay for the death of her sister. And if I'm right about it being Wendy, then she has our daughter in her van right now. If I was overreacting, I would stop this car and push you out into the middle of the road for patronising me, so no, I'm not overreacting, Kit.'

'Fair enough.' Kit cleared his throat. 'In that case, we need to work out where they're going rather than have you drive us straight into the sea. What's the most likely destination? Our house? Her house? I don't suppose she has a secluded lockup we don't know about. If we can contact the goons in the minibus behind us, perhaps we could divide and conquer?'

Holly's phone buzzed. 'Another message from Ken. Shit. I think I know where Wendy is.'

'Where?' said Eloise.

'I mean, I don't know for certain, but—'

'Where?' shouted Eloise and Kit in unison.

'The yoga studio is on fire.'

Chapter 46

Eloise

She could smell the fire long before she saw the glow above the jagged rooftops. The car wasn't fast enough, and the roads weren't straight or empty enough. Over and over in her mind she repeated, 'I'm coming, Meghan. I'm coming.'

She ran a red light, and as another driver extended his middle finger, she gave it back to him with interest. Access to the yoga studio was blocked, so she stopped the car in the middle of the road and ran the rest of the way. As she turned the corner, her steps faltered. The roof of the main studio had collapsed, but the kitchen block and café were still standing. As the flames were brought under control, the smoke turned black.

'Meghan!'

Wendy knew about the fire hazards, and she knew that the studio was closed. Who would question the place burning down?

Mimi and Jan stood a little way back, watching the black smoke plume into the sky. Eloise ran to them.

'Have they found Meghan?' she asked.

'No,' said Jan. 'There's no one in there.'

People were gathering at a safe distance. Some had their phones out and were filming. Eloise looked frantically around her, searching for a way to get into the building, but every way was blocked.

'It's okay,' Jan said. 'The fire brigade almost have it under control, and they say the building was empty when the fire started. Luckily a couple of women turned up for a cancelled class, and when they looked through the window, they saw smoke. It could have been so much worse.'

'But Meghan and Wendy—'

'The building's empty,' said Jan. 'It's okay.' She put her arm around Eloise's shoulder. 'What's going on?'

Eloise swallowed hard, unsure where to start. 'Wendy gave Meghan a lift home, only she didn't. I think she brought her here before setting fire to the studio. Meghan's in danger and we have to find her.'

Mimi turned to her with tears on her cheeks. 'Are you honestly making this all about you again when my studio has gone up in flames? Just like making the vigil all about you.'

Eloise blinked in surprise. 'What? Are *you* honestly more concerned about a building than my daughter?'

'We were a bit shocked that you hadn't told us you'd changed your name and stuff,' said Jan. 'That's all.' She cast a warning look at Mimi, then moved until she was standing between the two women. 'Everyone's upset,' she said. 'Now, what's all this about Meghan?'

'I don't have time to explain, but Wendy wants to hurt her to get back at me.'

'Ridiculous!' said Mimi. 'Joseph did it for the insurance money as soon as he got them to say it was a fire hazard.

Look at him standing over there pretending to be distraught. Surely no one is buying his act.'

Holly and Kit had caught up with Eloise. 'Are you absolutely sure that no one is in that building?' Kit said.

'Certain,' said Mimi. 'Seeing as you refuse to take my word for it, ask that man over there. He seems to be the one in charge.'

Kit went to do as Mimi suggested while Eloise frantically turned on the spot, looking for Wendy's van but not seeing it.

'What's going on, El?' Jan asked, stepping away from Mimi.

'Wendy is lying about who she is. She's lying about everything. About coming down here to be close to her daughter and grandson. I met her back when I was Elizabeth King, and if I'm right about who she is, her sister died the same night as mine. I think she's held on to their bodies for thirty years and is getting back at me by taking Meghan.'

'Are you serious? That's . . . Okay. I have a lot of questions, but let's start with this one. What do you need me to do?'

'I don't know. I just want to find my daughter.'

Holly's phone rang, and she moved away from them to take the call. Eloise watched her face, hoping for good news, a thumbs-up. She would be glad to be known as a chronic overreactor for the rest of her life as long as Meghan was safe.

Holly shook her head. 'There's no one at your house,' she said, covering the mouthpiece. 'Andy's there now. There's no sign of Wendy's van either. The hens have Wendy's address from Patty, and Sasha's almost there.'

318

Eloise nodded. She felt like she should do something, but she was powerless. If something had happened to Meghan . . . No, she couldn't let herself think that way. Everything she'd ever done was to keep her family safe.

'Ken is with the police,' Holly continued. 'But there's been a big accident on the A30, so they're struggling to send anyone else over.' She listened to the phone for a moment longer. 'Okay, they've got the van registration number and have instructed people to be on the lookout, but that's about as much as they can do.'

Kit rushed over. 'They're as sure as they can be that there's no one inside. Fire's almost under control.' He and Eloise locked eyes and stood motionless, then she collapsed against his chest.

'It's all right,' he said. 'We're going to find her. Listen to me.' He tilted her chin so she was looking at him. 'As far as we know, Wendy has never hurt anyone.'

'But she—'

'She hasn't hurt anyone. Deborah and Melanie were already dead. She kept hold of them. Kept their bodies safe. Unconventional? Yes. But violent? No.'

Eloise wanted to believe him. She needed to believe him, but the stakes were too high. 'Then why take our daughter?'

'Why do any of this?' he said. 'To get your attention. She wants you, not Meghan.'

'But the fire . . .' she began.

'Is a distraction. It's another sign that she isn't capable of hurting anyone. This is just a building.'

Mimi's head snapped around. 'It's not just a building. I poured my heart and soul into this.'

'Wind your neck in Mimi,' said Kit calmly. 'The woman you employed – without checking her references, I bet – has kidnapped our daughter. A bit of support wouldn't go amiss.'

Mimi looked like she'd been slapped. She opened and closed her mouth before saying, 'You're right. I'm sorry.'

Eloise looked at her husband – really looked at him. This was Kit at his best. She'd always loved his ability to calm her down and make her feel safe, but there was little he could do now to improve this situation.

'Sasha's just arrived at Wendy's house,' said Holly.

Patty Hansen

Switching to messaging on here so everyone can see what's happening in real time. Wendy (aka Sally Ann) has kidnapped the daughter of Eloise (aka Elizabeth King). They were last seen at the vigil. It appears that Wendy has set fire to a yoga studio where she worked to distract us. This lost us valuable time, so we must do what we can to track her down immediately. We don't know how dangerous she is, but we do know the bitch is wearing one of our T-shirts and she hasn't paid me for it.

Marsha Pirolo

I could tell by her aura that she was hiding a big secret. My spirit guides tell me that she is near the water.

Andy Pickford

Well that narrows it down, Marsha. In Cornwall. By the sea. FFS.

There's no sign of Meghan or Wendy at the Ford residence. The neighbours haven't seen anything suspicious. We're heading to the yoga studio now.

Patty Hansen

Sasha is at Wendy's house, but it's locked up and there's no sign of anyone at home.

Holly Bobs

Eloise says Wendy sometimes leaves the back door unlocked.

Sasha Walters

We're in! You were right about the back door. No one is here. The house is weird, though. There are no personal belongings. There's barely any furniture. I can look around if you like, but I don't really know what I'm looking for. There isn't anything particularly fishy. No wall of pictures with people's eyes cut out or anything. It's just a sad person's house. What do you want me to do? I could leave a note.

Patty Hansen

Are there any electronics in the house?

Sasha Walters

There's a television.

Patty Hansen

I mean like a laptop.

Sasha Walters

There's an iPad charging in the kitchen.

Patty Hansen

Perfect! If we can crack the code for it, we might be able to use the Find My Phone app to check her mobile. Holly, can you ask Eloise if she can think of any memorable dates? The date the sister died, maybe? Wendy's DOB from her employee records? Anything she might have used as a security code.

Sasha Walters

Or I could just use the code that's taped onto the back of the iPad.

Chapter 47

Holly

Patty jumped out of the car and waved her arms frantically. 'Here,' she called.

Eloise and Holly ran up the road towards her. 'Have you found her?' shouted Eloise.

'No, but we know where her phone is. Get in.'

Andy revved the engine as Eloise and Holly climbed into the back.

'Where is she?' Holly asked, grabbing Andy's seat and leaning forward.

'Listen, you've got to remember that we're tracking her phone, okay?' said Patty. 'The phone, do you hear me? Not Wendy. We're assuming that the phone and the phoney are together, but we can't be certain.'

'Unfortunately—' began Andy.

'No, I don't want to hear "unfortunately",' said Eloise.

'Well you're gonna. Unfortunately, her phone has either been switched off or ran out of juice about five minutes ago.'

'So we've lost her again?' cried Eloise, putting her hand to her forehead. Holly reached out to grab her other hand.

'Her last known location was back at the engine house where we held the vigil,' said Patty. 'And my guess is she's still there.'

'Why has she gone back?' said Holly.

'Like I said, she might not be there,' said Patty, turning around to look at her. 'She might have dropped her phone, or she could have left it there on purpose. This could be another misdirection.'

Eloise took a deep, juddering breath. 'No. She's there. Has to be. That engine house is the only one of the three I painted that she didn't get to put a body in. Maybe that's what she's intending to do now.'

She took her phone out of her pocket to text Kit, but her hands were trembling too much to type. 'Would you . . .?' she asked Holly.

'Sure. What do you want me to say?' Holly took the phone from her.

'Tell him we're heading back to the engine house.'

Holly started typing. 'Okay.'

'And tell him . . .' Eloise said, 'tell him I'm sorry for everything I've done that has led to this, for every mistake that I've ever made. Will you tell him that I love him so very much and I'm sorry for putting our daughter in danger?'

Holly paused her thumbs above the screen. She thought for a moment, typed a few more words and then handed back the phone.

Eloise looked at the display. The text message said, *Tracked Wendy's phone to engine house. Heading there now. Will call later.* She glanced at Holly, who just shrugged.

'Look, it says everything you need it to. I don't feel comfortable typing love notes to Mr F.'

'You do realise that these could be the last words he ever hears from me?'

'I know that you *think* that, but you're wrong. Tell him all that gushy stuff yourself later, when we've got Meghan back.'

Chapter 48

Eloise

The car park was almost empty, except for one white van.

'She's here,' said Patty. 'The bitch is actually here. The number plate matches.' She and Andy slapped their hands together in a high five.

'I'll call the police.'

'Okay,' said Andy. 'How do you want to play this? We don't want to spook her, so let's not go rushing in. She could be anywhere, so I suggest we each take a—'

Eloise pushed open the car door and took off at a run towards the narrow lane that led to the engine house. Though the evening wasn't yet fully dark and wouldn't be for another hour, the purple sky left the road in perpetual shadow, and she skidded on the gravel. She turned off onto the path and slowed as the slope dropped away. She could hear footsteps behind her.

'Wait up,' Holly hissed.

Though Andy had said that Wendy and Meghan could be anywhere, Eloise knew the engine house was the only place they could be. Deborah in one, Mel in another and Meghan in the third. A triptych of death.

She slowed even more and slid down the bank sideways. A leaflet from the vigil flapped in the spines of the gorse, and an empty water bottle rolled in the breeze. There was still no sign of life in the engine house. She had to hope she wasn't too late, but now that she was here, she wasn't sure what to do.

She came to a halt and felt Holly's hand on her back. 'Are you crazy?' she whispered.

'My daughter's in there,' Eloise said.

'And so is the woman who wants to hurt you.'

'I'll make lots of noise and let her know I'm coming. No sudden movements and no surprises. If she wants me to stop, she'll tell me. You to go back to the top path and see if you can drop down further along and get around the back of the building to approach it from below.'

'I hope you know what you're doing,' Holly said as she turned and scrambled back up the slope.

Eloise waited till she was out of sight, then called out, 'Wendy? Can you hear me?' She took a few steps closer. 'Wendy? Or do you want me to call you Sally Ann?'

There was no answer, but she was sure she could feel someone watching her. 'It's me, Eloise. You can call me Elizabeth if you like. That's what this is about, isn't it? About what happened back when people still knew me as Elizabeth King, the dropout and drug dealer.'

Still there was no answer. Eloise ducked under the fence. Past the faded notice warning people of danger and telling them to keep away. 'I'm coming in. Is that okay with you?'

She climbed onto the wall and flung her legs over the edge. It was dark inside the building, even though there was no roof. It took a moment for her eyes to adjust, but even then, all she could see was shadows.

'Wendy, are you in here?'

328

'You took your time,' said a soft voice.

Eloise peered in the direction of the familiar sound. 'You sent us off on a bit of a wild goose chase,' she said. 'Did you have to burn down the yoga studio? Mimi is quite upset.'

'Mimi needs to get over herself,' said Wendy.

'She treated you well and gave you a job. It was a poor way to repay her.'

'I had to lure you all away from here,' said Wendy. 'I didn't expect it to be so easy to get Meghan on her own. My plan was to take Mimi. You once told me she was like a sister to you, remember?'

'I remember,' said Eloise. 'It was at the open day.'

'An eye for an eye. A sister for a sister. When you arranged the vigil here, I thought I was going to have to abandon the idea of putting a body in the third engine house. I thought I'd have to leave Mimi in the studio to be overcome by smoke and flames, but then Meghan said she needed a lift home, and she had no concerns at all about getting in a van with a woman she'd only just met, all because I said I was a friend of yours. Everything fell into place. That's when I knew that God was on my side.'

'No one's on your side, Wendy. If you're lucky, you might find a sympathetic doctor or a lenient judge, but here, you're on your own.'

'Not completely on my own.'

Eloise peered into the shadows but saw no movement.

'Where is she?'

'Don't worry. She's here,' Wendy said. 'Safe and sound.'

'Meghan?' said Eloise.

A muffled sound came from somewhere in front of her.

'Meghan, are you okay?'

'She's all right,' said Wendy. 'But she can't move, and she can't speak.'

'Oh my God, have you drugged her?'

'No. Of course not. I've taped her mouth and tied her wrists and ankles, that's all.'

'Oh,' said Eloise, deflating with relief. 'I just thought . . .'

'What do you take me for?'

'This is no time to get defensive. You kidnapped my daughter.'

Wendy scoffed. 'Oh, please. She willingly got into my van and drank the water with the sleeping tablets in it.'

'So you *have* drugged her?' Eloise exclaimed.

'Only over-the-counter stuff. We can't all lay our hands on class-A drugs whenever we want them.'

Eloise sighed. 'Here we go. You want to blame me for your sister taking those drugs? Go ahead, but it's not my fault. Mel chose to do it.'

'She would never have taken them if it wasn't for you and your sister.'

Eloise slid off the wall and took a few tentative steps towards Wendy. She knew that there was a steep drop nearby and slid her feet across the ground cautiously.

'They stole those drugs off me, Wendy. I only sold them to make money to build a better future for me and Deborah, but I paid the ultimate price for that, didn't I? And I'll never forgive myself.'

'Well, weren't you a role model to be proud of?'

'I never pretended to be anything other than what I was.'

'Oh, but you pretend now, don't you? Miss I-own-an-art-gallery. Miss butter-wouldn't-melt. Lording it over us all with your posh house, your posh kids and your weekly yoga. You've become a walking stereotype of a middle-class, middle-aged average white woman. There is nothing special about you.'

'You want to talk stereotypes?" said Eloise. 'You've kept your sister's dead body for thirty years, clinging on to her. I bet you talked to her too, didn't you? Plotting to take me down one day, like a cliché from an American B-movie. Did you dress her up and put her in a rocking chair? You're sick, Wendy. You need help.'

'That's a fine way to talk to the woman holding a top-of-the-range kitchen knife against your daughter's throat in front of a sheer drop. It turns out Mimi was happy to let me keep those knives – or at least didn't notice me taking them.'

Eloise froze. She felt the sweat cool on her skin.

'You won't hurt her,' she said. 'It's me you want, so why don't you let her go?'

'Now who's talking in clichés?' asked Wendy.

Eloise twisted her head from side to side to release the tension from her neck. She slowed her breathing and told herself to remain calm. 'What do you want, Wendy?'

'I want you to suffer like I suffered.'

'You weren't the only one to suffer. I lost someone too.'

Wendy laughed. 'Are you honestly comparing your loss to mine? You took off at the first sign of trouble and found yourself a cushy life with a job, friends, a husband and kids. There were no consequences to what you did. Well, guess who *did* have to live with the consequences? Me. I was

331

fifteen years old. Mel was all I had. Mum and Dad had fucked off years before, and we didn't tell anyone. Mel pretended to be Mum whenever the school called, as well as running the house and doing everything as well as Mum had ever done. But even that wasn't enough. The things she had to do for money . . . Let's say you wouldn't wish it on your pretty young daughter here.'

'I had no idea,' said Eloise. 'I—'

'No, you wouldn't have any idea because you looked down on us. You! You whose dad had been inside. You whose mum sold knock-off stuff out of the back of Woolies. You've always thought you were better than everyone else.'

Eloise thought she heard movement outside and spoke louder to conceal the noises.

'Why didn't you tell someone she'd died?' she asked. 'You could have got help.'

'What? Foster care? Children's home? If they'd found out I was on my own, I'd have been another statistic in the system, and we know what happens to those kids. I had to keep up the pretence that all was fine at home, until I was old enough to get my own job and my own money. But I could never have friends around, not that I had any, because there were a couple of dead bodies in the house. Even after I moved them to the coal shed, I couldn't let anyone in. Couldn't have a relationship, because what if they went snooping around? And I couldn't move house either, so I've been stuck there alone for thirty years. And all this time, you've been living the life that I should have had. You owe me. And I *will* make you pay.'

Truth Seekers UK

Marsha Pirolo

I had to return to the hotel. I was overwhelmed by the events of the day. Where is everyone? What's happening? Have you found her?

Andy Pickford

I thought you'd already know, thanks to your psychic powers. Have your spirit guides gone home for the night?

Patty Hansen

Eloise is talking to someone in the engine house. We assume it's Wendy, but we don't know whether Meghan is with them or what kind of state she's in. Holly is in position behind the building, and I'm on the top path, looking down on them. We can't do anything until we know the situation and how dangerous Wendy is.

Andy is waiting in the car.

Andy Pickford

Whoa there! Don't make it sound like I've wimped out. The police will be here any minute, so I'm here to fill them in and/or stop Wendy from getting away in her van. You could argue that I've got the most important job here.

Patty Hansen

No, you really couldn't.

Sasha Walters

So bloody sorry. The minibus has broken down. Massive build-up of traffic. Will get to you asap. I hope the police aren't stuck behind us!

Ken Marchpane

Alas, we are in a traffic jam, which I can only assume has been caused by Sasha's minibus. Kind regards, Ken.

Patty Hansen

Looks like we're on our own.

Holly Bobs

I can hear two voices. Can't make out much of what they're saying, but Eloise's daughter is in there and I heard Wendy say she has a knife. I have to get inside.

Patty Hansen

Wait for the police!!

Chapter 49

Holly

Holly's palms were clammy and her lips were sticking to her teeth. Right now she could be on a plane to Cyprus, but instead, she was crouching behind an engine house, giving serious thought to confronting a knife-wielding maniac who'd held on to two dead bodies for three decades.

It wasn't how she'd planned to spend her Saturday night.

She could have turned around, walked away and returned to the car, and no one would have blamed her. In fact, she'd been told explicitly not to go in there. Patty had instructed her to wait for the police.

It was tempting.

But the police were delayed, and someone had to do something. Who was to say that they'd be more use than she was anyway? And there was no way she would leave Eloise to face this alone.

The soft wind was making it difficult to hear what was being said. Eloise's tone was calm, conversational even. Wendy's was sometimes loud, sometimes quiet. Holly didn't want to blunder in there and make things worse, but if she could distract her, maybe they could wrestle the knife off her and . . .

But knives were sharp, and Holly was soft all over, which wasn't a good combination. She slowly got to her feet and peered through the gap in the wall. She could see Eloise's silhouette, but she couldn't see Wendy, even though she could hear her clearly just to the right of the window.

She began counting down in her head. *Ten . . . nine . . .* She would leap through the window, waving her arms around like a madwoman, hoping it would distract Wendy long enough for Eloise to get Meghan out of there. *Seven . . . six . . .* But her legs were trembling, and every time she tried to picture Meghan, she saw Lisa's face. And that was why she had to do this. *Three . . . two . . .*

A whistle split the air, and another one. 'Buster! Here, Buster. Where are you, boy?'

Torch beams pierced the sky. A woman's voice, which she recognised as Patty's, called, 'Where are you, Buster? Buster? Come on. Here, boy.'

'Buster!' shouted Andy.

The lights shone into the engine house.

'Haven't seen our dog, have you, love?' said Andy as he shone the torchlight directly in Wendy's face. Holly leapt through the window and tackled Wendy from behind.

Too late, she realised that Wendy was holding on to Meghan, and all three of them fell forward into the pit before them with a sickening thud.

Chapter 50

Eloise

'Meghan!' Eloise screamed.

The torchlight went out momentarily, then flickered back on. One minute they were there, and the next, gone. Eloise was already running towards them, dropping to the floor and skidding on her knees.

Patty grabbed the back of her T-shirt to stop her from falling head-first on top of them.

'Wait,' she said.

She held her torch out in front of her, illuminating the hole in the centre of the room where Holly, Wendy and Meghan were lying in a heap. It was such a tangle of limbs that it was hard to see who was who.

Or who the blood was coming from.

'Shit,' said Andy.

Eloise dropped down into the hole and pulled Wendy aside by her shoulders, checking she wasn't holding the knife. Wendy blinked at her, but there was no fight left in her eyes. There was blood on her hand, and up her arm.

'Careful!' shouted Patty.

Andy landed with a thud and grabbed Wendy, pushing her so her face was against the wall. 'Don't move,' he said.

'Meghan,' said Eloise. 'Are you okay?'

Patty directed the torch at Meghan as Eloise cradled her daughter's face. Her eyes were open, and she had tears on her cheeks. Eloise peeled back the duct tape across her mouth, and Meghan gasped.

'Are you hurt?' Eloise asked.

Meghan shook her head. 'No. But I'll have a bastard of a bruise on my bum in the morning.'

'The blood . . .' said Eloise.

'Not mine.'

'Holly?' said Eloise.

'I'm good,' Holly croaked.

Eloise sank back onto her heels. 'Thank God. You're a maniac, Holly. Brave, but bonkers.'

'Yeah,' said Holly. The word came out slowly on the back of a sigh. 'I know.'

'Thank you.' Eloise reached for her and squeezed her hand.

'Where's the knife?' shouted Patty. 'Who's got the knife?'

'It's okay,' said Holly. 'I can see it.' She sat up and grunted. 'It's in Wendy's thigh.'

They all looked at the knife. Wendy seemed as surprised as anyone to see it there.

'Okay,' said Andy. 'Whatever you do, don't pull it . . .'

Eloise grabbed the hilt and pulled.

'. . . out,' finished Andy.

Blood bloomed black on Wendy's jeans as she cried out in pain. Eloise threw the knife out of the pit, and it skittered across the ground.

'What?' she said, seeing the shocked look on Holly's face. 'It's not a good idea for her to have a weapon, even if it is in her thigh.'

Andy was already applying pressure to Wendy's leg. Eloise stood up and joined Holly and Meghan in doing the same. She kept her eyes averted from the blood, and tried not to notice that there was some on her hands. She almost retched, but she breathed through it and waited for the nausea to pass.

They clambered out of the pit with Patty's help, while Andy tied a tourniquet around the top of Wendy's leg. Eloise didn't know why he was bothering. It wouldn't be the worst thing in the world if Wendy bled to death.

Holly and Andy stood over Wendy in the pit. It was too deep for her to get out of alone, even if she hadn't been stabbed in the thigh. The bleeding had slowed, and an ambulance was on its way. Eloise hoped they took their time.

She and Patty helped a limping Meghan back to the car park, Patty holding one arm, Eloise the other.

'Mum, I'm fine. I'm sure there'll be therapy in my future, but for now, I'm okay. I promise. Just achy and tired. That's all.'

They found a blanket in the boot of the car that smelled of dog and dirt, but it was warm and comforting nonetheless.

Eloise peppered her with questions. *Are you okay? Did Wendy hurt you? How's your head? Did you lose consciousness?* And while Meghan had plenty of her own, she kept coming back to 'What the hell just happened?'

'I've spoken to Dad to let him know you're okay, and he says he'll meet us at the hospital,' said Eloise.

'I don't need the hospital,' Meghan said. 'I've told you, I'm fine.'

'Shouldn't we wait for the police?' asked Patty. 'I feel like we can't just walk away from this without someone doing something official. I've never been in this kind of situation before. What are we meant to do?'

Eloise, who had been a staunch follower of rules for most of her adult life, realised that she didn't care what she was *meant* to do. If the police wanted to talk to her, they knew where she'd be.

'The most important thing is that I get my daughter checked over. And then I need an embarrassingly large glass of something strong.' She slid into the passenger seat and began looking for paracetamols or aspirins.

'Can't we just go home, Mum? It's not like it's an emergency.'

'You're hurt, so unless I can find some painkillers . . .'

'My mouth's sore from the tape. My hip's sore from the fall. And I'm hellish thirsty. But honestly, the worst thing is that you get to tell me "I told you so" because you always said to be wary of white panel vans.'

'Ken says the police are about fifteen minutes away,' said Patty, looking at the messages on her phone. 'They've passed Sasha's minibus now.'

Eloise climbed out of the car. 'I'll go and let the others know what's happening. If the police aren't here by the time I get back, they'll just have to talk to us another time. Patty, will you stay with Meghan?'

'You stay with your daughter. I'll go and speak to Holly and Andy.'

'No,' said Eloise, holding up her hand. 'If you don't mind, I'd like to see Wendy one last time.'

Patty started to object, but she took one look at Eloise's face and let her go.

Eloise made her way slowly to the engine house because she had no more energy in her legs. She could hear Holly and Andy chatting as she got close.

'. . . and then I saw your message saying you were going in, and I looked around the car for something to arm myself with, but all I could find was the dog's lead, and that's when I got the idea.'

EL

'That was lucky,' Holly said. 'Because I didn't have a clue what I was going to do when I got in here.'

She turned around as Eloise appeared at the window. 'How's Meghan?'

'Surprisingly fine,' said Eloise. 'Treating this like it's all one big adventure. Look, the police will be here in a minute. Is it okay if I . . .' She squeezed through the window and dropped onto the ground. 'Look, I need a minute alone with Wendy.'

'No chance,' said Andy. 'She's a bloody nutter.'

'Oi! Do you mind?' said Wendy from the bottom of the pit.

'Yeah,' said Holly. 'I don't think that's such a good idea.'

'Once the police get here, I'm not going to get a chance to talk to her alone again,' said Eloise. 'And there are a few things I need to get off my chest.'

'Are you going to give her a kicking?' Andy asked. 'Make her fall down the stairs or walk into a door? You know, I'm not convinced you didn't know what you were doing when you took that knife out.'

Eloise cuffed him around the back of the head. 'Get out of here. She can't escape that pit without help, and Patty took the knife, didn't she? I'll be fine. If there are any problems, I'll call for help. Okay?'

Andy and Holly looked at each other and nodded. 'You're shivering,' Andy said. 'Why don't you go up to the car?'

'Are you sure?' Holly asked.

'I'll stay and make sure Eloise doesn't waterboard her.'

'Thanks,' said Eloise. 'But you're waiting outside. What I have to say to Wendy is personal.'

Chapter 51

Eloise

'How did you work out that I was Elizabeth King?'

The torchlight illuminated the walls. The only witness, a bat, swooped and flitted overhead, but Wendy sat in the shadows in silence.

'Come on,' said Eloise. 'It's over. I think we can afford to be honest with each other now. We're not so different, you and I. We grew up on the same estate. We had to be responsible for our own upbringing from too young an age, and we both lost sisters we adored. You're probably the only person in the world who understands me.'

Still Wendy remained silent.

'If I'd known you were there that night, I'd have taken you with me. I would have looked after you, you know. I would never have left you behind to clean up my mess. In a way, I should thank you. I was waiting for someone to come after me when they discovered the bodies, but thanks to you, they were never found. You did me a favour.'

'Bollocks,' said Wendy.

Eloise smirked. At least she was speaking.

'Honestly, I would have done something. I just panicked

and thought I was the only one who knew. I didn't realise you were home that night.'

Wendy stood up and rotated her wrist. Hopping on one leg and grunting.

'It was the dragonflies,' she said. 'That's how I worked out you were Elizabeth.'

'Of course,' said Eloise.

'When I was a kid, they were all over our house because your Deborah kept giving them to Mel. They were planning to get matching tattoos of them.'

Eloise frowned. They were meant to be just for her and Deborah.

'I'd completely forgotten about them until this woman I cleaned for came back from her holidays in St Ives and put up these hideous paintings of old mines in the lounge.'

'Actually,' said Eloise, 'they're some of my bestsellers.'

'That says a lot about the rest of your work,' said Wendy. 'She had me dusting them like they were actual works of art . . .'

'Some people think they are.'

'. . . and I noticed this little dragonfly in the corner, and it reminded me of Mel. I mean, what were the chances, eh?'

'I bet you couldn't believe your luck,' said Eloise. 'Searching for me for all that time and then seeing those paintings . . .'

'Flippin' 'eck. Don't flatter yourself. I'd hardly given you any thought since the day you buggered off. I mean, I hated your guts and hoped you'd been knocked down by a bus, but mostly I was glad you'd disappeared before I could get my hands around your skinny neck.'

'Are you telling me you haven't been plotting revenge for thirty years?' asked Eloise.

'Christ on a bike. Are you up yourself or what? I was too scared that someone would knock on the door and take me away, but when the knock finally came, it was only your mum, looking for you and Debs.'

Eloise sat down on the cold ground. 'And? What happened?'

'I reckoned that if she was asking where you were, it meant you hadn't told anyone what you'd seen, so I told her that you'd said something about hitchhiking to Wales. At the time I thought it'd buy me maybe an extra couple of weeks to work out what I was going to do.'

Eloise nodded. 'Debs and I said we were going to go back again that summer,' she said. 'I was annoyed because she wanted Mel to come with us.'

Wendy nodded. 'Yeah, well, I told your mum you'd decided to go there early. Debs used to talk about the holiday you'd had there the summer before like it was paradise on earth. She said you'd met a lad there and you were planning another trip to see him.'

'How did she seem?'

'Who?'

'My mum.'

'She asked a lot of questions about how you were getting there and who you were staying with. She was dead worried about you. Sweet, really. I almost felt bad lying to her. I told her that someone had seen you all hitchhiking and that you were staying with that lad you'd met. She seemed annoyed but relieved.'

345

'And did she come back later to see if you'd heard anything else?'

'I don't know. I stopped answering the door after that. I wrapped the bodies up in carpet and plastic sheets and dragged them down the stairs and out to the coal shed. You know, it's funny how you get used to the smell after a while. The rubbish built up in the garden too. The neighbours complained, but they always moved on without doing anything about it. I spent a lot of time making my own plans to get away. I'd decided I'd live on the street rather than go into a children's home. I was bloody terrified. I lay awake at night, scared of being sent away, but no one checked up on us. And back then, we didn't get welfare officers asking about us or anything.'

'Did no one ever wonder what had happened to your sister, or your mum?'

'Don't you get it?' asked Wendy. 'No one gives a toss about people like me. They don't care if we miss a dentist's appointment or don't turn up to work. We're disposable. A drain on society. When people like us go quiet, no one notices. And if they do, they don't care. I heard you talking at the vigil about how many people disappear every year and all those bodies that have been found but not named. Do you think that's anything new? Do you think it would happen to people like you, with husbands and jobs and kids and friends?'

'It does happen,' said Eloise.

'Yeah, but your lot are found again. No one's even looking for people like me.'

Eloise hung her head. Despite her struggles, she'd been lucky that people had taken pity on her. Sasha's hen party had looked after her when she was distraught and freezing cold. If they hadn't come along, she might have just stayed in the bus station until she froze to death, and she wouldn't have minded. They'd always assumed she was heartbroken over Gavin, but she'd been devastated about the death of her sister.

The manager at Bertie's had given her a job – and a new name – when he'd seen her desperation. Strangers had let her sleep on floors and sofas when she had nowhere to live, and then Kit had taken a chance on loving a woman who had never been honest with him. Eloise knew that she was one of the lucky ones. It could have been so different.

'When did you decide to come after me?' she asked.

'When I saw those godawful paintings,' said Wendy. 'I was being forced out of the house anyway so it could go to a more needy family. Ha! More needy than me? I don't think so. I knew it was only a matter of time until someone looked at what I was keeping out back. When I saw your paintings, I thought, "Look at that cow, living in Cornwall, pretending she wasn't responsible for ruining my life." I went home that night and tried to search for you online, but there was nothing, because you weren't called Elizabeth King any more, were you? I couldn't stop thinking about you. I'm not ashamed to say it, I got obsessed with what you were doing down here. I decided the only way to flush you out was by plastering your name everywhere.'

'So you put Debs and Mel in your van and came down here?'

'Yep. But when I found out who you were . . .' Wendy threw her head back and laughed. 'You were right under my

347

nose all along, giving me toys for my imaginary grandson. I needn't have bothered with the whole charade of planting the bodies and giving anonymous tip-offs to the police. I gambled everything, and why? Why am I always the one taking the risks while you're swanning around? It made me even angrier, and I wasn't just content with exposing you any more, I wanted to take something from you like you took something from me. I wanted to destroy your family.'

'And so you took my daughter,' Eloise said.

'Hold on,' said Wendy. 'I didn't know she was going to be here. Like I said, I was going to take Mimi.'

'I don't believe you would've hurt her,' said Eloise.

'Yeah? Well you're a mug then. You ruined my life. It only seems fair I ruin yours.'

'You'll never get the chance,' said Eloise. 'You kidnapped and drugged my daughter. The police will see a crazy woman who has kept hold of her dead sister's body for thirty years. I think that's probably against the law, don't you? You might have fought to stay out of institutions as a kid, but now you've guaranteed you'll be spending a long time in one.'

'They might go easy on me,' said Wendy. 'Maybe they'll see I was a scared kid with no parental support who hid her sister's body rather than be taken into care. Maybe I'll be out after a few months, and you'll be forever looking over your shoulder.'

'Maybe,' said Eloise. 'But maybe I should make sure you don't get the chance.'

Wendy sighed. 'I wouldn't blame you if you did, but you're one of those weird people who has a conscience, and you know that you owe me. Do you know why I made up a daughter and a grandson? It was because that's all I ever wanted. A family. And because of you, I never had one. In these last few weeks, I've been the happiest I've ever been. I've enjoyed my job, and I quite liked the person I was pretending to be. I made some lovely friends, and, before I knew who you were, I would have counted you as one of them.'

'Am I meant to be flattered?' asked Eloise.

'This whole vendetta has given me a purpose, you know. I don't think I've had one of those before – a purpose or a vendetta – and to be honest, it's a relief to get rid of those bodies. I could never go on holiday or anything. It's worse than having a dog.'

'I can imagine,' said Eloise. 'But it's a shame you'll never get to tell your side of the story.' She reached into her sleeve and slid out the knife she'd taken from the glove compartment, where Patty had put it for safe keeping. 'Now get out of that pit.'

Chapter 52

Holly

Everyone seemed to arrive at once. A police car and ambulance narrowly beat Ken's battered Ford Fiesta. They skidded into the car park just as Eloise and Andy appeared beside the car arm-in-arm. Andy appeared to be propping Eloise up.

'You took your time,' said Patty.

The ambulance headlights made everyone ghostly pale. Eloise looked like she could have fallen asleep standing up, and there was an unnerving stillness about her. Suddenly she darted to the side and threw up.

'Is everything okay?' asked Holly.

Andy looked at Eloise, but neither of them responded.

'Eloise,' said Holly. 'I asked you if everything was okay.' She didn't like how quiet Andy was being. He wasn't the kind of person who usually kept his thoughts to himself.

'Hmm?' asked Eloise, wiping her mouth. 'Oh, yes, thank you.'

'Have you cut yourself again?'

She looked down at her hands. 'Why do you ask?'

'Because last time I saw you throw up, it was at the sight of blood.'

'Oh. No. I'm fine.'

350

Ken was doing his best to fill the police officers in on what had been happening. Fire, he said. Kidnap. Patty explained what had just happened in the engine house and pointed them to where they would find an injured and most contrite Wendy. However, no one seemed to know what had happened to Wendy's knife. Patty swore it had been in the car a minute ago.

There was a flurry of activity as the paramedic and two police officers hurried towards the engine house, talking on their radios.

'Isn't this a bit over-the-top?' said Meghan. 'I just want to go home for a cup of tea and a nap. Honestly, Mum, I came home to escape the drama.'

Another car bumped into the car park, coming to a halt at an angle behind the police car. Kit jumped out and ran to Meghan. Another figure getting out caught Holly's eye. She couldn't see his face, but she'd recognise those skinny legs and rounded shoulders anywhere.

'Mum,' Eddie said, pulling Eloise in for a hug. 'Jesus, woman, I can't leave you alone for a minute, can I?'

'What are you doing here?' Eloise buried her face in his shoulder.

'After talking to you this morning, I had a pang of home-sickness, or it might have been jealousy that Meghan was going to get one of your Sunday roasts. I got a lift off another lad going home to Bristol for the weekend and caught the train the rest of the way. Dad picked me up from Truro station and explained everything.'

Eloise stepped away from him, and Holly saw that she was crying.

'I'm so sorry to have dragged everyone into this,' she said. 'I always wanted you and Meghan to be proud of me, and then I almost got your sister killed.'

'It's about time she realised that I'm your favourite,' Eddie said, producing a tissue from his pocket and handing it to her.

Eloise laughed. 'I don't have the energy to give you a thick ear, so would you do it to yourself?'

'Consider it done,' he said. 'Seriously, though, is Megs okay?'

'She's fine. Or she's in shock. I guess time will tell.'

'Mrs Ford?' a police officer called.

As Eloise went to talk to them, Eddie turned to Holly. 'Hey,' he said. 'How have you been?'

'Like you care,' Holly said. 'You haven't responded to any of my messages.'

'I wanted to, but Mum said it would be kinder to you if we had a clean break. Don't tell her, but I've struggled to settle in. I thought that talking to you would have me running home. I am literally the thickest person on my course.'

'I doubt it,' said Holly.

'No, I am. And I've realised, maybe a little too late, that I'm a bit of a homebody. I like my own bed and my mum's cooking. I've really missed home. I really missed you.'

Holly folded her arms. 'Shut up, you idiot.'

She was looking at him, wondering what to say next, when she became aware of a commotion.

'What's going on now?' asked Eddie.

'She's gone,' said the police officer. 'We're trying to get a helicopter here to search for her. She can't have got far.'

'What?' shouted Patty. 'You have got to be kidding me. You left her alone? Eloise, what were you thinking?'

'Well, no one is more surprised than me,' said Eloise. 'I didn't think she would have been able to get out of that pit on her own, not in the state she was in, and she swore she'd stay put, didn't she, Andy?'

Andy looked up at the sky, pretending he was anywhere but there. 'What? Yeah. That's what you told me. She must have been stronger than she looked.'

Holly went to Eloise and threaded her arm through hers. 'What did you do?'

'I did what I had to.'

Truth Seekers UK

Patty Hansen

Well, I may never fully recover from last weekend. I've had a few days to think about it, and on balance, I'd call it a success. We discovered the truth about what happened to Elizabeth King, identified the two sets of remains in the engine houses, and found out who was behind it all. On the downside, Eloise and Andy let the suspect escape, and she's still at large. I guess you can't win them all.

Andy Pickford

How many times do I have to say this?? I did not let her get away.

Patty Hansen

Then why won't you tell us exactly what happened?

Andy Pickford

Let me take you out to dinner, and I'll explain everything.

Patty Hansen

I would rather starve.

Ken Marchpane

No sightings of Wendy have been reported since the vigil. The police believe the most likely explanation is that she fell or jumped into the sea. Nonetheless, the conclusion of this case was most satisfactory. I sincerely hope to work with you in the future. Kind regards, Ken. ✓

Sasha Walters

OMG, guys, that was one of the best weekends of my life! I've been telling my kids about me breaking into Wendy's place and using the iPad to track her phone. They think I'm the coolest mum ever!! And the girls from the hen party have decided that we're going to have a reunion in Cornwall every year now. It has honestly brought us all closer together. I haven't seen some of those ladies since Amy's wedding. I tell you, it's been an absolute joy. And then when you think about the fact that we probably saved Eloise's daughter's life . . . ✓

Marsha Pirolo

Not to mention that we freed two souls by identifying them and releasing them from their torment. ✓

Andy Pickford

Marsha, I can't decide whether you believe what you say or whether this is one big act. ✓

Marsha Pirolo

Why are you so resistant, Andy? Oh, wait. I see her now. A larger lady. Is this your mother? Grandmother? She says you were always obsessed with bosoms. You wanted to breastfeed far past when it was acceptable. What age were you when you stopped? Four? Five? This was the beginning of your love–hate relationship with women.

Andy Pickford

Lucky guess.

Holly Bobs

Thank you all for coming down to Cornwall. I can't begin to tell you how much I appreciate it. As some of you already know, it looks like my sister is in Cyprus. I don't know if she's still there, or even if it was her, but this is our best lead. She seems to have been working in a bar out there. I'll check it out as soon as we can get flights, but it's no longer tourist season, and there's a chance she'll have moved on. BUT, I'm feeling hopeful for the first time in a long time. And I only went and got a job. I start next month!!

Sasha Walters

Did someone say Cyprus? I bloody love Cyprus. Do you need company? I wouldn't mind a bit of winter sun. Pissing it down with rain here.

356

Patty Hansen

Give me everything you've got on the place where Lisa was working. I'll see what I can find on social media. People will have tagged the bar in their drunken holiday photos. I can see if she's in any of the pictures. Sometimes the bars themselves have pictures. Do you want me to contact them? It pays to do some background research before you go. It might take some time to go through all the pictures. Andy, mind giving me a hand?

Andy Pickford

You want me to spend hours on the internet looking at pictures of scantily clad women? I've been training for this my whole life.

Two months later

The new building had an old building smell. It had started life as a school before becoming the shell for which Eloise had co-signed a twelve-month lease. She breathed deeply and was sure she could smell school dinners, glue and wet paper towels above the paint fumes. She breathed out and saw her breath make silent speech bubbles in the air.

'I can't teach yoga in these temperatures,' said Mimi. 'We'll need double-glazing and heaters.'

'It'll warm up once we've blocked the gaps in the window frames,' said Eloise.

The building was big enough for two studios, a therapy room, and a café that would double as an art studio for local artists, but it wasn't yet fit for purpose. Even so, Eloise was more excited about this than she'd been about anything in a very long time.

They'd finished the second coat of paint for the therapy room and the studios. New flooring was being fitted on Monday, and furnishing would come later.

'Do you need me for anything else?' asked Mimi. 'I said I'd meet Arthur and Joseph this evening and I need to get cleaned up first.'

'No, you go. I'll lock up.'

Mimi pulled Eloise into a lingering hug.

358

'I'm so glad I get to do this with you,' she said.

'Me too.'

She picked up her scarf, winding it around her long neck like a maypole. Eloise grabbed the stack of mail that she'd been ignoring and walked to the window, from where she could see the mist-heavy harbour.

'I was talking to Joseph about Kit's proposal to have an adults' school disco here,' Mimi said. 'He thinks it's a great idea.'

Kit was desperate to return to DJing but wanted to play his old favourites rather than new music. He'd only realised how much he missed it when he discovered that Holly had sold his vinyl collection.

'Yeah, me too,' Eloise said. 'You're spending a lot of time with Joseph at the moment. And don't tell me it's all about Arthur.'

'So? He's hot, and I'm recently single.'

'Isn't he a fair bit younger than you?' Eloise asked.

'I know. Glorious, isn't it?'

They were still a few months away from being able to run art classes and yoga classes, but more than anything, Eloise wanted the place to be a community space where anyone could drop in if they were having a tough time at home so that no one would feel alone. Nothing too big. A small pond. A safe, reliable life where surprises were few and safety was a given.

Holly's sister had moved on by the time she got to Ayia Napa, but the bar owner confirmed that she had been working there, so at least they knew she was still alive. Holly had started her new job helping with events for the National Trust, and she and Edward were giving their relationship another go.

Eloise was surprised at how thrilled she was by this turn of events, and she was getting to see a lot more of Holly.

Meghan had a new job, too, even further away from home this time, but she said she'd be back for Christmas. Edward had agreed to stick with his university course, so the house was quiet again. Eloise and Kit had decided that she needed a project, and that was how she and Mimi came to take over the draughty old schoolhouse and how Kit came to want to run old-school discos for people who'd hung up their uniforms long ago.

'Right, I'm off,' Mimi said. 'We still having lunch at Jan's on Monday?'

'Yep.'

Eloise looked at the mail. Some were bills, some were reminders of bills, but one hand-written item caught her eye. She checked the stamp on the front and frowned. She didn't know anyone who lived in Scotland, did she? She slit it open and saw a postcard with a painting of the Scottish Highlands. She turned the card over, but it was blank. She was about to throw it in the bin when she noticed something in the bottom right corner.

'Don't tell me that's another bill?' asked Mimi.

Eloise stared at the card for a moment longer. Then she ran her finger over the ink – a small but perfectly drawn dragonfly.

'No,' she said. She stuffed the postcard back in the envelope and the envelope deep into her bag.

'Actually, it's quite the opposite,' she said. 'It's confirmation of a debt paid in full.'

360

Acknowledgements

FIN=

I've been staring at this page for a good twenty minutes now, wondering how to acknowledge everyone who has helped with *The Vanishing Act*. You'd think I'd be better at this by now. Many people have worked hard to bring this book to life and I want to convey my immense gratitude to all of them. From the inspiration of my writing pals to the encouragement of my family, the belief and support of everyone at Constable and the opportunities provided by Jericho Writers and Curtis Brown Creative – each of you has played a crucial role. Forgive me if I've missed anyone!

This book is the result of opportunities and choices stretching back years. First, my agent, Imogen Pelham, for taking on an enthusiastic, if slightly clueless, writer. Jericho Writers for staging the Friday Night Live competition I won in 2016. Curtis Brown Creative for helping me get on the right track in my writing, and my tutors and fellow students on the MA in Writing for Script and Screen who have helped me develop my work. All have inspired and motivated me, and I have tried not to let a single opportunity pass me by.

I'd like to thank everyone at Constable for their belief in and support for *The Vanishing Act*, especially my editor, Krystyna Green, who helped shape this story, and Jane Selley, the copy-editor, who saved me by picking up the inconsistencies in the text. The publicists, cover designers and everyone else at Constable are superheroes for taking my scribbles and producing a book from them.

Writing can be a lonely job – but not when you have the kind of writing pals I do. Thank you, Ladykillers. You are the most talented, kind-hearted and hilarious bunch of women I know, and I'm not sure what I'd do without you.

And to the Cornwall writing contingent of Roz Watkins, Emma Cowell, Liz Fenwick and Claire Peate. Each of you has allowed me to vent my frustrations and buoyed me when I've felt overwhelmed. Thank you for the support. And the cocktails.

This book is dedicated to my husband, James, and my sons, Alex and Danny. Their unwavering support, endless love and patience during the hours spent at my desk juggling writing and coursework have not gone unnoticed. Thank you for keeping tea and snacks coming when I 'vanished' into another world for weeks on end.

All of this would be pointless if it weren't for the fantastic bookshops who promote my books (a special shout-out to Falmouth Bookseller!), and every reader who has read this or any of my books. Thank you all for being a part of this incredible journey, and see you for the next one!